Karina Halle is a former travel writer and New York Times and USA Today bestselling author of The Pact, The Artists Trilogy, and other wild and romantic reads. She lives in a 1920s farmhouse on an island off the coast of British Columbia with her husband and her rescue pup, where she drinks a lot of wine, hikes a lot of trails and devours a lot of books. To find out more about Karina and her missable books, visit www.authorkarinahalle.com, find her on Facebook, and follow her on Twitter @MetalBlonde.

Why you should lose yourself in a Karina Halle novel:

'Karina Halle has done it again with this violently beautiful tale of love, pain, revenge, and loss, that will rip you apart, piece by piece, and put you back together again'   S. L. Jennings

'A story that just about jumps from the pages directly onto the big screen. Fans of suspense and twisted romance will be overjoyed with Halle's talent'   Romantic Times

'Full of twists, surprises, action . . . This book was spectacular, unique and made me feel all sorts of raw and deep emotions'
                                  Bookish Temptations

'Halle's writing is flawless. She writes with so much passion that you can't help but fall in love with her characters'
                                  Four Chicks Flipping Pages

'the right mix of intense emotions: love, hate, anger and sadness'
                                  Romance at Random

'Fiercely unique. Bold. Riveting. Gritty. Stressfully intense. Evoking an exceptionally wide range of emotions, this action-packed and thought-provoking story left me breathlessly tense'
                                  Vilma's Book Blog

'She dares us to fall in love with the bad'   Smexy Books

By Karina Halle

The Artists Trilogy
On Every Street (e-novella)
Sins & Needles
Shooting Scars
Bold Tricks

Dirty Angels Trilogy
Dirty Angels
Dirty Deeds

Dirty DEEDS

Karina Halle

headline
ETERNAL

Copyright © 2015 Karina Halle

The right of Karina Halle to be identified as
the Author of the Work has been asserted by her in accordance
with the Copyright, Designs and Patents Act 1988.

First published as an Ebook in Great Britain in 2015
by HEADLINE ETERNAL
An imprint of HEADLINE PUBLISHING GROUP

First published in paperback in Great Britain in 2015
by HEADLINE ETERNAL
An imprint of HEADLINE PUBLISHING GROUP

1

Cataloguing in Publication Data is available from the British Library

ISBN 978 1 4722 2886 4

Typeset in Electra by Palimpsest Book Production Limited,
Falkirk, Stirlingshire

Printed and bound in Great Britain by
CPI Group (UK) Ltd, Croydon, CR0 4YY

HEADLINE PUBLISHING GROUP
An Hachette UK Company
338 Euston Road
London NW1 3BH

www.headlineeternal.com
www.headline.co.uk
www.hachette.co.uk

For Scott and Bruce MacKenzie.

A NOTE FROM THE AUTHOR

Thank you for wanting to read *Dirty Deeds*. Though this book is not as dark or disturbing as the previous book in the series, *Dirty Angels*, it does contain violence, coarse language and sexually explicit scenes. Reader discretion is advised.

Speaking of *Dirty Angels*, though *Dirty Deeds* is the second in the series, it can be read as a standalone. The third book in the series, *Dirty Promises*, can also be read as a standalone. While all the stories are connected, I do write them with the mindset that each reader is a new audience unfamiliar with the other books. So, no, you don't need to read the whole trilogy but, of course, I personally think it's more fun if you do.

CHAPTER ONE

Derek

The call came at 6:30 a.m. from a voice I recognized but couldn't place. The fact that it sounded familiar was surprising, though. The turnover rate for these guys was exceedingly high. They were shuffled around to different *sicarios* like a game of musical chairs. Sometimes I wondered if the ones giving me the orders – the *narcos* just underneath the bosses – ever lasted more than a few weeks. Did they go on to have long careers doing the dirty work of the *patrons?* Or were they so good at getting the job done that they were employed for a long time, even promoted, just like any assistant manager at McDonald's?

It didn't really matter. I took these calls, I carried out the orders, and I got paid. I was at the bottom of their food chain, but as long as I wasn't tied to just one cartel then I didn't have to worry about long-term security. You didn't want long-term security when working for the *narcos*. You wanted to stay as distant – as freelance – as possible. You wanted a way out, in case you ever had a change of heart.

That was unlikely for me. But I was still a bit of a commitment-phobe. Freedom meant everything, and in this game, freedom meant safety.

The girl next to me in bed moaned at the early intrusion, pulling the pillow over her head. She looked ridiculous considering she was completely naked on top of the sheets. Was it Sarah? Kara? I couldn't recall. She was so drunk last night that I was amazed she even made it to my hotel room. Then again, that's why I was in Cancun. I could pretend to be like everyone else, just another dumb tourist on the beach.

I took the phone into the bathroom and closed the door.

"Yes," I answered, keeping my voice low.

"I have a job for you," the man on the other line said. His English was pretty much perfect but relaxed, almost jovial. Sometimes they gave me orders in Spanish, sometimes in English. I felt like this man was trying to extend a courtesy.

"I assume I've worked for you before," I said.

"For me?" the man asked. "No. For my boss? Yes. Many times. But this has nothing to do with him. Let's just say this is coming from a whole new place."

None of that concerned me. "Tell me about payment."

He chuckled. "Don't you want to hear about the job?"

"It doesn't matter. The price does."

"One hundred thousand dollars, U.S., all cash. Fifty now, fifty upon completion."

That made me pause. My heart kicked up. "That's a lot of money."

"It's an important job," the man said simply.

"And what is the job?"

"It's a woman," he said. "In Puerto Vallarta. She should be very easy to find for someone like you."

"I need a name and I need her photo," I told him. Though the price was quite higher than normal, the man was ignoring the basics. It made me wonder if he had ever done this before. It made me wonder a lot of things.

"I have the first, not the second. As I said, she should be easy to find. You might even be able to Facebook her."

I waited for him to go on.

He cleared his throat. "Her name is Alana Bernal. Twenty-six. Flight attendant for Aeroméxico. I want a bullet in her head and I want it front page news."

Bernal was a very common name, which is probably why it sounded familiar. I wondered what she had done, if anything. Usually when I was sent to kill women, it was because they were involved with a *narco* and had overstayed their welcome. They knew too much. They had loose lips in more ways than one.

I was never really given time to think about it. You weren't with these types of things. There were a few minor alarm bells going off in my head – the high price for someone minor, the greenness in the man's voice – but the price won out in the end. That amount of money could get me away from this business for a long time. I saw a lengthy hiatus on my horizon, one that didn't include fucking drunk chicks on spring break just because I was horny, a hiatus that didn't include bouncing my way from hotel room to hotel room across Mexico, waiting for the next call.

I told the man I agreed to his terms, and we worked out the payment plan. I wouldn't get the other half until she made the news. Considering how rare shootings were in Puerto Vallarta, I had no doubt it would happen. And I would be long gone.

I hung up the phone feeling almost elated. The promise of a new life buried that worm of uneasiness. One more job and then I'd be freer than ever.

I came out of the bathroom to see the chick sitting up in

bed and looking extremely nauseous. Once she saw me though, her eyes managed to light up.

"Wow," she said. "You're fucking hot."

I tried to smile, hoping she didn't find me enticing enough to stay. "Thank you."

"Did we have sex last night?"

I stood beside the bed and folded my arms across my chest. Her mouth opened a bit at my muscles. I still had the same physique I had back in the military, and it still got the same reactions from women. They never knew the real me – knew Derek Conway – but at least, with the way I looked, they thought they did. Just another built, tough American boy, a modern G.I. Joe.

They had no idea what I did.

They had no idea who I was.

"No," I told her, "we didn't have sex. You stripped and then you passed out."

She looked surprised. "We still didn't . . ."

I gave her a dry look. "Sex is only fun when you're awake, babe." I stretched my arms above my head and she stared openly at my stomach, from the waistband on my boxers to my chest. Okay, now it was time for her to go.

I told her I had stuff to do in the morning and needed her to move along. I could tell she wanted to at least take a shower, but I wasn't about to budge.

I had a plane to catch.

❥❦

Alana Bernal was extremely easy to find.

At least for me. She had a Facebook page under Alana B.

Her privacy settings were high, but I was still able to see her profile picture, dressed in her Aeroméxico uniform. She had a sweet yet beautiful face. Her eyes were light hazel, almost amber, both stunning and familiar at the same time. They glowed against her golden skin, as did her pearly white teeth. She looked like a lot of fun, and I could imagine all the unwanted attention she got from unruly passengers in the air. She looked like she could handle them with a lot of sass.

Once again I found myself wondering what she had done.

And once again I realized I couldn't care.

That wasn't my business.

Killing her was my business.

I drove to the airport, and for the next two days I began to stalk the employee parking lot, using a different rental car each time. Most of the flight crew I saw looked a bit like her but lacked the certain vitality she had. So I waited in mounting frustration, just wanting this job to be over with.

On day three, just as I was driving past for the forty-second time that morning, I spotted her getting out of a silver Honda, wrestling with her overnight bag. I quickly pulled the car around again and parked at the side of the road, plumes of dust rising up around me. There was nothing but a chain-link fence between us as she began the long walk toward the waiting airport shuttle. Her modest high heels echoed across the lot and she tugged at the hem of her skirt with every other step. Not only was she beautiful, but there was something adorably awkward about her.

What had she done?

No, I couldn't care.

I looked down at the bag in the passenger seat and took

out the silencer, quickly screwing it on the gun that I was holding between my legs.

She only had a few seconds of life left before I put the bullet in her heart.

I got out of the car, moving like a ghost, gun down at my side. In three strides I would make it over to the fence where I would take quick aim and shoot. She would go down and I would be gone.

I was one stride away when it happened.

A golden sedan pulled out of a parking space in a hurry and slammed right into Alana, knocking her to the ground. She screamed as she went down, tires screeching to a halt, and people started shouting from the shuttle.

The sedan reversed then sped around Alana's crumpled body, not stopping to check on the woman they had just hit.

I've been in a lot of situations before that smack you square in the face – abrupt and brutal scenes that change the course of the day, the course of a life. They come out of nowhere, but you adapt, you roll with them. You refuse to be shocked. I should have been able to collect myself better than I did.

But seeing that car speeding away toward the parking gates and crashing through them as it fled the scene, well I seemed to lose all logic. Before I knew what I was doing, I was getting back into my car and driving after the hit-and-run sedan.

As I passed the broken gates to the parking lot I could see people – employees – emerging from the shuttle, one of them pointing at me. I had been spotted. Maybe as a witness, maybe as someone that was a part of the crime.

Only it wasn't the crime they thought it was, but the one I didn't get to commit.

I was fucking everything up for myself and I knew it. But seeing that car gun her down then keep going, as if the driver thought they could get away with it, brought back every debilitating moment from Afghanistan. I watched a lot of people get killed before I became the killer.

I would like to tell myself that I was going after them because they fucked up my potentially perfect assassination. That would make more sense than the truth – that I felt like a helpless soldier again, watching the world around him crumble from senseless acts. I was angry, angrier than I had been in a long time.

I'd snapped. I guess I had it coming.

I drove the beat up car I'd rented from a cheap agency right on his ass, following him in heated pursuit. I wasn't thinking, I wasn't even breathing, I was just reacting to some long-forgotten, deep-seated need for vengeance.

The sedan screamed down the road, tires burning on hot asphalt, heading for the highway. I was going to stop him before that. I didn't know what I was going to do after that, but I had an idea.

I pressed the gas pedal down as far as it would go and willed it to catch up, muttering expletives as it shuddered beneath me. The rental car was a pile of shit to look at, but it turned out the engine worked well enough to let me catch up with the sedan that was sputtering erratically, a tire having blown out as it fought for control on the rough road.

I couldn't get a good look at the driver, but through the dust I could see him thrashing around in his seat, panicking at the wheel. He wasn't a professional by any means. Then again, I was supposed to be one and I was trying to kill his fucking ass for no reason at all.

No reason except that it felt one hundred percent right.

His car suddenly shifted right and I took that moment to gun it until my front end clipped his back. The headlights shattered, and with a screech of metal, the car went spinning to a stop.

Before I could comprehend what was going on, I was jumping out of the car, gun at my side, and running to his door. I threw it open and aimed it right at the man's head.

The dust blew around us, and through the haze he looked at me, mouth open, the whites of his eyes shining as they stared at me with fear or shock or regret.

I didn't care which one it was.

He raised his hands, screaming out in Spanish, "It was an accident, please, it was an accident!"

"Who are you?" I asked, my voice more steady than I felt.

"It was an accident," he cried again. For a brief moment he took his frightened eyes off the gun and looked behind him, at the parking lot in the distance and the commotion that was gathering there. Soon they would be heading our way. "Is she all right? Please, please, the girl, is she all right?"

"No," I told him, and pulled the trigger.

Because of the silencer, the sound of his brains and skull splattering on the window – a bright burst of red – was louder than the gun.

I quickly got back in my car and drove away. There was no time to stand around and figure out who the man was, if it was truly an accident or something else. Questions would come later, as they always did, only this time I'd be the one doing the asking.

I spent the rest of the day inside my hotel room, cleaning my guns and watching the local Puerto Vallarta news, trying to see if the accident would be mentioned. It was at the end of the segment when they finally reported on it. It was the usual shoddy shot of the serious reporter standing in front of the smashed gates to the parking lot. Alana, as it turns out, wasn't killed or even critically injured. She had been admitted to the nearest hospital. The bigger part of the story was the part that had my hand all over it. It was that someone had caught up with the driver and shot him in the head. The news wasn't sure whether this was a botched hit-and-run or vigilante justice.

I didn't know what to think of it myself. One minute everything was going to plan, the next minute I was putting a bullet in the head of someone else, acting out of pure, untrustworthy instinct. That lack of control scared me. I hadn't responded like that, so loosely, so foolishly, since my wife had been killed.

Regression was not a good thing in this business.

It was just after nightfall when my phone rang. I waited a beat, trying to read my gut before it got compromised by the voice on the phone. My gut was telling me to back out.

"Hello," I answered.

"Hola," the man said in that light tone of his. "I think we may have gotten our wires crossed here. I heard you were the best in the business. I'm a bit confused as to why you killed someone else instead of the woman you were paid to kill."

"No time for pleasantries," I noted.

"No," the man said. "Not when she's in the hospital and you've jeopardized this whole operation."

I cleared my throat. "It was all lined up. Before I was even able to take my shot, she was hit by a fucking car. Everyone saw it. What was I supposed to do, still go through with it with everyone watching me?"

"That still doesn't explain why you shot the driver."

No, not really, I thought.

"I guess I lost my cool," I told him.

"I didn't think that was possible with you."

"Maybe you've heard wrong about me."

"They've called you soulless."

"Maybe I'm getting tired of this game."

"Ah," he said. "The game, but not the money, hey?"

"Maybe money gets you killed in the end."

"No, no," he said. "Money is what gets other people killed. By you." He sighed long and hard, and I tried to picture who this man could be. So, so familiar. And so, so wrong.

"Listen," he went on, "I know things are more complicated now, but the job still has to go through."

"I don't think so."

"No?"

"It's more than complicated. There were witnesses there that could have seen me."

"No one has come forward."

"How would you know that?"

"Don't you worry about it. Just trust me when I tell you that you are clean. The only real complication is the fact that you'll have to get into the hospital. She's being guarded, will be for some time. But I know you've handled dicier situations than that before."

I frowned. "How much *do* you know about me?"

"Enough," was his dry answer. "The price is now two hundred thousand dollars. You can keep that fifty we gave you. This is on top of that."

Fucking hell. Two hundred and fifty thousand dollars would end all my problems forever. But that was way too much money for just a girl, unless she was more than just a girl. She was a death sentence.

Something was terribly fucking wrong here, and I would be an idiot to stick my nose in it for one minute longer.

"No," I told him with steely resolve. "I haven't survived this long to know when there's something more at stake. I'll meet your people somewhere, give you your deposit back if you want, but this is where we part ways."

There was a heavy pause on the line. "Don't be foolish."

"I'm being smart," I told him. "Whatever game this is, I don't want any part of it."

"I suppose raising the price wouldn't help."

"No. This is a job I don't want to touch."

"But you've already had your hand in it," he said, and finally there was an edge to his voice, a warning. "It's too late for you to back out now. You accepted the job, and now you have to finish it."

"You're telling me that the fact that the target was hit by a seemingly random car isn't a warning sign to you? Right before I pulled the trigger? The fact that the dead body of a fucking flight attendant has a two hundred thousand dollar price tag on it? If you want her out so bad, there are plenty of other people you can pay to do your dirty work. This one though, I'm no longer a part of."

More silence. I could hear his breathing. "Have you ever backed out of a job before?"

I swallowed. "No," I said thickly. "I haven't. But there have been jobs that I shouldn't have taken, only I didn't listen to my instincts. I'm listening to them now. This isn't the job for me, and this is where we part ways." I took a deep breath, feeling the monetary sting already. "Just tell me where to meet your people. I'll give you the deposit back, I haven't touched a single bill. I don't want any trouble, we'll just forget it all and move on."

"Oh, you'll be moving on," the man said. "And so will she."

The line went dead.

I stared at my phone for a good minute, feeling absolute dread coursing through me. I was trusting my gut on this one – I had made the right decision, hadn't I?

Within an hour, I was out of the hotel room and booked into one of the swankier all-inclusive resorts close to downtown. I used my fake Canadian passport – Derrin Calway – and credit card. I tossed my phone and got a new one at a street-side kiosk. I still had an email address and a pager number that most people knew, and though many of the cartels didn't possess the same high-tech tracking systems and surveillance the movies would lead you to believe, it never hurt to be careful. I was constantly getting cheap new phones, constantly changing names, constantly on the move.

Most people just called me The American. They never really knew my name was Derek, and the ones that did, they assumed it was a fake name. But my name was really the only real thing about me.

I tried to fall asleep that night, but the sound of people partying it up at the sprawling hotel pools was too much for me. Sometimes, only sometimes, the normalcy of the world around me hurt. This was one of those times.

When dawn finally colored the sky tangerine pink, and the only sound was the crashing of the Pacific outside my balcony, I finally fell asleep. My last thought was of Alana, lying on the pavement, her body broken by intent or circumstance.

I wanted to find her.

CHAPTER TWO

Alana

"Alana." I heard a voice cut through the darkness. A firm hand shook my shoulder as the screams and cries started to fade away and only the fear, that deep, desperate fear, was a film left behind.

I blinked slowly, the white light filtering in through my eyelashes. The nightmare was hanging around in the back of my pounding head, and the living nightmare was before me.

Fuck my fucking life. I couldn't believe I got hit by a goddamn car.

"Alana," the voice said again, and I knew it was the nurse, Salma. "Are you all right, dear? You were crying in your sleep."

I brought my eyes over to her without moving my head. I'd gotten pretty good at that over the last few days. If I moved my head at all, I'd be hit with a wave of nausea. The doctors assured me that I probably wouldn't have a concussion, but I didn't believe them. I felt like my brain had been demolished.

The nurse had a kindly face, full-cheeked like a chipmunk. So far she was the only one in the hospital who had been doting on me. The doctors and surgeons were so brusque and professional. I was used to that being with the airlines and all, but it was nice to have someone that acted as if they really cared.

"Sometimes I do that," I said carefully. "I . . . have nightmares."

She gave me a sympathetic smile. "I can tell." Luckily she didn't press it any further. My childhood wasn't something I liked to talk about.

"How are you feeling, otherwise?" she asked, trying to adjust my pillow. I winced at the movement but was relieved that it didn't hurt as much as it usually did.

"I still get dizzy when I move my head," I told her. "But it's getting better now. Thank god. My arm is really itchy." I looked down to the thick bandage around my wrist, going from palm to mid-forearm.

"It will get better as your skin gets used to it," Salma said. "You were incredibly lucky, Alana. Not many people walk away from a hit-and-run accident with only a broken ankle and fractured wrist."

"And the bruising and the pain and the head that feels like it is going to explode," I filled in.

"That, too, will go away," she said. "All you need to do is rest."

I swallowed hard. It felt like I had a lump of coal in my throat. "Have they caught the guy yet, the guy who did this to me?"

A funny look passed over her eyes, and I knew she knew something.

"Tell me, please," I told her. "I hate being kept in the dark."

She sighed and cast a quick glance over to the open door

leading out into the rest of the hospital. The bed next to me in the semi-private room was thankfully unoccupied the whole time I had been there.

"I haven't talked to the police," she said in a low voice. "It's just what I've been hearing. But the guy who hit you, he's dead."

My eyes widened. "Dead?"

"Someone killed him . . . he was murdered. Not too far from where you were hit."

"What does that mean?"

She shrugged. "I don't know. I am sure the police will talk to you about it as soon as they can."

My thoughts automatically went to my brother. Javier was protective over me, even more so lately, and this seemed like something he would do.

"How was he killed?" I asked with trepidation.

"He was shot. In the head."

"That's it?"

She shot me a funny look.

I quickly fumbled for my next words. "I mean, that's terrible."

That meant it wasn't Javier. Javier wouldn't just shoot whoever did this to me, he would take them and make them suffer for a very, very long time. My brother might be twisted – as all drug cartel lords are – but family always came first.

"I'm not sure how terrible it is," the nurse said. "This man hit you with his car and took off. Some might say it's his comeuppance."

Some might say all of this was too weird. "I guess I don't have to worry anymore."

She shook her head. "You don't. But there is still a police officer stationed on this floor, for at least tonight. They can't tell whether the hit and run was intentional or not."

"I'd seen that car before," I told her, just as I had told the police. "I got glimpses of the man from time to time. I think he was a mechanic for the airlines."

"That's what they say. No record of criminal history either, but then again it's Mexico, so that doesn't mean much, does it?"

I wanted to shake my head but didn't risk it. "No, it doesn't." I closed my eyes. "When do I get out of here again?"

"The doctor wants you under observation for a few more days. The fact that you are still dizzy isn't good, although that can be a side effect of the pain medication."

"Do you have anything to help me sleep?" I asked, and when I didn't hear her reply, I opened my eyes to look at her pleadingly. What I wanted was something strong enough to knock me out and keep my nightmares at bay. Usually I had them about once a week, but ever since the accident – which happened, what? Four, five days ago? – I had been having them more. Perhaps because for the first time in a very long time I was afraid again.

And perhaps because being here in the hospital made me realize how little I had in my life. My brother hadn't come by to see me yet, but I hadn't called him either, and I hadn't talked to my twin sister Marguerite. Everyone else – my other sisters, my mother, my father, they were all dead. I had no children, no husband, no boyfriend. Nothing. I only had my job and my friends Luz and Dominga.

Salma gave me a conceding smile then left the room.

When she came back she was holding two pills and a glass of water.

"This will make you rest for a long time," she said, and gently helped me up so I could take them. The room spun and my head hurt, but I managed to get them down.

It wasn't long until I felt good, sublime, floating on a cloud, and everything went black.

It was ten o'clock at night and the hospital was quiet. Luz sat on the corner of my bed while Dominga stationed herself at the door, watching for anyone who might try and stop my escape attempt.

I'd been at the hospital for a week in total and yet the doctor still wanted me to stay for another night or two. I was sick and fucking tired of just lying in bed, watching terrible soap operas and flipping through magazines. Luz and Dominga came to see me when they could, but since Luz was a flight attendant like I was and Dominga was a maid at one of Puerto Vallarta's largest resorts, they couldn't always find the time during visiting hours.

Finally I'd had enough and told them to come and rescue me the first chance they got. Luz had the spare key to my apartment and went in to get me some clothes to leave in and helped me get changed into my dress while we waited for Dominga to finish her shift.

We weren't going far. I couldn't really fathom it in my condition. I was no longer dizzy, but I was still on pain medication, my left forearm was bandaged tightly, and my left foot was in a cast from below the knee down. When I officially left the hospital I would have crutches, but for tonight I would just rely on my friends. The only people I really had.

I had finally called Javier and Marguerite and told them what had happened. Javier said for me to call him as soon as I was discharged, and Marguerite had whined about not having any money to fly down from New York to see me. But the fact was, my only two living family members still weren't here.

"Is the coast clear?" Luz asked, drumming her fingers excitedly on the bed. She had this crazy sparkle in her eyes that she got when she was feeling particularly hyperactive. Luz was tall with long dark hair down to her butt that she almost always wore in a bun, which only added on extra height. She was a force, a powerhouse, and was just as good at putting drunken passengers in their seats as she was at being the life of the party. Luz was a ball of energy and very hard to ignore, and I knew she would get me out of this dull hospital room as if her life depended on it.

Dominga raised her finger to shut her up and kept staring down the hallway. She was about my height, 5'6", but runway-model thin and had this quiet air about her that most people mistook as snobbishness, but I knew it was because she would just rather listen than talk. She also didn't smile much because she hated the gap between her teeth, something we all – especially her husband – found adorable.

Then there was me, Alana Bernal. Sister of one of Mexico's most powerful drug lords. Queen of meaningless one night stands. Flight attendant who couldn't seem to get the routes she wanted.

Forever alone.

And hit by a fucking car.

"Okay, *now*," Dominga said, and Luz immediately got to her feet, helping me off the bed. I had put on a simple black dress that showed off a lot of cleavage – I needed something to distract from the bandages and cast. On my good foot was a sparkly flat sandal for stability and Luz had covered up my body with mounds of concealer to mask all the bruises which were now fading to an ugly yellow purple, like a rotting plum. I definitely didn't look as good as I normally did, but I was still high on pain medication, so at least I felt pretty good.

With all my weight on Luz's shoulder, we hobbled over to the door and looked down the hall both ways. It was totally empty. Thankfully I knew that there were no more policemen stationed on this floor to look after me. They had all been called off once it was ruled out that the hit and run had been a crime but not a deliberate one, and that the man who had shot the assailant had been a vigilante of sorts. At least, that's what the cops had told me. It was hard to know the truth when it came to them.

The three of us scampered down the hall toward the stairwell, away from the nurse's station, and with an awkward, clumsy descent, we made our way down the stairs and out into the hot night.

I nearly collapsed into Luz's arms, bursting into a fit of giggles. I hadn't felt this rebellious since I was a little girl, stealing candy from Violetta. But at that thought, my smile began to falter, as it always did when I thought about my poor sister. She hadn't died long ago.

"Now what?" Luz asked, giving my shoulders a squeeze.

She could always tell when I was being held in this violent melancholy and did her best to get me out of it. "What's the plan?"

"I think that was the plan," Dominga said, brushing her hair out of her face. "Get Alana out of the hospital."

"Get Alana a drink," I said quickly. "Did you think I got all dressed up to stand in the parking lot?"

"Are you sure with your medication?" Dominga asked as she eyed me suspiciously.

I waved her away. "I'm fine. Just get me to a bar, get a beer in my belly, get some fucking hot men with big dicks, and I'm happy as can be."

Luz and Dominga exchanged a look above my head. Finally Luz said, "There's a bar down the road, but you know it's going to be filled with hospital workers that may just haul your ass back here, not your usual hot men with big dicks."

"I'll take my chances," I told her, nodding to the road. "Now let's go before someone pulls me back in."

We got in Luz's car and drove a couple of blocks until we saw a bar with a pink and green neon palm tree outside. *Lolita's*. It looked a bit rough around the edges, but the people standing outside smoking seemed like your average Mexican twenty somethings in Puerto Vallarta.

"We can do better," Luz said with a discerning gleam to her eyes. "I'll keep driving."

"I don't think I should go too far from the hospital," I said quietly. "Just in case." Even though I was feeling fine, I was still afraid that a rogue concussion could spring up out of nowhere. I was also afraid that Salma would discover that I had escaped. Lately she hadn't been checking on me until just about one o'clock in the morning, but I felt bad about possibly disappointing her.

Still, freedom felt divine.

"All right," Luz said, and pulled her Toyota into the lot behind the bar.

If there were any nurses celebrating the end of their shift, I didn't see them. As Dominga and Luz helped me into the bar, we were met with smiling, drunk faces and spilled drinks. The music was loud and booming, bass thumping into my bones, and I couldn't help but grin back at the rowdy patrons. I had needed this, badly.

While Luz went to the bar to get us beer, Dominga and I managed to score a booth in the corner. We pushed away the stacks of empty drinks that were left behind and settled in to do some hottie watching. Well, I was the one who was always looking for someone to catch my eye. Dominga took her marriage very seriously and wouldn't even admit whether a guy was hot or not.

"I'll get the next round," I said to Luz as she came back with the beers.

She waved her hand at me dismissively. "You are always buying us drinks, Alana. It's time for us to treat you for a change."

I raised my beer in the middle of the table. "Well, I think I owe you something for your excellent escape plan." I clinked their bottles. "So cheers to that. And thank you."

"And thank you for not dying," Luz said, her features growing stern. "When I saw it on the news . . ." She trailed off and took a quick sip of her beer. I wasn't used to her acting emotional and it was throwing me off. "I'm just so glad you're okay."

I gave her a look. "I'm not exactly *okay*. I am a bit banged up."

"But you're here now with us," Dominga said. "And that's something."

I nodded. It was true. I really had no right to complain about the fact that I would be off work for at least another month. I was going on disability, but even with the airline funding it, that didn't equal the full amount of pay I would normally receive. I was going to be on a budget for the next month as my bones healed. And because I wouldn't be able to do my yoga or pilates or go for my daily runs, I was going to be bored out of my mind.

But it could have been worse. I know that in my life, the worst possible thing was always lurking in the background, ready to strike.

I turned my attention to the bar. I was ready to be distracted, and a man was usually pretty good for that. Unfortunately there weren't a lot of men here to do a good enough job. I wasn't even that picky, I just wanted someone that made my head turn, my heart skip a few beats, my thighs squeeze together. That didn't mean I never settled for less – I often did, and usually with the wrong man (don't get me started on the pilots I'd had affairs with, always a mistake) – but I still hoped for someone a bit extraordinary.

You would think that with my past and family I would want the safe and mundane, and I guess I craved that in most aspects of my life, but when it came to love, I wanted to be blown off my feet. Hell, I think I just wanted to feel what love was, period.

It looked like I wasn't going to find it here.

"Are you doing okay?" Luz asked, giving me that concerned look again. "Should we take you back?"

"I'm fine," I said before I knocked back the rest of the beer. With the painkillers coursing through my system, it was all hitting me a little fast, but I didn't care.

When they both just stared at me, I rolled my eyes. "I said I'm fine. Really. Hit and run aside, I'm fine."

Luz raised a brow but didn't say anything. I took out a few pesos from my wallet and plunked them down on the table. "I'd go up and buy the next round myself, but I don't exactly feel like crawling on my hands and knees in this place. Do you mind getting me a refill?"

She got up but left my money on the table. It was true, every time we went out I was usually the one paying for their drinks and food and little gifts. It's not that I made more money than them, both Luz and I were paid the same, I just liked to do nice things for them. Who else would I spend my money on?

"Are you really okay?" Dominga asked quietly after a moment.

I gave her a look. "Is this just about the accident or is there something else?"

She rubbed her lips together in thought before saying, "I'm worried about you. About . . . who did this."

"The police said it was a random event . . . shit like this happens."

"First of all," she said, "the police can't be trusted. Second, shit like this does happen, but it rarely ends up with the driver being shot in the head. Don't you think that's weird? It has to be connected."

Of course I thought it was weird, but I'd spent the last week in the hospital thinking about it, and I wanted to put it to rest.

"Even if it is connected, the guy who hit me is dead. Don't you think that means someone is looking out for me? If anything." I caught her eye and quickly added, "It's not Javier. Believe me."

Luz and Dominga knew all about my brother. I mean, everyone in Mexico knew about him, but only they knew that we were related. I didn't talk about him much, mainly because I didn't have much to say – Javier kept his life very separate from mine and for good reason. They weren't exactly happy that I was connected to someone so notorious and regarded him with constant suspicion and disdain, even though they had never met him. Though, for all his charm, I think they'd be even more scornful if they had met him.

"So then who?" Dominga went on. "It just can't be an accident. And if it is, why would this other person shoot him? It makes no sense and you are being way too cavalier about all of this."

"I'm not being cavalier," I told her. Suddenly I felt very tired. "I'm worried, very worried. But for tonight, I don't want to be worried."

"Yeah, Dominga," Luz said, giving her the stink-eye as she appeared at the table, placing our drinks down. "Give her a break." Luz grinned at me and slid my beer over. "You've got us both tonight. You're safe. Let loose."

"Oh, so now I'm allowed to let loose?"

She looked me up and down. "You can't get too loose with the way you are."

I took a big gulp of beer, challenged. "We'll see."

An hour later, I was feeling a lot looser. Two more beers had helped with that as well. They also tipped my bladder over to the breaking point.

I pushed back my chair and attempted to stand up, but suddenly Luz was beside me, holding me by the arms.

"Where do you think you're going?" she asked.

"I'm trying to go to the bathroom," I told her. "You don't need to come with me."

The two of them exchanged a look. "I won't go with you into the stall, but you should probably have some help getting across the room."

The bar at this point was completely packed, and people were being rowdy, drunken idiots. I nodded and leaned on her, not willing to risk it on my own. I'd probably be bounced against the wall and stepped on by dancing jackasses.

Eventually we made it to the washroom. It was dirty with wet floors and no paper towels, and had a line of slurring girls with smudged makeup waiting to use the two stalls. Luckily someone took pity on me and let me use it ahead of the line, even though there were a few disgruntled murmurs in the crowd. Even totally beat-up and obviously injured didn't mean I got a free pass.

When I was done, Luz was still in line, so I washed my hands and told her I'd wait outside the bathroom. No way in hell did I want to be in there, especially now as some chick was puking her brains out. I went out into the dark hallway and leaned against the wall. I was drunk, but my body was slowly starting to ache, and I wondered if the pain medication was beginning to wear off.

Suddenly some loud morons rounded the corner from the men's washroom and bumped into me hard. I let out a cry and flew to the side, the ground rushing up to meet my face, when an arm came out of nowhere and caught me.

Before I knew what was happening, I was pulled back up by someone who was very strong. I looked at the large, muscular forearm around me then followed it up to the fitted white t-shirt which belonged to a tall, insanely built guy. His blue eyes were sharp and filled with concern, his jaw wide and stern, his stance fierce.

He was Caucasian. Ripped. And hot as hell.

And he was holding on to me like he wasn't about to let go.

CHAPTER THREE

Derek

I t was probably a big mistake. I'd been making nothing but big mistakes since the moment I answered my phone in Cancun. I should have listened to my instincts then, but the goddamn need to escape this life loomed much larger than I thought. I never knew how badly I needed that chance and how much money could buy it until I heard it offered.

But no amount of money, no amount of change, is worth it if you end up dead in the end. If I've learned anything from the people I've killed, it's that.

I was certain that whoever had been on the other line, the one giving the orders, wouldn't let me go so easily. It's not unheard of to back out of a job. Usually the *sicario* gets to keep the deposit and then fucks off somewhere. Usually that *sicario* is not hunted down, but they also aren't used again.

I would definitely have a black mark against me, but that was better than ending up dead. The money, the persistence to have this girl killed even after being hit by a car, the heightened stakes – it wasn't worth it. I'm never told the whole story when it comes to my job. It isn't my business. I carry out the orders for the right price. But when the orders don't add up and things don't make sense, you're a fool if you don't get out of it.

As far as I know, I've never been on anyone's hit list myself. It doesn't work that way. Revenge is never taken on the assassin, but on the one who pays the money, who orders the hit. That's the real bad guy. You still have to watch the ground beneath you for traps, though.

After the phone call and after I woke up the next day from a fitful sleep, I tried to write everything off. If they wanted the deposit back they could get it – the guy knew my email – but if they didn't, I was going to wipe my hands clean of this. Normally I'd get out of dodge as a second safety measure – switching hotels was the first one – but the last place anyone would expect me to stay is Puerto Vallarta.

The truth is, I wanted to see Alana. There was a voice in the back of my head, one that I've been trying to ignore over the years, that told me if she was valuable dead to someone she might be even more valuable alive to someone else. She meant *something*, and those were the people I usually had to kill. No one pays a *sicario* to assassinate the worthless.

For the first time in years, I was intrigued, curious, interested in the world before me. I was fascinated by this mystery woman, this flight attendant with a big smile. Why her? Who was she and what had she done?

And so it was probably a big fucking mistake that I slipped a gun down my cargo shorts before slipping on shades and a wife-beater. I looked like your typical tourist down here to party – no one would look twice at me. Then I headed out the door, taking the bus to the hospital where I knew she was staying.

It's funny how much I stick out like a sore thumb in Mexico. Though I'm as tanned as a motherfucker after being here for so long, I'm obviously not a local. My Spanish is excellent, though I dumb it down more often than not. It's better that way. When you speak the language too well you raise questions, and even though everyone always noticed me, they never noticed what I was doing. That was the big difference.

On the bus, for example, I was just another tourist trying to go somewhere. People looked; an older gentleman gave me a discerning glare, but then they forgot about me. I was different, but not interesting. They would never in a million years know what I really did, how my trigger had, time and time again, changed the course of the cartels, and as a result, the citizens' lives.

Normally, though, I would be cool and calm, but this time I wasn't. On that bus, I was nervous. Just enough to make the palms of my hands damp. I had no fucking idea why I was nervous, except that I was doing something I shouldn't have been.

I didn't *know* what I was doing. And that was a first.

When the bus finally let me off at the hospital, I didn't waste any time. Even without a plan, I knew it was best to keep moving. I waited by the side doors to the building until a nurse went back inside from her smoke break, and then I followed her in. I got looks in the hallway, but again I looked like someone just visiting their sister that had gotten roofied at one of the downtown clubs, or had broken a leg in a parasailing accident.

One doctor ended up stopping me, asking me what I was doing, and after I quickly explained, in English, that I was visiting family, he let me go. When an orderly on the second floor asked me the same, but in Spanish, I answered back in rapid-fire English. That was enough for me to confuse him, and he let me walk past. My size and strength probably had something to do with it as well.

Finally I found her floor. It was a big hospital and slightly chaotic. I used the disorder – the bustling staff, the patients wheeled to and fro, the opening and shutting of doors – to my advantage as I walked down the hall with purpose.

I knew her room because there was a plain-clothed policeman standing outside of it. It wasn't very subtle, but I guess that was the point. To scare away people like myself, people who wanted to harm her.

I still couldn't be certain what she was to me yet, or in what direction I would go.

I slowly walked past and quickly glanced through her open door when the cop wasn't looking. It was a fast look but I had been trained to notice details. I saw her, lying down and all bandaged up with her leg in a cast, a nurse talking over her at a doctor. Even though I could only see a bruised cheekbone, she appeared to be asleep.

I kept walking.

Over the next week, I kept a close eye on her. Sometimes I was parked in a new rental car across the street, watching people come and go. Other times I walked down the hall, stealing glances when I could. Any time someone asked

me where I was going, I explained the same story about
my sister. To the hospital staff, I was harmless. Frequent,
but harmless.

While I watched over her, I toyed with my options. What
was I going to do with her? So far there had been no one
else around watching and waiting. Not like I had been.
Every day it became more and more obvious that the hit
and run was just that – no one else was coming by to finish
the job.

Unless that meant I was still the only one *on* the job.

Perhaps my clock was still ticking.

The buyer was still waiting.

There was a bit of comfort in that. If they thought I
would still go through with it, I was buying her some time.
Even though her time consisted of lying in a hospital bed,
wondering what had happened.

But after a few days, her spirits lifted. I could hear her
laughter in the halls sometimes, so bright and infectious,
as her friends visited her. It was always the same women.
A pensive looking thing with long hair, and a tall one that
was about as subtle as a battering ram.

That was it, though. There was no man – no husband,
no boyfriend, no father, no brother. There was no mother.
There were those two friends and that was it.

I don't know why I found myself relating to her, this
woman I was supposed to kill, but I did. Maybe I always
had. Maybe that's why I watched and waited, unsure of
what to do, but feeling like I eventually had to do
something.

Then one night I saw her and her friends leave the

hospital. I ducked down in the car but they weren't even paying attention. I was in the dark, just a shadow, and they were giggling as they helped her into a Toyota. This was the first time I had seen Alana fully dressed since the day I was supposed to kill her. Though she was limping and needed help, she looked beautiful.

That was something else that surprised me. The rush of blood to my heart and my dick. Feelings were rare, unwarranted and unwanted. I swallowed them down like acid.

When their car started, I waited until they left the parking lot and then followed. They didn't go very far. A tacky-looking dive bar a few blocks away pulled them in like a siren.

So, Alana was escaping for a night of drinking. Part of me thought this wasn't very wise and that her friends should know better, not just because of her injuries but because I was there, I was watching, and I was the man who had been hired to kill her. Didn't they know just what kind of danger she was in? The fact that they had no clue made the whole thing even more puzzling.

But part of me was impressed, too. Car accident or no car accident, assassination attempt or no assassination attempt, she wasn't going to let anything hold her back.

I waited in the car outside for an hour, listening to the rhythmic thumps of music and the drunken laughter floating through the humid air, before I decided I'd had enough. I wanted to watch her up close. I wanted to get to the bottom of everything, and that included her.

Once in the bar, I ordered a beer and quickly surveyed the room. It was a riotous mess of people having fun in

ways I never really could. Once upon a time, when I was
eighteen, before I was deployed, before I lost everything
again and again, I had the same sense of naivety and immor-
tality, like the world really wasn't that bad and it was waiting
at my feet. I laughed at all my options. Now I was older,
and I knew the truth. There were no options. There never
were.

The world was bad.

Alana and her friends had secured a table, and were
drinking, laughing, and looking like everyone else. I tried
to study her as subtly as I could, but from the way she kept
looking around the room, I was too afraid to get caught.
She wasn't looking around, eyeing people as if they meant
to harm her. She was sizing up the men like she wanted
to eat them for dinner.

Eventually I removed myself from the bar and went to
hide in the shadows. It was safer this way, even though a
small part of me was tempted to see her face when she
noticed me. I knew the effect I had on most women. That's
not even my ego talking, it's just the truth. I don't really
take a lot of pleasure in the fact that women seem to gravi-
tate toward me. Being good-looking means nothing. They
just want a hard fuck and big muscles. They wouldn't feel
the same way if they got to know me.

The more I stared at Alana, the more I was struck by
how familiar she looked. I knew that was nothing to ignore
– there was a chance that I'd seen her somewhere before.
But I couldn't place when or where. Though she looked
familiar – it was something about her amber eyes or smile,
which alternated between fun and feminine carnality – it

was like she possessed this kind of life to her that I know would have made a permanent impression on me if we had happened to meet before.

It was later in the night when she got up to use the washroom. Her friend had to help her navigate the rowdy crowd, and before I knew what I was doing, I was walking after them. I waited by the men's washroom, staring at my phone, pretending to be occupied.

All I could think about was *why*? Why was I doing this? Why didn't I just get the fuck away and go live out the rest of my life? Why was I here? The gun burned against my skin, but I already knew I wasn't going to use it on her.

Then there was movement. I looked up to see her come out of the washroom, alone, and lean back against the wall. She shut her eyes and winced. Time seemed to stretch as we both stood in the dirty hallway. If she looked my way she would catch me staring at her.

Do it, I thought. *Look.*

But she didn't. She seemed like she was in pain. Now she was the accident victim, broken and bruised. Vulnerable.

It was almost enough to make me move toward her. I don't know what I'd say, if I'd even say anything. I just wondered if I could tell who she was by her looking at me, if her gaze would show me why all of this happened. Why I had been sent to kill her.

I barely noticed the two douchebags who barged out of the men's bathroom, bumping against the walls as they passed me, slurring and laughing. I could see they were about to collide with Alana, and before I knew what I was doing, I was there beside her. One guy's shoulder collided with hers and she let out a yelp of pain as she stumbled forward.

My instincts were quick and probably wrong.

I grabbed hold of her arm then quickly brought her up toward me, and from the moment she looked into my eyes, hers wide with shock and pain, I could tell who she was.

A wildcat.

I swallowed hard and immediately forgot about wanting to ram my fists through the two drunk boys' heads. She was staring at me so intently that I knew I could never fade into the background after this. I could never observe her from a distance again. I could never watch from the shadows. From now on, this all had to be out in the open.

"Thank you," she said to me in perfect English, her voice lightly accented. I guess it came with the territory of being a flight attendant.

"You're welcome," I said, immediately relaxing into my role. Without fail, this was the role I'd always fall back into. Dumb tourist jock, Derrin Calway.

However, I failed to relax my fingers. I slowly released them from her arm before I made her uncomfortable.

From the way her lips pouted slightly, I could have sworn she wanted my hands to stay where they were.

A long, heavy moment passed between us as we stared at each other. I tried to take her all in – her hair as it stuck in places to her damp forehead, the faint bruising still evident around her eyes, the stiff way she held her battered limbs, the soft swell of her cleavage – not knowing if I would get the chance again.

Then the door to the bathroom swung open and her tall

friend came out. "What a mess in there," the woman said
to Alana in Spanish. When she didn't get Alana's attention,
her eyes swung over to me.

"Who is this?" she asked, an edge of suspicion to her
voice. That actually made me feel relieved. Alana needed
protective friends.

"I don't know," Alana mumbled briefly in English. She
gave me a crooked smile. "Who are you?"

I tried on an easy grin but I wasn't sure if it was sitting
right. I wasn't used to smiling. "Derrin Calway," I told her,
extending my hand.

"Alana Bernal," she said, shaking mine. Her palm was
hot, her grip firm. Somehow it grounded me. "Thank you
for saving me, Mr. Calway. This bar is full of fucking idiots."

She didn't seem apologetic over her language at all. I
liked that.

I gave her a nod. "No problem. Bars are always full of
them." I eyed her friend. "*Tu nombre?*" I asked her, butch-
ering the language just enough.

She raised a strong brow. "You speak Spanish," she said
dryly. "How impressive. My name is Luz. Where are you
from, Derrin?"

"Calgary, Alberta," I answered. "It's in Canada."

"I know where it is," Luz said quickly. "The whole of
Puerto Vallarta is full of you Western Canadians."

I shrugged. "What can I say, it's a good place. Your
English is very good, by the way."

"We're both flight attendants," Alana said, leaning briefly
against her friend in an affectionate way. "We have to know
English to deal with drunken white boys."

"Especially those who get too close," Luz added, although this sounded more like a threat. From the way she was staring at me, I had no doubt it was.

Time to play it cool.

"Well, have a good night," I told them both with a quick nod and turned to head back to the bar. I'd only walked a few feet before Alana called out after me.

"Hey!"

My heart stilled. It had been a gamble.

I turned and looked at her inquisitively.

In the dim light it was hard to tell if she was blushing or not. She attempted to walk over to me, but Luz immediately helped her along. "I was wondering if I could buy you a drink."

I feared the smile on my face was actually genuine. "I'd love that. But I'll be buying you a drink. You're the one all bandaged up." I pretended to look around the bar. "What will you have and where are you sitting?"

Alana jerked her head in the direction of their table. "Beer would be great. Any kind. And don't forget Luz here."

"How could I?" I asked playfully before heading toward the bar.

As I walked away I heard Luz mutter something to Alana and Alana say, "But did you see his muscles?" in response.

Once at the bar, I put in an order for four Pacificos, knowing there was a chance that her friend at the table would want one too, and took a moment to compose myself. The new plan was working, but I still wasn't sure what the outcome was or why I was really doing it. A tired voice in my head told me to be careful, to bring them drinks, and at the end of the night walk away. Another voice wanted me to keep tabs on her and figure out her importance and how I could make it work to my advantage. Yet another voice told me to take her out back and do away with her like I was supposed to and collect on the rest of the money.

But I didn't want to listen to the voices for once. I wanted to run on instinct, and my instincts were telling me to take this slow and cautious, one step at a time. Eventually the purpose would become clear, like a diamond underneath.

When I brought the beers back, the three of them were looking up at me with wide smiles. Actually, Luz had more of a discerning sneer and the other girl's smile was strained and polite, but Alana's was big and wide. It was the kind of smile that made you stare longer than you should, the kind that made even the deadest men feel alive.

Thankfully I was too dead for even that.

"Here you are, ladies," I said, placing the beers on the table.

"Did you drug them?" Luz asked as she carefully slid the beer toward her.

"Not enough time for that," I told her as I pulled out a seat. "Besides, I know better than to tangle with Mexican girls."

"You got that right," Alana said. She raised her beer toward the middle of the table and said, "Here's to our new Canadian friend." She looked me in the eye, so direct and unnerving that I had to fight the urge to look away.

I clinked the neck of my bottle against theirs, making

sure to look all of them in the eye. "And here's to such friendly women in Puerto Vallarta."

And with that, the conversation came relatively easy to us. I found out her other friend was Dominga, a hotel maid, who didn't say much, but was a lot more welcoming than Luz was. When the questions turned to me and what I did and what I was doing here, I told them a bunch of half-truths. My whole life seemed to be built on half-truths.

"Well," I said between sips of my beer. "I used to be in the military."

"The Canadian military?" Luz asked.

"Yes. I was shipped off to Afghanistan. After that . . . I wasn't sure what I was going to do, so I became a personal trainer. Might as well do the one thing that I was good at."

Alana almost fluttered her eyelashes at that.

Luz folded her arms, not impressed. There was something commendable about her obvious dislike for me.

"And so what are you doing in Mexico?"

I shrugged as casually as possible. "I like it here. The people are friendly. The weather is perfect. The girls are nice." I flashed Alana a smile. "I wish I could stay longer."

"How long are you here for?" Alana asked.

"It depends if I have something to stay for." I was really laying it on thick now. "I was going to spend a few weeks here in Puerto Vallarta, I was thinking of maybe buying a condo here, a vacation home or something, so I wanted to really get to know the city. Maybe I'll be here a month if it suits me."

Alana gave me a half smile. "Well, this town may seem

like a dream come true to tourists, I'm sure, but it has its
bad side too."

I jerk my chin at her. "When you say bad side, does it
have something to do with what happened to you?" I hadn't
asked her earlier about her appearance; I wasn't really sure
what to say.

She pursed her lips, thinking it over. "Yes. I was in a car
accident."

"Oh no," I said, hoping my shock was coming across
as genuine. I at least knew my concern was. "What
happened?"

She paused. "It was a hit and run. I got hit, he ran."

"Shit."

"Yeah it was shit."

"Did they catch the guy?"

She nodded. "They found him." But then her lips
clamped together, signaling that the conversation was over.
Interesting how she didn't divulge any further. I wondered
if she just didn't want to get into it with a stranger – it
wouldn't be easy to talk about how the man who hit you
ended up shot in the head – or if she just didn't know.
Both were possible.

"When are you getting out of the hospital?"

Luz fastened her eyes on me. "How did you know she
was still in the hospital?"

Fuck.

I lifted one shoulder. "I just assumed. Her arm still has
the tape from where the IV goes in."

They all looked down at Alana's arm. Sure enough, over

her vein in the crook of her elbow, the clear sticker remained.

"Playing hooky?" I asked, turning the question on them.

She blushed then coquettishly bit her lip. "Promise not to tell anyone?"

I made the sign of the cross over my heart. "Hope to die."

Her brows furrowed for half a second before she eased back into her sex kitten grin. I wondered what that was about. She cleared her throat. "They said any day now. It's what they keep telling me."

"Well, I'm no doctor, but if you're well enough to be out at a bar accepting drinks from strange Canadians, then you're well enough to be out of the hospital."

"I agree," she said, raising her beer. "Let's all drink to that."

We all raised our beers and clinked again. I held eye contact with her the whole time, trying to read her while trying to tell her something. Mainly that I was a good guy. That I could be trusted.

Even though, at the heart of it all, those were both lies.

We sat there for another half hour until it became apparent that the mention of the hospital had taken the wind out of their sails. Dominga kept eyeing the clock on her phone and Luz monitored Alana's alcohol intake. All the while, Alana was trying to talk with me, asking me question after question. It was a good thing I came prepared and I knew my fake history as if it were my own. It was a lot easier that way. Some days I even lied to myself about what once was.

"Well, I think we should get Alana back to the hospital

before she gets in trouble," Luz said as she and Dominga got to their feet.

I rose too, hoping to help Alana out of her chair. "If anyone gives you any trouble, you report them to me," I told her with a wink.

"I will," she said, then gave a resigned sigh as Luz darted over to help, beating me to it. Then the two of them started arguing in Spanish, Alana saying she wanted to stay and talk to me, Luz telling her there were other boys when she's good and ready for them. For some reason, what Luz said rankled me, and I had no idea why. Jealousy was not my thing. Caring wasn't either. Couldn't have one without the other sometimes.

I walked with them as far as the door – walking them to their car seemed borderline stalkerish – but just as they were about to leave, Alana leaned into me and whispered in my ear, "So if someone does give me trouble, like a mean old nurse, how am I going to get a hold of you?"

This was unexpected. Alana was flirty and forward from what I'd seen so far, but I didn't think this would continue beyond tonight. I don't know what I really thought would happen after, but it wasn't her basically asking for my number.

Little warning flags started going off. They weren't as bold or urgent as the ones I'd gotten when dealing with her arranged assassination, but they were telling me my life would be a lot easier if I let Alana Bernal go and I went on with my sorry little life.

But I guess my sorry little life felt like it was missing something.

Stupidity, perhaps.

So I told Alana where I was staying and the room number. And when her friends helped her hobble away into the dark parking lot, she shot me a look over her shoulder that told me I was in for it.

If only she knew.

CHAPTER FOUR

Alana

I could not get that man out of my head. For once, instead of thinking about pain and injustice, I was thinking about a 6'2" man with tree trunk arms, caveman shoulders, and the most sculpted, masculine face I'd ever seen. His wide, strong jaw, straight nose, slicing cheekbones, and piercing blue eyes became my drug of choice to keep the aches at bay. Even his buzz-cut showed off a perfectly-shaped head.

But of course when I told Luz this, I was met with a scowl.

We were sitting in my apartment, having hot chocolate. I sprinkled a bit of cayenne pepper onto mine, liking the burn more and more these days. Making hot chocolate – or any beverage, really – was about the extent of what I could do around the apartment. Luz had to come over and help me clean since I couldn't move my body very well.

"Perfectly-shaped head," she repeated with a sound of disgust. "Will you listen to yourself?"

"Maybe he has a perfectly-shaped dick too," I teased her, though somehow I knew he did. Men like him had to.

"Alana, please get a hold of your hormones. Goodness, woman, you've been out of the hospital for three days now. You think you'd forget about it and get back to your life."

I folded my arms across my chest even though I winced as I did so. "Maybe my life isn't so fun anymore."

She tried to give me a sympathetic look but failed at it. That little bit of Luz hardness showed through her dark eyes.

"Look, it's just temporary. All of this. Every day you're getting better. The doctors told you so."

"Every day is another day away from my job. Luz, you knew that was my life. *Is* my life."

"Well, did you ever think that perhaps this accident was God's way of showing you what's important?"

I rolled my eyes. "Don't start with that God crap." Though it didn't seem like it, Luz was a pretty earnest church-goer. That's par for the course in Mexico but sometimes she comes across as preachy. And by preachy, I mean bossy, because that's the Luz way.

"It's not crap. Don't say that," she chided before taking a hearty sip of her drink. "Besides, I think I'm right. Why not take this time to reflect a little?"

I snorted. Like hell I'd want to reflect on anything except the massive, gorgeous white dude I'd met the other night. Derrin Calway.

I guessed Luz caught the dreamy look in my eyes because she said, "You still haven't called him, by the way. So if you're going to get all smitten kitten on me, you should at least do something about it instead of pining away here like some forties American housewife whose husband is off to war."

I gave her a look. "First I'm all hormonal, now I'm a forties housewife. Make up your mind, you're slipping a little."

But truthfully, she was right. After I saw him at the bar and he told me he was in room 1600 at the Puerto Vallarta Sands

Hotel, I had every intention of contacting him. But then I got back to the hospital, was caught as I was sneaking into the room, and got lectured by the night nurse Salma, and then again the next day by the day nurse, and finally was discharged by a very disapproving doctor (apparently news around the hospital traveled fast), and I kind of lost my nerve.

As much as I fantasied about Derrin and his thick forearms and strong hands, as much as I wanted someone like that to take my mind off of things, I was too scared to follow up on it. Normally I didn't have a problem with chasing a man, but then again, normally I didn't have to. But Derrin . . . I felt like he would have let me walk out that door and out of his life. That's usually how guys on vacation are. They don't bother pursuing anything beyond one night, and if one night doesn't even happen you're pretty much out of luck.

Besides, what would he really do with a cripple like myself? Throw me against the wall and fuck me crazy in my condition? No, I didn't think so. I didn't even know how I'd go down to see him, not without someone like Luz driving me, and I didn't see a chance in hell of that happening. Luz was always a bit suspicious of the men in my life and seemed especially suspicious of everyone since the accident. I couldn't really blame her. I needed to borrow some of that suspicion myself.

But maybe I didn't have to go to Derrin. Maybe he could come to me, at least halfway. I'd never know unless I picked up my phone and gave the hotel a call. Hell, there was even a chance that he'd already checked out and left. Or maybe there never *was* a Derrin Calway, and it was a decoy to throw me off the scent. Stranger things have happened.

Luz was staring at me with a perfectly raised brow and reading my mind again. "Look, either you call the gringo or you forget about it. If you're choosing to forget about it, then let's start now. How about we add some rum to the hot chocolate?"

Now she was speaking my language. But I wasn't choosing to forget.

I picked my cell phone off the table and waved it at her. "If I call him, if we make plans, can you help me get to him?"

Her eyes sought the ceiling for an exaggerated minute, but she managed a thin, stubborn smile. "Fine. As long as it doesn't interfere with work, I'll be your chaperone."

"Oh, you are so not being my chaperone," I warned her as I Googled the number for the hotel. "Let's just call you a chauffeur."

"Great."

I dialed the number and put the phone to my ear while I shot her an overly sweet smile. "You're a doll." She stuck her tongue out at me.

While the phone rang on the other end, my heartrate doubled. I had no idea how nervous I was until the front desk agent answered, and I fumbled over my words. Meanwhile, Luz was looking at me like I'd lost my damn mind.

The clerk paused over the name, and for a minute I thought maybe he had given me a fake name. But then he corrected himself and told me he'd ring Mr. Calway.

My chest tightened, all my functions pausing while I was on hold.

Then Derrin answered. "Hello?"

His voice was even raspier on the phone – he almost sounded dirty. I was focusing so much on that, that I didn't realize he was waiting for me to respond.

"Hello?" he said again, his voice harder this time, almost panicked, and that spurred my lips into flapping.

"Uh, *hola!*" I blurted out while I heard a sigh of relief come through the phone. Better relief than regret. "Derrin, it's Alana. We met at the bar the other night. I was the one—"

"All bandaged up," he filled in. "Yes, I remember. Glad you called. I was starting to think I'd never get a chance to tell you how beautiful you looked in a cast."

Wow. He was a lot smoother than I remembered.

"Well this cast is, what is the English word, *hindering*. Definitely hindering me. I could barely use the phone until today." A bit of a lie but I enjoyed provoking the damsel in distress reaction in men.

"Then I'm honored you chose to call me."

There was a pause and I thought he'd go on, but the line went silent instead. Okay, maybe this was just a tad awkward. Guess I was going to be the one doing all the talking. Actually, when I thought back to the other night at the bar, I did all the talking then, too. I thought maybe it was because I was drunk – I often rattled people's ears off – but maybe Derrin was the strong, silent type. I could definitely work with that.

"So, um, I was wondering," I started, realizing I didn't have any idea at all what to say next. I looked over at Luz for help. She picked up the mug and mimed drinking it.

"Uh," I continued, "I know you're not in town for long, but I thought we could grab a coffee somewhere. I bet you're sick of all the tourist places and I know some really good ones. You know, local flavor."

"As a matter of fact, I am sick of the tourist shit. But I don't want you to travel too far in your condition. Why don't I come to you?"

I eyed Luz again who was looking resigned, like she knew she was at my bidding no matter what. Personally, I wouldn't have minded bringing Derrin back here, but there was a small, instinctual part of me that insisted that I meet him in public. As much as I liked to have fun, I rarely met men at my house. There was something a bit foolish about that.

"We can meet halfway," I told him. "There's a really good café by Nuevo Vallarta. Do you know how to get there? The buses run there every half an hour or so."

When he told me yes, I gave him more extensive directions before Luz cleared her throat with a very well-placed, "Ahem."

I looked at her expectantly before remembering that it had to go around her schedule. Luckily she had tomorrow afternoon free and wasn't flying out until the evening, so as long as I was back at home by dinnertime, it would be fine.

After I hung up with Derrin, I said to her, "Jeez, I guess you might as well call me Cinderella."

"It's for the best," Luz said. "This will prevent you from sleeping with him. Though if you ask me, I have no idea how you're going to manage that in the near future with the way you look."

"Hey, I look just fine. Besides, my one hand and mouth work great."

She gave another disgusted snort, waving me away. "Okay now, that's enough." She pursed her lips. "I don't know if I trust you with this boy, Alana."

"Why? You think I'm going to break his heart?"

She frowned for a moment and a serious look came across her eyes. "No, I don't think so. I think he's going to break yours."

"That'll be the day," I told her. I'd never fallen in love before. I never did those big relationships with big feelings. My life was all get in and get out and have fun along the way. That's the only thing that was safe.

She shook her head slightly and tapped her blood red nails against the clay mug. "I've got a feeling about this one."

Seeing her so serious always made me pay more attention. Still, I tried to shrug it off.

"You say that about everyone who's not from Mexico. Racist," I joked.

She glared at me. "This one is different. He's . . ."

"Hot," I supplied, before she could fill me with paranoia. "Built as fuck. Nice. Mysterious."

"Yes," she said, leaning forward. "Mysterious. And sometimes that's not a good thing. Sometimes people are mysterious because they have something to hide."

"We only just met him. I think it's a bit too soon to be making these assumptions. Besides, I'm the one going after him here."

She seemed to consider that before polishing off the rest of her drink. As she delicately wiped at the chocolate above her lip, she shrugged.

"You're right. But just be careful, that's all I'm saying. I'm not going to stop worrying about you for a long time, you know that, right? Dominga and I . . . we're going to be your little watch dogs, whether you like it or not. Not until this," she waved her nails at my brokenness, "is just a memory. Until then, everyone is a suspect."

"Are you sure you weren't supposed to be a detective instead of a flight attendant?"

"When you're stuck thirty five thousand feet in the air with a bunch of idiots, you become really adept at reading people. You should try it sometime."

Even though Luz and I rarely flew together – airline crew was a lot more spread out than most people think – when we did, she was always the "bad cop" of the cabin while I was the good one. She'd be the one cutting people off from the liquor while I was giving free drinks to the well-behaved passengers.

Later as I was lying alone in bed, trying to ignore the aches and pains that were spreading through my bones and wanting to avoid taking any more pills, I thought about what she'd said. Maybe I did need to be more suspicious of everyone. My whole life seemed geared to make me that way, hard and jaded. Perhaps I needed to start thinking more like my brother.

My only fear about that, of course, was that if I started thinking like him, I might become like him. And there's nothing scarier than that.

I shivered at the thought and pulled the covers over me, despite the thick humid air that settled in my room, remembering the last time Javier had involved me in his business. I had picked up his wife Luisa's parents from the docks, them having come over on a private boat all the way from the Baja.

I took them into my apartment, which operated as a kind of safe house until Javier and Luisa came to get them. It was a nail-biting, paranoid two weeks, made even worse when I discovered the thing he wanted me to take out of a cooler and put in the freezer was actually a human head.

Yeah. A human head, not a fucking frozen thing of lettuce like I'd assumed. I wanted to take scalding hot showers for weeks after that.

Surprisingly, there was still a bit of a dull ache inside me. Not because of the accident, but because of Javier. Though we spoke on the phone the other day, briefly, he still hadn't come down to see me. I wondered if I told him that I was scared if he'd visit or at least say something comforting. But I put up a brave front with him, and I guess he did the same with me.

I was a young child, trying to sleep. It was impossible. On one side of me was Marguerite, who had this way of snoring like she was a purring cat. Some might find it cute, but when you're trying to get rest for the night, it was annoying as hell. On the other side of me was Violetta, who always curled up under my arms like a doll. Even though our mama was lovely, she was hardworking, especially with Father gone. Sometimes she just didn't have the time to give Violetta – who was the youngest – any attention. For whatever reason, that usually fell on me.

We had two beds in our tiny room. It was supposed to be me and Marguerite, the twins, on one, and Violetta and Beatriz on the other. But as Beatriz got older, she wanted her own space, so the three of us ended up sharing. Mama had her own room, of course, and Javier didn't really have a room. When he was younger, there used to be a cot pushed between our beds, but now Javier slept on the couch. Even as a child, I'm not sure that he really slept at all.

He didn't that night, and it saved our lives. All of our lives, except my mother's. But in my dreams, sometimes I was the one that died instead. I'm not even sure I'd call it a nightmare, because despite the dark and the terror and that horror, there was something about death that I welcomed. Every now and then, as I hid in the closet with my siblings and that door opened, the guns pointed at our heads, I didn't scream or cry as the *sicarios* gunned us down. I smiled. I wanted it. I wanted peace, that safety that comes with death. Once death takes you, nothing can hurt you ever again.

Death takes away your life. But it also takes away your fear.

When I woke up from the dream covered in sweat, I was disappointed to see the room was still dark. There was something so dreadful about waking from a nightmare in the middle of the night, with the adrenaline still coursing through your veins, only to see you have half a world of darkness, to go. Suffice it to say, I couldn't go back to sleep. Even though I sometimes wanted death in my dreams, I didn't when I was awake. When I was awake, I was governed by fear, through and through.

I carefully pulled my covers back up since they were usually kicked off as I thrashed in the throes of my dreams. I stared up at the ceiling, my body still sore and aching. Maybe that's why I was so attracted to Derrin. He looked like the sort of man who could protect me, who could take care of me. He was a soldier. Those were the type who never showed fear, who never ran from anything. For the most part they were honest and noble and brave.

I stayed awake like that for a while longer, accepting the fact that I wouldn't fall back asleep, thinking of him. I thought about him to the point where I was sure I was obsessing which wasn't new for me – but I let myself do it without judgment. It was a distraction and a most welcome one.

At some point I fell back asleep.

CHAPTER FIVE

Alana

"That's what you're wearing?" Luz asked as I opened the front door to her.

I looked down at myself. I was wearing cut-off jean shorts and a faded yellow tee with a vintage Coca Cola slogan on it. "What's wrong with it?"

"Nothing," she said adamantly. "It's just that I've never seen you so dressed down and casual before."

"Yes you have."

"But not for a date."

She was right about that. "This isn't a date."

She rolled her eyes. "Goodness, just own up to it. It's a date, sweetheart. Even if it's coffee, in the middle of the day, with no sex, it's a date."

"Says you on the no sex thing."

"Are you really going to fuck him the way you are? At a café?" She gave me a look then shook her head and her lip curled in disgust. "You know what, don't answer that. You've already told me your options."

I grinned at her, quickly setting the alarm, and locked the apartment behind me.

It was a Monday and traffic was crazy congested as usual. I started to fret a bit, wondering if I was going to be late, and how long he would hang around for, or if he thought I was standing him up. The skin beneath my cast began to itch like crazy, and I was flipping open the glove compartment to see if Luz had a pen or something.

"Will you calm down, you crazy girl?" she said, eyeing me out of the corner of her eye while laying on the horn in protest of whatever driver did something stupid up ahead.

"You calm down," I retorted. "My arm is so itchy and you're taking forever."

"I'm taking forever," she repeated, waving at the sea of cars on the highway and at the thick dust that choked the side of the road.

In the distance, the jungle green mountains rose up from the dryness, offering respite. The area around the Bay of Banderas was always an interesting mix of the wild and the urban, the wet and the dry.

"Do you want me to drive over the traffic? Because I totally would, you know, if I had a bigger car."

I sighed, blowing a strand of hair out of my face as the car inched along.

Finally when we reached Nuevo Vallarta, we were already fifteen minutes late. All my sighing and foot tapping (the good foot, of course) couldn't change that fact. I could only hope Derrin would understand.

We parked right outside of the Dos Hombres Café, and Luz helped me out of the car as quickly as she could. From the street, I couldn't really see inside, but it looked like the place was packed as always. It had simple décor, a ton of indoor palm plants, and the best breakfast burritos, banana flan, and spicy mochas that one could hope for.

It seemed we had caught the workweek lunch rush, so it took us awhile to actually get into the café and look around. If I didn't have to lean on Luz – crutches were far more awkward to use than I had thought, and I rarely used them – it would have been easy to do a quick sweep of the place.

But even so, he wasn't there.

"Maybe he's in the washroom," Luz suggested hopefully.

Another heavy exhale escaped my lips. We were too late. Derrin was gone. Although there was a chance that he'd never been here to begin with.

"There you two ladies be," a rough male voice said from behind us, speaking in broken Spanish.

We craned our necks to see Derrin coming toward us holding three hot drinks in his large, capable hands. He was wearing knee-length cargo shorts and a grey wife-beater that showed off every single tanned muscle and plane on his body. I had to make sure my mouth wasn't gaping open.

"Sorry we're late," Luz said, switching to English. "The traffic was really bad."

I found my voice. "Yeah. Sorry. I thought we'd missed you."

He gave me a half-grin, something that made his face change from hard and masculine to soft and boyish. I liked both parts of him.

"Like I would leave so easily. I'm used to everything running on Mexican time by now. *Mañana* and all that."

"Such the typical tourist thing to say," I teased him.

"We only say it because it's true," he said, and handed me

my drink. "And you know it. I got you just a plain coffee, by the way. I didn't know if you were lactose intolerant or on a diet or what."

I thanked him, and Luz muttered something along those lines as she took her coffee.

Derrin looked around the café. "It seems there is nowhere to sit."

"There's a park around the corner," I said, but even then I wasn't too keen on the idea of having our date on a park bench surrounded by pigeons. Derrin didn't seem as if he liked it either. His smile sort of froze.

"Oh, look," Luz said, pointing to the corner. "Those people are leaving."

"But there are only two seats," he said.

Luz gave him a look. "Nice try, but you know I'm not staying with you. I agreed to be a chauffeur, not a chaperone." She eyed me, a hint of warning in them. "I'll be back here in three hours. Any change of plans – and I really hope there aren't any – and you text me, okay?"

I nodded. She squeezed my shoulder affectionately, raised her coffee at Derrin as her way of saying goodbye, and then she was gone.

"Come on," he said, stepping closer to me. "Let's get you over there before someone else takes the table." He put his arm around my waist so I put mine around his shoulder. His skin was so taut and so warm that it was hard to hide the shiver that went through me.

"Not a fan of crutches?" he asked as we hobbled between the tables.

I tried to ignore how close his mouth was to my face, and

the way his voice shot right through me and right between my legs.

"No. Have you ever had to use them before?"

He nodded. "Yes. Broke my leg in Afghanistan. It's why I was sent home. Tried to use them for about a day until I threw them out the hospital window. It was better to hop around on one foot than to knock over everything you came in contact with."

I wanted to take that moment to ask him more about the war – something I was very curious about, but I knew it wasn't coffee shop kind of talk.

He eased me down into the seat. I was amazed I hadn't spilled half of my coffee during the maneuver. I was frustrated at being so helpless and awkward these days, but I guess it wasn't so bad when you had a man like him helping you.

"So," he said, when he adjusted himself in his seat. He leaned forward on his elbows, his eyes staring warmly at me.

"So," I said right back, my chest fluttering with anxiety. "Tell me about the war."

Ah, fuck. So much for "don't mention the war." *Jesus, Alana, you're a mess*, I scolded myself.

To Derrin's credit, although his brow furrowed, making his eyes seem intense, he didn't seem offended. "All right," he said. "What do you want to know?"

"Well, how about how you broke your leg? Trading hospital stories might be fun." But I regretted it the moment I said it. How could what I went through compare to what he had? A hit and run, as traumatic, scary, and damaging as it was, was nothing compared to honest to god war.

"It was silly, really. We were going down one of the roads – which are nothing more than faded tire tracks in the dirt – when a bomb went off." I gasped and he went on, his voice monotonous. "It caught the front of our transport and flipped us. The driver died – so did another one of us. I broke my leg from the flip. We all broke something, everyone that survived."

I felt like a hand had squeezed my heart. Just the mention of a bomb – the very thing that killed my sister – was a sinister reminder of Violetta's violent death.

"How could you say that was silly?" I whispered.

He exhaled sharply. "Because we should have known better. We should have seen it coming from a mile away. The road hadn't been checked, and we weren't using due diligence."

"Why not?"

"Because we were young kids. Because we'd seen so much, every day, that after a while you become desensitized. You stop caring. And you think you're invincible. Until it happens to you."

"How old *are* you?"

"Twenty-nine," he said. "This was a long time ago. I use due diligence now."

"But you're no longer in the army."

He shook his head. "No. I'm not. But it doesn't mean life isn't waiting out there to catch you unaware."

I took a long sip of my coffee while I mulled that over. He was sounding a lot like Luz. Perhaps they had more in common than I thought.

"So how old are you?" he asked, seeming to want to change the subject. I couldn't blame him. I was sorry I had brought it up to begin with.

"Twenty-four," I told him. "Going on forty."

He smiled but it didn't reach his eyes. "What makes you say that?"

I shrugged. He may have brought up his battles, but I sure as hell wasn't going to bring up mine. The fastest way to scare a guy off is to tell him your brother is the leader of one of the most powerful drug cartels, and aside from your twin sister, the rest of your family was murdered in related incidents. Violent, messy, disgusting incidents.

"I've always felt older, that's all."

"No boyfriend? No husband?"

I tilted my head and gave him a wry look. "Do you think I'd be out here with you if I had either of those?"

"I don't know," he said, leaning back in his chair. His chest muscles moved smoothly under his tank. "Maybe you're in one of those open relationships. You never know with you Mexicans," he added jokingly.

"Hey," I warned him. "If I wasn't so crippled, I'd reach over and smack you right now."

"Good thing you're a cripple then. You seem to be part wildcat."

I made a clawing motion with my good hand. "You have no idea."

That got a smirk out of him so I turned the tables.

"All right, hotshot," I said to him. "What about you? Girlfriend? Wife?"

His lips twisted sourly, and for a heart-stopping moment I was afraid he actually did have one or the other. But he said, "No, I don't."

Yet there was more to it. I quickly glanced at his hand and

didn't see a ring or even the tan line of one. I knew already he didn't wear a wedding ring – it was usually one of the first things I noticed about a man – but I had to double check.

He caught me looking but still didn't say anything.

"Ex-wife?" I asked.

He hesitated, and by doing so was already telling the truth. I think he knew this because he looked down at the coffee in his hand and exhaled.

After a moment's pause – which felt like eternity – he said, "Yes. I was married once."

And it was quite apparent he didn't want to talk about it. But like the bumbling, stubborn fool that I was, I pried further. "Are you divorced?"

There was a barely visible shake to his head. "No. She died."

And once again, I was an idiot. This poor fucking man.

"Shit," I swore. "I'm so sorry. How did she die?"

At that he looked up and stared me dead in the eye. "Car accident," he said, completely emotionless. Somehow, maybe because the way he was staring at me was almost a challenge, like he was calling me out on lying about something, I knew it wasn't the truth. But I guess it didn't really matter. When someone was dead, they were dead.

"I'm sorry," I said, and suddenly it felt like all I'd done so far was apologize. It served me right for bringing up such horrid topics.

"It's not your fault," he said. "It was a long time ago. I was a different person then."

But have you moved on? From the darkness in his eyes, it was hard to tell if he had.

"I'm also sorry I'm not so good on dates," I told him. "Or talking in general. And that *is* my fault."

He managed a smile. "You're direct. I like that about you."

"What else do you like about me?"

"You look very pretty in a cast."

I felt my cheeks flush. "What else?"

"You have the sexiest eyes and lips I've ever seen."

My cheeks grew even hotter. I guess this meant he was into me after all. It was kind of hard to tell with him so far.

I decided to take the plunge. This emotionally wounded soldier boy was strumming all the right chords with me. I leaned forward slightly and looked at him through fluttering lashes.

"After coffee, did you want to come back to my place? Luz could drive the both of us."

No, I couldn't be more forward than that.

He seemed caught off guard. He blinked at me, his body stiffening, and I was so certain he was going to take me up on it. Then his brow softened and he said, "Sorry, I can't."

So, big fat no. Score one for rejection.

"Not into crippled chicks?" I joked, but I knew he could tell I was smarting.

"It's not like that," he assured me quickly. "I'd love to. But I have an appointment with a realtor at four-thirty to see an apartment. You know, I told you the other day I was looking to buy something here."

That was true.

"How about we take a rain check?" he asked. "Better than that, maybe you can come down to the resort I'm at. I'll ride out in a cab to get you. Your friend doesn't even have to be bothered."

Okay, this was soothing the embarrassment a bit. "Okay, when?"

"Tomorrow evening," he said. "I'll take you out for dinner."

"Aren't you staying at an all-inclusive place?" Those hotel restaurants weren't exactly known for their good cuisine.

"Yes, but there's a great little fish restaurant tucked away a few streets over. Looks fancy. It should impress you."

"Little do you know that I'm easily impressed."

"Then that's another thing I like about you."

It wasn't long until our time was up, three hours having flown by in flirty giggles and stories and glances, and Luz was honking her horn from outside the restaurant. I looked over at her and waved, even though I knew she couldn't see in properly.

"Is she always so impatient?" he asked as he got to his feet and came around to my side.

"Yup," I said. He held an arm out for me, his muscles strained, the veins in his thick forearm bulging as I grabbed hold of him. He lifted me to my feet like that, as if I weighed less than air. With ease, he helped me across the café and outside to the car, and I relished every second of his warm skin against mine, his bracing, ocean-like smell. For those few moments, I felt completely protected.

He helped me into the passenger seat then shut the door. I quickly rolled down the window.

"So tomorrow?"

"I'll give you a call in the morning and let you know the time."

I grinned up at him. "See you then."

He nodded and raised his hand.

Luz stepped on the gas and we burned rubber away from the sidewalk.

"Where's the fire?" I asked, glaring at her and trying to put my seatbelt on.

"In your pants, I'm guessing," she said.

"Ha-ha, very mature."

"So I guess you have another date tomorrow?"

"Yes, but don't worry, you don't have to be involved. He's coming in a cab to get me. We're going out for dinner."

"I'm surprised you didn't try to eat him already," she commented dryly as we cruised down the street toward the highway exit.

I bared my teeth at her playfully. "That will come later."

We were silent for a while as she drove, the traffic momentarily lighter, an American pop star singing to some bouncy beat on the radio.

Eventually Luz said, "So how was he?"

"Nice," I told her.

"That's it? Just nice?"

I shrugged, staring out the window while secret butterflies danced in my chest.

"That can't be it. What did you guys talk about? Tell me something about him."

"He grew up in Winnipeg, Manitoba, and was going to go into the NHL for hockey. Then he decided to join the army instead."

"And . . .?"

"Nothing else," I told her, not wanting to divulge the personal stuff. "We talked about this and that."

"And did you mention your family?"

"Of course I didn't. I talked about the airlines. That's always a safe topic. People always want to know about crazy passengers, or the time you were hit by lightning or the scariest landings."

"And did he want to know?"

"Probably not but I told him anyway."

She laughed, and her eyes darted to the rearview mirror. She frowned. "And do you trust him?"

"Do I trust him?" I repeated. "What does that mean? I barely know him."

"I know." Her eyes were still focused on something behind us. I looked in the side mirrors but couldn't see anything unusual except for cars.

"What do you keep looking at?"

"I don't want to alarm you," she said in a way that made me immediately alarmed, "but I think there is someone following us."

Now I managed to twist in my seat and get a good look behind us. It was hard because the back window was so dusty.

"What is it? What car?"

"There's a white truck two cars behind us. It's been two cars behind us before we even got on the highway."

Now I could see it, the top of the truck poking up above the traffic, but it was too far away for me to get an idea of who was driving it.

"Do you think it's Derrin?" I asked, feeling this incredible sense of dread creep up on me.

"I don't know."

"What are we going to do?"

"Take the next exit," she said determinedly. "If someone is following us, we don't want to lead them straight to your apartment."

Jesus. So much for thinking all my paranoia was put past me.

Luz put her signal on for the next exit, one that led to an outdoor market permanently set up in a parking lot. We both held our breath as we exited the highway, and soon after the truck followed.

Shit. Shit. Shit.

We exchanged a nervous glance.

"It's going to be fine," she told me, though she didn't look like she believed it. For once I found myself wishing I had a gun. I'd always been so against owning a gun, telling myself the minute I had one was the minute I became my brother, but considering everything, it made a lot of sense. Too much sense. Maybe Derrin knew something about them and could help me out. He was a Canadian, but he had been in the army, so he at least knew how to handle one.

Luz kept driving past the market stalls, and finally pulled into a parking spot right beside a bunch of other people. Safety in numbers and all that.

We waited, still as ice and with bated breath as the truck slowly crept past us. There was some older man driving – Mexican – with a thick mustache but no real discernable features. He didn't even look our way and kept driving until he parked further down.

I let out the largest puff of air and nearly laughed from relief. "Luz, you are crazy."

"You thought he was following us too!"

"Only because you told me. Besides, he was following us but not in the way you thought." I shook my head and sank further into the seat, my heartbeat slowing. "I think I've had enough excitement for one day."

"Agreed," Luz said. She started the car and we drove back onto the highway. We never saw the white truck again.

CHAPTER SIX

Derek

H er name was Carmen. She had been the love of my life.

When I first came to Mexico, all those years ago, I wasn't sure what I was looking for. I had grown disillusioned with the American government, destroyed by the war. My leg still hurt from the explosion in Afghanistan, and I hurt somewhere deep inside. It was so needless, so senseless. I had lost too much, we all had, over something that was never meant for our benefit, just to pad the pockets of those in the country that mattered most. I'd seen villages burned, young children dead and torn up on the streets, parents wailing, grandparents dying. All for nothing, not really.

The day the Humvee blew up was the day that everything changed. I guess that's the sort of day that *should* change a person. I was one of the lucky ones – one of my buddies lost both of his legs, another had half his body burned to a gruesome crisp. But I would never consider myself lucky because I was burdened with survivor's guilt. More than that, I was burdened with guilt, pure and simple.

When I returned home to Minnesota and was finally healed, I said goodbye to an ice hockey career – or at least the promise of one – and I said goodbye to friends and family. Both of those were easy. My father, a cruel, terrible man, had died while I was overseas. My mother, weak and helpless, couldn't seem to exist without his cruelty. She barely noticed I was gone.

As for my friends, they'd all pulled away once they got to know the new me. I barely spoke. I stopped drinking with them, going out, finding chicks, playing hockey. It was all over. I worked out and hated every single minute I had to be a veteran, a survivor, a pawn.

One day something in me snapped. I'm not sure what it was, maybe someone cut me off driving or perhaps I saw an advertisement for Mexico somewhere. But the next morning my bags were packed. I got in my car and drove for the border.

It took days to get there, and once I crossed over through Texas, time seemed to stop. Though I would never completely fade into the background, there was anonymity here that seemed to shake loose what little soul I had left. I felt free from everything – who I was, where I came from, the baggage I carried.

For a year I bounced around from place to place. I started with the resort towns on the Caribbean side before heading to the ones on the Pacific side. Veracruz, Cancún, Tulum, Mazatlán, Puerto Vallarta, Acapulco. When I got tired of the tourists, I moved inland and stayed in different cities, then towns, then villages. Each place had something special about it, and in each place I met people who seemed to think I was of some use to them.

It wasn't until I started running out of money that I found

myself reaching for these people. It was also then when I met Carmen.

I was in a town just south of Manzanillo. It was a small resort town, a bit down at the heels but popular with Mexican tourists, which suited me just fine. I'd met a man once called Carlos, and of all the people I'd met, he not only was the most genuine but also the most ambitious. Though cordial and generous, he was also a realist who made things happen. He had connections – none of which he held lightly – and success in his sights.

When I first met him I was sitting in a bar in a rustic but authentic establishment, sipping tequila, which the bartender gave me on the house for no real reason, and reading a book. Some John Grisham thriller, something to pass the time. I read a lot that first year in Mexico.

Carlos was there with two buddies of his, conducting business in the corner. At least I assumed it was business because when I would look over there, their faces weren't laughing and no one except Carlos was touching their drinks.

Suddenly there was a yelp and a fight broke out. Before I knew what I was doing, I was in the middle of it, holding back a man who sneered like a dog and seemed hell-bent on ripping Carlos's face off with his own veneers.

I don't know why I got involved – instinct, I guess. But after the two gentlemen were escorted out of the bar, Carlos bought me a drink. He wanted to know where I was from and what I was doing there. He wanted to know where I had learned to move like that, if I knew how to handle a gun, if I knew how to fight.

I didn't tell him much beyond the fact that I had been in the American military. He seemed happy with that. He said there was a lot of work here for someone like me, and then he gave me his card, patted me on the back, and left.

I kept in touch with him via email after that, just a few messages here and there. Advice. Where I should go next. Every time he told me I should look him up if I was in the area. And sometimes his area moved around, too.

One day, I was out of money and in the same place that he was.

We met up at a bar, and a casual deal was made. I'd accompany him on a few transactions, sort of like a bodyguard. It was easy work and he paid me well. He trusted me and I trusted him.

But soon I did more than just stand around and give people the stink-eye. I started doing him favors. Nothing terrible, but I knew Carlos was a drug lord and whatever package I was delivering, dropping off, handing over to numerous nondescript people either contained drugs, weapons, money, instructions, or a combination of the four.

And still I did my job.

And when I discovered Carlos's sister was moving back to town, and I first laid eyes on Carmen Hernandez, I realized I had more than this job keeping me in Mexico.

I fell in love and fell in love hard. I don't know if I ever picked myself off the ground.

We married. We made plans. We talked babies.

We had a blissful year together.

And then she was dead.

And I lost the last parts of me that were human.

I think it's too late for me to get them back.

Alana Bernal was doing something to me and I wasn't sure if I liked it. Actually, if I was being honest with myself, I was loving it, but that reaction in itself spurred on one of the opposite nature. I wasn't used to being excited, to being intrigued, to feeling remotely good. I was used to the coldness inside of me, to the life of monotony and that growing numbness that reached into everything I did.

Change was frightening. Change made you weak. And I didn't want any part of it.

But I wanted part of her. That was a problem.

Of course, when I met her for coffee yesterday, I had to act like I hadn't been following her for days. It wasn't so much that I was interested in what she was doing with her time the moment she was discharged from the hospital – because let's face it, I was – but that I wanted to make sure I hadn't been replaced.

Thankfully, from following her and watching her apartment I came to the same conclusion that I had while watching the hospital. There was no one else still, only me. It was wishful thinking that whoever ordered her assassination had just forgotten about her. They hadn't. Not for the price on her head. They were just biding their time. But there was no one else on the job, not that I could see.

I told myself that's why I was hanging around, that I was watching out for her. And I was. I was curious, and after talking to her over coffee, I was even more confused as to what she could have done in her life to warrant such a thing. Such death. Such money.

As a result, I was more or less honest while answering her questions, hoping that if I opened up a bit she would do the same for me. So far though, that hadn't seemed to be the case.

When she invited me back to her place afterward, my first thought was to obviously say yes, and while my mind was trying to figure out her mystery, my body was responding to her gorgeous face and slim limbs like any hot-blooded male would. Plus there was the chance at some answers, as well as sex, if I got a chance to look at her surroundings.

But I couldn't do it. My instincts were telling me to wait until I was in control of the situation. At her place, there were too many variables. In my hotel room, we were safe.

My plan was pretty simple. I didn't need to impress her, so it seemed, but a little wining and dining wouldn't hurt. The emphasis would be on the wining. I know it's pretty backwoods to get information out of someone by getting them drunk – I've done a hell of a lot worse to get what I needed – but it would still be effective.

And, because of the company, somewhat fun.

I couldn't remember the last time fun had ever entered the picture.

I called Alana in the morning, telling her our reservation at Coconut Joe's was at seven and that the cab and I would come get her at six. I thought about using the new rental car I had just picked up but thought better of it. I'd already driven past her place too many times in it.

Even the sound of her voice over the line – how buoyant

it was, despite all the shit and pain she still had to be going through – did something peculiar to me. I tried not to dwell on it but it was there, lodged in my chest and growing. I wondered if she was becoming more than a curiosity to me – a mystery to be solved. I wondered if she was someone I was actually starting to care for.

Was it possible to care for someone you didn't know?

God, I hoped not.

The hotel called the cab and made sure the driver agreed on the price and the return trip before we started out. Cabbies are known for ripping you off, and Alana didn't live near the downtown area – and soon I was knocking at the door of her first floor apartment.

That was one thing I didn't like about her living situation. Though the apartment building was fairly new, Mission-style with white paint and a red-tiled roof, it was on the ground floor, opening to a small gravel yard that was accessed through a wrought-iron gate. There were bars on her windows, which was the norm here, but that didn't mean it was hard to get inside. All the apartments also seemed to back into an inner courtyard, probably with a pool, which meant there might be another door and easy access point into her place. It never slipped my mind that while I had been watching the front, someone could have been slipping through the back.

It was taking her a while to get to the door, so I tried to look in through her barred windows to get an idea up close without seeming too suspicious about it. But when the door flung open, I was caught somewhat red-handed.

"*Hola*," she said, leaning against the doorframe. "Wasn't sure if I was home?"

She looked absolutely stunning in a white halter-neck dress that showed off her perfect breasts, thin waist, and full thighs. I barely even noticed her leg in its cast.

"Just noticing your bars on the windows," I said evenly. I frowned. "Is this a bad neighborhood?"

She smiled at me like I was a little boy. "It's not the best but it's not the worst. Most places worth anything have bars. Mexico has more crime than you would think."

I nodded, not letting on what I knew. "Well then, it's good you're well-protected."

"Yup," she said, placing her clutch purse under one arm and reaching for something against the wall. I heard the electronic beep of buttons being pressed. "I'm all alarmed here. Just in case."

I looked over her shoulder to the back of the apartment, but it looked as if there was no entry from the back. That gave me a bit of peace.

I took her arm and most of her weight, and helped her out of her small yard and to the waiting cab. She smelled like flowers and hot sunshine, and I was tempted to kiss her bare shoulders to see if they tasted like the tropics. As usual, though, I brushed the urges away and kept myself in control.

Once in the back of the cab, she was sitting with her thigh flush against mine. I was somewhat dressed up – dark jeans, white and blue pinstriped dress shirt – and yet I could feel her heat through my clothing. That and her smell, and the way her hair fell across her face, highlighting the coy glimpses of her eyes and smile, was driving me borderline insane. Though we made small chat throughout the ride, my mind was elsewhere, concentrating on keeping that well-earned control I had. I had to focus on the task at hand, which, of course, was her. But not in that way. I needed in deep, for her own safety and my own sanity.

It took a long time to finally get to the restaurant, located in the old town of Puerto Vallarta, despite the driver cutting everyone off along the way. You either drove aggressively around here or you didn't drive at all.

"Thank you," she said to me as I took her arm and helped her out of the cab. When she straightened up, she looked at the place and made an impressed face. "Wow. You know, I've never been here before and I've lived in PV for a long time."

"First time for everything, then."

I picked the place because it looked a bit different from the tourist traps in the downtown area. There wasn't much to the outside except for a tall stone fence topped with green, strangling vines, and flowers that bloomed like white and magenta cotton balls. But what was on the other side of the cast-iron gate was a different story.

I helped her over to the fence and a waiter opened the gate, giving us a hearty welcome to Coconut Joe's. I gave him the reservation name and he led us around tables with ivory-lace tablecloths, past a clear blue pool with koi fish and a waterfall, under dramatic palm fronds, all the way to a table in the back corner with a candle on it. The place wasn't anything too outrageous or stuffy; it was just classy enough.

"Again, wow," Alana said as I helped her into her seat. I was starting to like being her nurse. She looked around, her cheeks glowing beautifully in the candlelight. "This is something."

"Something good?" I asked as the server poured us bottled water.

"More than good," she said. "The guys I date never bring me places like this."

Something pinched in my chest. "Oh? They take you to McDonald's?"

She gave me a look. "Most of the men I dated were pilots. They would take me somewhere really snobby and expensive to try and seem better than they were." She took a polite sip of her water and straightened her napkin on her lap. Every day, her pain seemed to be easing, her movements becoming more fluid. "Then the next night they would take some other stupid flight attendant to the same place."

As much as I felt an unjustified hit of jealousy, she was giving me some information, something I could work with.

"So I guess there's a lot of drama in the workplace, huh?" I said casually, eyeing the waiter who was approaching us with menus in hand. In the background "Morena de Mi Corazón" started to play from the speakers. "Spurned lovers and revenge in the air."

She laughed. "No, not really. It was my fault. Rookie mistake to date a pilot, even though I did more than a few times." She looked away, embarrassed. "Most guys I date are a mistake, but no one seems to get hurt."

So that probably ruled out the whole spurned lover angle. Not that I thought an ex-lover could or would attempt to have her taken out for that amount of money. Love made people do crazy fucking things, but that would have been a first in my books. Besides, if she did have an obsessed ex-boyfriend I was sure I'd find out about him sooner or later.

The waiter came by and told us the specials. I ordered for the both of us – seared Ahi – because I'd never done that before, not even with Carmen, and made sure he kept the bottles of wine coming.

She was about three glasses of wine in, giggly and eating her fish with gusto when I started pressing her.

"So do you have any siblings?"

The smile seemed to vanish right off her face. There. I had something there. No matter what her answer was, I'd hit a nail.

"I have a twin sister and a brother," she answered simply.

"Oh? And where do they live? What do they do?"

She relaxed her jaw a bit and took a bite of her rice. "My sister, Marguerite, lives in New York. Goes to film school."

Hmmm. That placed her out of range and a student at that.

"And your brother?"

"He lives around here."

"In Puerto Vallarta?"

She shot me a wary look. "Around here. But he's an asshole and I'd rather not talk about him."

I raised my brow. "An asshole? What makes you say that?"

"I just do," she said stubbornly. Then she sighed. "He just is. Every family has a black sheep, right? Well that's him."

"What's his name?"

She bit her lip and said, "Juan."

I didn't know her well enough to tell if she was lying or not. But I'm not sure why she would lie about her own brother.

I pressed it further. "What does he do?"

"He's in importing and exporting. Trade with America. That sort of thing."

Well, we all knew what that meant down here. Running drugs, like everyone else. Still, that gave me something to go on. Of course the name Juan didn't help me much.

"What's his last name?" I asked, knowing that sometimes the men in Mexico took their mother's maiden names.

"Bardem," she said without hesitation. "Why all the questions?"

I shrugged and leaned back in my seat. "Just want to know more about you."

Her brows knitted together as she eyed me suspiciously. "Maybe so, but you're asking with this look on your face like you're all David Caruso."

"David Caruso?"

"*CSI Miami*. It's still my favorite. I don't care for the other ones."

"Well, I'm sorry to disappoint you, but I don't have the hair to be David Caruso, nor do I have the sunglasses and quippy one-liners."

She took a sip of her wine but couldn't hide her smile. Good, she was back to trusting me again. I wanted to ask her about her parents, but I thought that would be pushing my luck. Whether she was close with them or not, they were either dead or out of the picture. They had never come to see her in the hospital, and the truth about her brother and sister explained why they hadn't either.

What the hell have you done, Alana? I asked in my head as I stared at her across the table, the light illuminating her in an almost angelic way. *Why would anyone pay me two hundred thousand dollars to have you killed?*

And how the hell would I ever know the answers to those questions without incriminating myself?

To help her relax a little more, I turned our conversation to TV shows since David Caruso had proved to be such a good segue. There was nothing that got the passion flaring in this country like *Telemundo* and poorly translated American dramas.

By the time we had finished two bottles of wine, it was getting late and I had no idea where the evening was going to take us. I had gotten her drunk – a little too drunk – and she was looking wistfully at the area by the pool where couples had started slow-dancing to sad mariachi music.

"Care to dance?" I asked her.

She shot me a sloppy smile. "Yeah right. The way that I am?"

I got out of my chair and held out my hand. "We can make it work, I promise."

She didn't look convinced but let me get her out of the seat anyway. She was extra wobbly on her feet now, particularly since she really only had one foot to stand on, but somehow I managed to help her hobble over to the edge of the dance floor.

We weren't quite in there with the crowd of couples – I had visions of us falling into the pool – but we were close enough to feel like a part of it.

"Here," I told her, peering down into her eyes. "Put your arms around my neck and hold on."

She did as I asked, an impish smile on her lips. Her arms around me felt impossibly good.

"What do I do with my feet?"

"Step on my foot with your good one and keep it there. Wrap your other calf around mine."

"Are you sure about this?"

"Trust me," I implored, and her hold around my neck tightened as she placed her sandaled foot on top of my boot and then hooked her lower leg that had the cast around my other calf.

"I'm not breaking you?"

"Are you kidding? You weigh a hundred pounds soaking wet."

"My thighs and ass weigh more than that," she pointed out.

Taking the opportunity, I slid one of my hands down to the small of her back, my fingers just brushing against the top of her curves. "I can't be the judge of that yet."

She grinned up at me, her cheeks flushing. "Yet, you say."

I returned the smile. "The night is young."

She pressed herself into me. *The night is also hard*, I thought to myself. There was no point hiding it though. I couldn't imagine any straight man who wouldn't get an erection with this woman pressed against them.

Focus, Derek, I told myself.

But maybe it was the muggy night air, or the way we moved together to the slow waltz of a broken-hearted band, or the way she looked at me and the way she felt, so soft and so close, that made me lose focus. Just this once, I wanted to be able to feel something without thinking it through. Just this once, I wanted to feel something more than ice inside me.

Alana was heating me up, one beautiful smile at a time.

We danced for three songs until she rested her forehead against my chest and seemed to doze off for a minute.

"Okay," I whispered into her ear. "Time for bed. Let's go."

I thought that would get a reaction out of her but she pulled away and nodded, her eyes still shut. I couldn't help but grin at her, glad I could do so without her noticing.

I paid for dinner and got us in a cab. It didn't feel right sending her off to her own place. She was drunk and vulnerable, and I wanted her in my sight for the night.

The cab dropped us off at the hotel, and I helped her up to my room.

"You don't mind staying the night?" I asked her as we paused outside my door.

She giggled to herself but didn't say anything.

Once inside, I left her on the couch and went into the bedroom. I had cleaned it up earlier, knowing there was a strong chance I'd bring her back here after dinner. All my guns and weaponry were tucked away, and it looked like the hotel room of your average tourist, albeit one on an extended vacation. In fact, if anything I should have had more stuff than just a duffel bag. I was so used to traveling light.

Once I pulled back the covers for her, I got one of my t-shirts out of a drawer, one I worked out in but was freshly washed, and laid it on the bed. Then I went back into the room where she was dozing and scooped her up in my arms, carrying her to the bed. I gently placed her down on it then held her up while I placed the shirt in her hand.

"Put this on," I told her softly. "I promise not to look."

She looked at me through glassy eyes. "You do it. I'm too tired."

"All right," I said, swallowing hard, and reached behind her neck to untie the straps of her dress.

She watched me closely as I did so, her gaze daring me to meet it. So I did. The straps came loose and the front of her top floated down like tissue paper, exposing her breasts.

Fuck. They were so fucking perfect. Beautifully round with dark rose nipples that tightened in the air. Suddenly all I wanted to do was run my tongue under their soft curve then take the nipple in my mouth and suck until she moaned.

My erection strained against my jeans and my breathing deepened. All the while, Alana kept staring at me, almost asking for it. Her eyes were heavy-lidded, her mouth open and wet. I was so close to kissing her hard, to letting my tongue run down that vulnerable throat and to her breasts.

I took a deep breath and looked away from her for a moment, composing myself. I may be a lot of horrible things but I wasn't about to take advantage of her when she was this drunk, even if she seemed to want it. She couldn't know what she wanted right now.

Before I could think better of it, I took the shirt and motioned for her to raise her arms.

She blinked at me, shocked, I guess, but did as I asked. I slipped my t-shirt on over her head then gestured to the bottom of her dress. "I guess you can keep the rest on," I said.

"Don't you find me attractive?" she asked, slurring her words a bit but still sounding hurt.

I took her good hand and placed it on the bulge in my jeans. "I think I do." Then I took her hand away and put my arm around her waist, scooting her back into the bed where I quickly undid the straps on her shoe. "But you're drunk and I'm tired, and it's not going to happen like this."

"But it will happen," she said, her head leaning back into the pillow. She closed her eyes and yawned.

"I'll see you in the morning," I told her. Then I went to the washroom, filled up a glass of water, and left it on her bedside table.

I closed the door just in time to see her dozing off, then I settled onto the couch in the other room. I pulled extra blankets from the closet, the nightly battle against the air con, and tried to get some rest.

No way in hell was sleep coming to me in my state. I took my dick out and jerked off in minutes flat, biting down my cries as I came onto my stomach. I didn't know what relationship I had with Alana right now and my own motives seemed to be changing by the moment, but I knew better than to make her aware I was getting off to her.

Once my heartrate slowed and the hazy warmth of orgasm flooded my limbs, trying to take me down into sleep, my thoughts became clearer.

I needed to focus. I needed to find out why she was a target and who had ordered the hit.

Things couldn't get complicated. I couldn't get involved. There was no way any of this could end happy if I did.

But maybe, just maybe, her staying alive was happy

enough. Even if I had to walk at the end to protect my involvement, to protect my truth, maybe if she got through this safely, that would be enough.

I had to protect her.

CHAPTER SEVEN

Alana

I awoke to yelling from the other room. It wasn't the type
of yelling that made you jolt out of bed, but the unnerving,
haunted yelps of someone having a nightmare. I should
know, of all people, what that sounded like.

Because the light was dim and the sky outside the hotel
windows was the hazy grey of pre-dawn, I carefully got out
of bed, feeling out of sorts. My head was pounding from all
the wine at dinner and I felt ridiculous in Derrin's t-shirt with
my dress around my ass. My god, had he seen me naked last
night?

I shook away the embarrassment, recalling bits and pieces
and that sting of rejection yet again and then hopped as
delicately as I could over to the door that separated the
bedroom from the main room.

I opened it a crack and peered inside. Derrin was on
the couch, half-covered by a blanket, and twitching. For a
horrible second I thought perhaps he was sick or having a
seizure, but then in the grainy light I saw his brows come
together in a look of pain and he softly cried out, "Carmen
. . . Carmen."

Carmen? I wondered if that was his ex-wife, the one who

had died. Poor guy. He obviously wasn't over her yet. No
wonder he wasn't throwing himself at me. Not that I expected
him to, but when you've got a drunk naked chick in your
bed it's hard not to dwell on it and feel slighted.

I watched him for a moment, unsure of whether to wake
him or not, but when his yelps grew deeper and more pained,
I couldn't stand it anymore.

I hopped over to him and stood at the foot of the couch.

"Derrin," I called out. "Wake up."

He didn't. I said his name again, louder, then I grabbed
his leg, giving it a squeeze. I didn't want to get any closer
than that when it came to waking someone from a
nightmare.

I chose wisely.

Suddenly he bolted off the couch, practically leaping sideways
until he was standing on the ground in a crouch, a gun drawn,
his eyes focused stiffly on the blank space in front of him.

Actually there was no gun at all – his hands were empty
– but he had made the motion as if he was pulling one out
from under his pillow.

Okay then. Maybe he knew more than something about
guns.

"Derrin?" I said softly.

He slowly turned his head to look at me, chest heaving,
and blinked a few times as he took me in. Then he looked
down at the way he was posed and slowly straightened up.

"Sorry, I . . ." He trailed off and pressed his hand against
the back of his thick neck, looking behind him at the couch.

"You were having a nightmare," I told him. "I heard you
in the other room. I didn't want to wake you up, but . . ."

He nodded and licked his lips. "Some nightmare," he said, looking visibly shaken.

"Did it involve guns?" I asked, nodding at his hands that were clenching and unclenching.

He shook his head slightly. "No."

"Did it involve Carmen?"

He looked at me sharply. In the dim light his eyes looked like black holes. It scared me a little, but I stood my ground.

"How did you know?"

I gave him a shy smile, feeling awkward over it all. "You were calling for Carmen."

He sighed and sat down on the couch, his face in his hands.

I gingerly hopped over and sat down beside him. "Want to talk about it?" I asked hopefully.

"Not really."

I chewed on my lip for a moment, considering my options. I guess I could tell him the truth about me for once, at least one little slice of the truth. "I have them too, you know."

He cocked his head to the side and peered at me inquisitively. "Really?"

I nodded. "Yup. Usually the same ones, though in the past they were less frequent. Now I get them all the time. Ever since the accident."

"The accident," he repeated.

Shit, I'd forgotten I'd only told him so much about that.

"Yeah. The hit and run. I guess it triggered something."

"That kind of trauma would do it. What do you dream of?"

And here's where things got complicated. I hemmed and

hawed about it for a moment then decided to just bite the bullet. Sorry little pun, but there it was. I wasn't about to tell him everything, though.

"It's usually me and my brother and sisters in our house in La Cruz. It's a little town, just north of here on the curve of the bay. We're sometimes in bed and then my brother comes into the room and tells us we all have to hide. Sometimes it starts when I'm already in the closet. Sometimes I'm alone, sometimes it's all of us. Sometimes I'm under a bed. Sometimes I'm out on the street and watching it all happen."

His leg pressed against mine. "What happened?" he asked gently, his voice low. "In the dream."

"Some men come to kill us. They kill my mother. My father is already dead at this point. We're all spared because we were hiding, and the cops come soon after. But in the dream, sometimes we all die."

He frowned, his body stiffening. "What do you mean in the dream you sometimes die? Did this happen in real life?"

I took in a deep breath, trying not to choke up over it. I so rarely talked about it because tears often came after. It's like it wasn't real unless I was saying it out loud, as if my words could conjure it from the air.

"When I was young, yes, it happened. I'll never forget it, even though I've tried. It's like my brain won't let me forget. It keeps bringing it up in my dreams."

"What happened?" His full and rapt attention was on me now, those intense blue eyes pouring over every inch of my face. "I mean, why?"

Here came the hard part. "My father was mixed up in some

bad business. I guess they took out my mother for revenge, I don't know. But it left us all orphans. My brother had to step up and take care of us, along with my older sister Beatriz."

"Your brother, Juan," he said.

"Yes," I said hesitantly. Javier's fake name felt wrong.

"And Beatriz. I thought your sister was Marguerite. What happened to Beatriz?"

And here came the can of worms.

"Beatriz died later. So did my other sister Violetta."

"How?" Derrin seemed almost hyperactive over this information. Now I was really scaring the poor guy away.

"They are long stories."

"I have time."

"You're a tourist," I reminded him. "You're leaving soon. You don't have time."

He put his hand on my arm and squeezed lightly. "I've met you. I'm not going anywhere."

There was something so kind and sincere in his voice, in his eyes. This tough soldier who had been through so much, yet he was trying to comfort me.

"They were both murdered. Horribly. Brutally. That's all you need to know."

He frowned as he took that information in. "And your father was the same way?"

"Yes. The cartels shape our lives here. The cartels can take it all away."

I knew this was a lot for someone like him to understand. I knew Derrin wasn't naïve – the defensive moves he'd just used springing out of bed told me he was far from that. But Canada didn't have the same problems as we did in Mexico.

Neither did the States. Mexico was as backward, corrupt, and Wild West as a second world country could possibly get. The poor were destitute. The rich were rich beyond their wildest dreams. The rest of us struggled in the middle, assured that the only way to get higher was to become like the rest of them. Drugs ruled our lives. It was a fact we had accepted, along with the violence that came with it.

"If most of your family was murdered," he said slowly, deliberately, "wouldn't that mean that you're at risk too? You, your other sister, your brother?"

I grimaced. "Marguerite is safe. My brother . . . probably safer than I am. And me . . . well, I can't live my life in fear."

"But you have been, haven't you?" He was staring at me so intently, but I refused to meet his eyes, afraid he might see more than I wanted him to. "The accident," he went on. Exactly what I was afraid of. "When you were hit. There is more to that, isn't there?"

I dipped my chin to my neck and nodded. "I still don't know who hit me. The police think it's someone who worked for the airline. A mechanic. He certainly looked like one I would see. The car might have looked familiar too, but I don't know. They told me it was a hit and run, an accident . . . and I believe them. I guess. I mean, no one has come after me now. I'm here, aren't I? But the weird – the weirder – thing about it all, is that he's dead. Someone shot him in the head moments after he ran me down. They just caught up to him, stopped him, killed him. And no one can figure that part out. If it was vigilante justice, why hasn't the person come forward?"

"Because the person has blood on his hands," he suggested gravely.

"True. But it doesn't make sense. I've seen some horrific things. I've never heard of someone acting this way. I think it's all related, but I don't know how."

"You could be in danger, Alana," he said.

I rubbed my lips together and sighed. "I know. But I just . . . I want to ignore it. I want it to go away. I want to pretend it's all over." I looked at him with hope. "This could be all over, couldn't it? If the accident was on purpose, the guy is dead. He's not coming after me again. If it wasn't an accident, then I have a guardian angel out there looking out for me."

"Or maybe the guy botched the job – because it wasn't a fatal hit and he knew it – and someone else was hired to take him out and make sure he didn't leave a trail."

I frowned at him, unease gripping my heart. "There you go, acting all David Caruso again."

He didn't smile. "I'm worried about you."

"I'm worried about *you*."

"Why?"

"Because you're scaring me. And you're a nice Canadian boy. If what you're saying is true, and I have reason to be scared, then I'm a target and you'll be put in danger because of me."

"Don't worry about me," he said. "Don't ever worry about that." He paused. "I know how to take care of myself. And I can take care of you."

Those last words were music to my soul.

Still, I said, "That isn't your job."

"It shouldn't be anyone's job. But I'm making it mine." He

brushed a strand of hair off my face and I closed my eyes at the rough brush of his fingers. Damn, he could take care of me all he wanted.

"Now, do you know why you were hit?" he asked, soft enough not to break the spell of his fingers on my face. He ran a thumb under my bottom lip and I nearly lost it.

"No," I said quietly, sucking in my breath.

"Everything that happened to your family didn't happen recently. You have no idea why someone would do this to you now?"

I shook my head. Everything in the past had been done to hurt my father or to hurt Javier. But honestly, I didn't know if that was it. If someone really wanted to make a statement, they would kidnap me, not try and take me out. If they kidnapped me they could get Javier to bend to their will.

I wasn't certain that Javier would do that, however. Sometimes I felt like I wasn't even related to him. Though he always said how important family and loyalty was, sometimes I wondered if he would let me die in the streets if it suited him. Family came second to the cartel, to the drugs, to the money, to the power. It always had. He was just good at fooling people.

"What are you thinking about?" he asked, inching closer to me.

"About all the ways there is to die."

"None of them are going to happen to you."

"You sound so sure." And yet I believed him. At least, I wanted to. I wanted so much from this man. I could feel the intensity burning off of him, infecting me, making me feverish from head to toe.

His face was so close now, his eyes half-closed with lust and focused on my lips.

"Are you going to kiss me?" I whispered.

"Yes," he murmured.

"Are you going to fuck me?"

"Oh yes."

A small, brief smile flashed across his lips and then he leaned forward. The kiss was soft for a moment, just enough time for me to luxuriate in the dreamy fullness of his lips, the way they covered mine, wet and warm and wanting. It pulled me in, stirred something deep inside, like a small candle flame that was growing with each feathery stroke of tongue against tongue, each long, lingering taste.

He pulled his lips away a millimeter to catch his breath and it felt like he was stealing mine.

Then his mouth came back onto my own, hard and fast and urgent. His large hand gripped the back of my neck, the other wrapped around my waist as he tugged me toward him. My nipples immediately went hard, brushing against the inside of the baggy shirt I was wearing. Heat pooled between my legs, throbbing for him already.

Damn, he was good at kissing. Each passionate melding of our lips and tongue was stoking the fire inside until I felt ready to self-combust. I moaned against him, trading in the ability to breathe for the ability to be fucked by his mouth. He was so needing, probing, greedy. I loved it, wanted more, wanted everything.

He slipped his hand under the shirt, finding my breast. He gasped, raspy and deep, as his fingers found my nipples, rubbing over their stiffness.

I loved a bit of foreplay. Making out was a long lost art.

But I needed this man inside me, and badly. I'd needed him for a few days now. From the stiff bulge in his boxer briefs, I could tell he felt the same way.

"Fuck me," I whispered as his lips found my neck and sucked there. "Don't be gentle."

He paused for a moment, probably remembering my injuries.

"Don't be gentle," I repeated, my good hand holding the back of his head, his buzz cut both rough and soft against my palm.

"I won't," he mumbled against my neck. Then he pulled away and got up. In a second he got his strong arms under my body and was lifting me up in the air. So effortless. I really felt like I was going to get fucked by a superhero or something. He definitely had that whole Captain America thing going on.

He put me down on the bed and pulled the rest of my dress off as I tried to shimmy out of it. There I was lying naked, legs open on the bed, bare for him to see. And boy, did he seem to see it. He stared down at my body, his eyes roaming over me in such a way that I could feel their heat on my skin.

"You're gorgeous," he said, voice raspy and dripping with lust as he slid his large rough hands down the sides of my body.

"So are you," I said, trying not to feel bashful. That wasn't like me at all. "Take off your clothes. It's not fair that I can't do it myself."

He gave me a cocky grin then pulled his shirt over his

head. I propped myself up on my elbows and admired the
sight of him undressing between my legs.

His chest was a work of art. Everything about him was a
work of art, like a living breathing sculpture of what a real
man should look like. His pecs were so hard and wide you
could bounce pesos off them, his shoulders broad and
muscled, his abs a perfect, grooved six-pack leading down to
the flattest stomach imaginable. Most impressive of all were
his arms. Obviously I'd been admiring them before, their
thick, veiny example of Derrin's brute strength, but now with
his shirt off he was the total package. He looked like a killing,
fucking machine.

"All of it," I told him, my intentions bold even though my
voice was barely above a whisper. I was so fucking eager for
him I could hardly stand it.

He kept up that arrogant grin – one very rightly earned
– and pulled down his underwear, stepping out of them.

Against the virile strength of his thighs, his erection jutted
out like a mast. I had been right when I assumed perfect
head equaled perfect dick. This man was all man and definitely didn't use any steroids. His cock was thick, long and
dark with want. He even had a nice set of balls that I wanted
to wrap my lips around.

He stepped to the edge of the bed and I quickly remembered I had condoms in my purse.

"Condom," I told him. "I haven't been taking my pill
properly since the accident."

He nodded, almost looking a bit sheepish for not suggesting
it, and went over to the chair and fished a foil packet out of

my purse. He ripped it open and slid it on himself, and I couldn't help but bite my lip at the sight.

He came back to the edge of the bed and took a hard hold of my thighs and yanked me toward him.

"I need to be inside you," he said, his voice sliding over me like rough silk. I agreed and wrapped my legs around his firm, tight hips. I winced slightly at the sight of my cast, knowing it couldn't feel too nice against his skin, but he didn't even seem to notice. He positioned the head of his cock at my opening and moaned as his fingers drifted over my slickness. Then he grabbed my thighs even harder, holding them up as he thrust into me.

I gasped from the welcome intrusion, his stiff length as it struck deep. He felt so good inside me, so full, so thick. My fingers grabbed the edges of the blanket, holding on as he pulled in and out, so slowly, so deliciously, and I expanded again and again to take him all in.

"Yes," he hissed as he pumped into me. I stared up at him, at this mammoth man, my legs looking so small in his capable hands. There was a sheen of sweat over his hard body, his muscles flexing as he fucked me harder and harder, his hips swiveling and driving in as deep as he could go. When he was pushed in to the hilt, he paused and then started to rub my clit with his thumb, even though I was so close to coming without it.

He stared down at me as he brought me to orgasm, his eyes filling with lust and want and maddening desire. There was something else in them though, some kind of sadness or loneliness that would have hit me in the heart if he hadn't just pushed me over the edge.

I came violently, my body screaming with the release of it all, the release of everything. I writhed and spasmed, feeling no pain, no weight, no shadows. It was all just light, and I was warm and fuzzy and in an angel's hands. An angel who was coming himself with a few loud grunts and a well-placed, "Fuck, Alana, fuck."

I moaned happily, feeling satisfied like nothing else. That was one hell of a fuck.

He pulled out of me, disposed of the condom, then climbed into bed, pulling me up so I was beside him. I wanted to get up to go to the washroom, to have some water, to wash my face, but before I knew it I was succumbing to his arms once again.

We must have dozed off for a few hours because when I woke up cuddled into him, the sun was shining bright and relentless through the window. I turned to look at him and was surprised to see him staring at me, blinking at the light.

"Hi," I said softly. I couldn't help but smile, and it danced on my lips. I couldn't remember the last time I had woken up with a man beside me. Usually one of us left during the night.

I also couldn't remember feeling this warm and secure before. For once I wasn't waking up with a pit of loneliness inside me.

"Good morning," he said. "Did you sleep well?"

I nodded. "How long was I out for?"

"Hours."

"Did you sleep?"

He smiled stiffly. "I rarely sleep."

Right. The nightmares.

"Listen," he said, adjusting himself on his side and trailing his fingers along my collarbone. "I've been thinking. I think you should stay with me."

I raised my brows. This was new. "What, here?"

"Yeah. Just for the time being."

"You don't trust me?"

He gave me a steady look. "I don't trust anyone, and especially not around you. I told you I wanted to take care of you. I want to protect you. I can't do that when you're injured and living all the way out there by yourself."

"My friends . . ."

"Your friends are wonderful, but they're busy with their own lives. And they're women. No offense, but unless one of them has some special training up their sleeves, they're going to get hurt in the process. Except for maybe Luz. She seems like she'd be brutal."

I bristled at that. "They'd protect me. You don't know them."

"I know they'd try, and that's admirable. But I'm a strong man and I have military training. I have ways of protecting – real ways. You know these people aren't playing, that this isn't a game. If there's a chance that someone is still out there, wanting you dead, then I have to do what I can to ensure they don't touch you."

"But we don't know that."

"And I'm not willing to chance it. You're off work now, and you obviously need help, even if there wasn't anything going on. Let me do this for you."

I blinked at him. "But why?"

"Well, if you can't already tell, I like being around you.

With you. Inside you." He put his hand under my chin and pulled it up so I was looking at him. His gaze was so focused. "Maybe some of this is selfish. I want you for myself."

Butterflies scattered in my stomach.

"Okay," I told him. "I'll stay here. Just for a bit. Until you get tired of me."

"Never," he said, and kissed me.

CHAPTER EIGHT

Derek

E ven though Alana had agreed to stay in my hotel room for a while, we still weren't in any rush to get out of bed. In fact, we stayed there all day, only taking a break to have room service.

We were both wrapped in hotel robes after enjoying a shower together. She'd gone down on me in there. She couldn't drop to her knees because of her cast, but the shower seat worked just fine. The woman certainly knew how to fuck with her mouth. She also had this uncanny ability to fuck you with her eyes at the same time.

When Carmen died, everything had changed for me. Her brutal, haunting demise, right in front of me had changed the course of my life. It was all my fault. The two cartels, she never should have been caught in the middle of it. I never should have been involved. They said she was in the wrong place at the wrong time, but I knew it was more than that. Carlos had shown such little compassion for his sister before, the fact that she was there at all during that transaction was a sign. He didn't care who got hurt, who died. Neither did the other side.

She was gunned down in front of my eyes. I can still see

her running for me from across the road, the fear so rampant on her delicate face. She was telling me to get out of there while I stood there dumbly with my mouth open. I think I was yelling at her to do the same. I can't really remember. One minute I had been waiting in the car, the next I was trying to reach her. It was all a blur. But I do remember the rose shade of her lipstick, the way her long red and white dress flowed behind her, and how, somehow in that terrible moment, she looked more beautiful than she had on our wedding day.

Then it was all erased by gunfire. Hot blasts. Bullets bouncing off the pavement. Smoke.

Blood.

She was shot on both sides. She was riddled with bullets from her brother, from the people I worked for, and ripped apart by the Gulf Cartel.

She was the first victim. And the only innocent one.

Seconds later, others died. The cartels faced off, both meaning to leave no one alive.

I don't know how I didn't run into the middle of it all, to go to Carmen's lifeless body as she lay face down in the street, the blood pooling around her and creating new abstract patterns on her dress. I knew at that moment I wanted to die. I wanted to join her.

But after everything I'd been through, my survival instincts were stronger than my soul. I removed myself from the scene. I drove back to our house. I packed up everything I had that was important. It all went in a gym bag.

Then I got back in my car and drove.

I drove for days and days, my eyes burning behind the wheel during the day. At night I cried and grieved.

Nearly everyone had died in that battle. Everyone except for Carlos.

It didn't seem fair.

I didn't want anything to do with the Gulf cartel – I blamed them as equally as I blamed Carlos. So I went to the Zetas. I had a few contacts there, and I gave them everything I had on Carlos. Then I offered my own brand of services.

They paid me a large amount of money. The next day I killed Carlos, three shots into his head while he was sleeping in his leather armchair. The maid knew me, and though she was surprised to see me back, she let me in.

I had to kill her, too.

I had blood on my hands. But I didn't care. When Carmen died, I lost the ability to care about anything except blood and vengeance. I became a murderer for the first time. I lost my humanity.

Over the years I moved deeper and deeper into the circuit of cartels. I was loyal to no one except those who paid me the most. I became quick and efficient. There were better *sicarios* out there – there still are – but the cartels seemed to love the fact that I was white. They called me their G.I. Joe. They liked that no one paid much attention to me, that no one ever looked for me. They liked that I didn't care for politics or drama or fame. I did the job I was paid to do.

Well, except for that last one.

I was a lone wolf. I operated alone, and I usually went to bed alone. If I was horny, finding a chick to fuck wasn't hard. I always treated them nice enough, but they never got anything from me other than a handful of orgasms.

I certainly never took them out on dates, or ordered room

service in the afternoon with them, or invited them to stay in my hotel room for an indefinite amount of time.

I never cared about them, not even a little bit. But I cared about Alana.

She was getting under my skin. She was awakening that dead husk inside of me.

She was becoming my second chance.

I couldn't protect Carmen. But maybe, somehow I could protect her.

I started by getting to know her body thoroughly.

While she sat there cross-legged on the messy bed, sipping on a black coffee, I leaned forward, and with one swift move, I undid the sash around her robe so a bronze line of skin from her chest to her pussy was exposed.

"Smooth move," she commented, putting the coffee down.

I moved the plate of food to the side. "Lie down," I told her.

She raised her brow, inquisitive, but lay back on the duvet. I reached over and pulled her robe to the sides, exposing her more. She was so fucking amazing, a body built from the heavens.

I reached for the small metal pitcher of cream that came with the coffee and held it above her breasts.

"What are you doing?" she asked with a smile.

"I'm going to enjoy you and my breakfast at the same time," I said.

"That sounds a bit greedy."

"That I can be."

I grinned at her then tipped the pitcher so that just a bit of the cream poured out in a single stream, splashing between her breasts. She let out a gasp and a giggle, and my dick twitched hungrily. The sight of the white creamy liquid spilled against her dark skin was hot as fucking hell. I wanted to come right on top of her to add to it, but I ignored my urges for now.

I ran my finger between her breasts and licked it. Then I massaged it over her breasts and nipples before lapping the cream up like a cat.

"That was the appetizer," I told her as I pulled away, my fingers still rubbing the rest of it into her skin. "Now for the main course."

"Are you like this with every woman?" she asked me, and though I could see in her bright eyes that it was a joke, it kind of dug deep.

"No," I said quietly. "Not every woman. Only you. You've been the only one who has mattered in a very long time."

She blinked, perhaps taken aback by my honesty. I certainly was. I flashed her a smile and picked up a jar of honey. "Now, I can stop if you want me to," I said, waving the jar at her.

"Don't you dare stop."

So I didn't. I dipped my finger in the honey and began painting suns all over her skin. That's what she reminded me of, the sun, shining always so bright and bold. The darkness was always behind her, waiting to take her out, but most of the time she was this ball of warmth that seemed to melt everything bad away.

"You better get it all," she said, closing her eyes and moaning as I stroked the honey between her legs. "Or else I'll be left sticky."

"Don't worry about that. I'm going to lick you clean then fuck you hard."

Her eyes flew open, even more aroused now.

I ran my tongue all over the honey art on her body, making sure there was nothing too sticky left, just enjoying the sweet taste of her and the nectar in my mouth. Then I put my head between her legs and lapped up the rest of it, sucking on her sweet folds and teasing the swell of her clit until her moans were so loud and I was drowning in salty sweet.

She came quick and hard, her legs gripping my head and holding on tight while she pulsed beneath my lips and tongue.

"*Ay dios mio,*" she swore as she continued to writhe, breathless and panting. Eventually her legs loosened and I pulled away. She lifted her head up, her eyes glazed, and looked at me. "Wow. Just wow. If that was the main course, what's for dessert?"

I grinned at her and opened my robe, my dick like a thick piece of steel. I stroked it once. "This. Served any way you want."

She bit her lip and leaned forward to grab my robe, pulling me down on top of her.

It was a long time before room service could take the tray away.

Finally we decided to get a move on things. I got her in a cab and she was off to her apartment to pack up some of her stuff. I would have gone with her to watch over her, but while she was gone I wanted to go get a new rental car.

I dropped off the old one and picked up a black mustang convertible at a new rental agency. It was the sexiest thing they had, and I knew how to drive it well, even if they weren't all that practical for the area. But in terms of a getaway car, it worked. After she told me everything about her family, I had a clearer picture of what I was up against.

While I drove the mustang back to the hotel, I had time to think. Her father had been involved in one of the cartels long ago, and he was killed. Her mother came after. Then her sisters. She, her twin, and her brother were all that remained. I needed to find out more about her sisters, when they had died and how. I knew she didn't want to talk about it, but it was crucial to understanding this. The way they had died could tell you a lot about who was doing the killing. From what it sounded like, the deaths of her parents were a pretty rushed, amateur job. Anyone can storm a house in the night and shoot a woman in bed. That doesn't take any skill at all.

It just didn't make any sense to keep going at someone's family. Unless, of course, there was more to it. And I was sure there was. Either Alana or one of her siblings was still involved in something and hanging with the wrong crowd.

Her brother was the obvious choice, considering he was involved with drugs in some way. But so was everyone. Was her brother part of the same network that her father had been? If so, why would they still bother going after the children?

Unless Alana did something, even if she didn't realize it, or knew something she wasn't supposed to. Though she'd been open last night, she was still playing her cards pretty close to her chest. I had more questions for her, but now that it was out in the open that people could be after her, now that she had admitted her accident might have not been an accident at all, I was confident we would get to the bottom of things, especially now that she would be staying with me.

As soon as I gave the car to the valet, I went up to the room and started rearranging things for her arrival. It was a weird feeling knowing I'd be sharing my space with a woman. Not only on an intimacy level, but because I wasn't sure how much of "Derek" I could show her. She only knew Derrin, and parts of me were hard to hide.

For one, I knew she was a bit suspicious of the way I woke up the other day. I couldn't help it. Normally I was a very light sleeper, except when I was dreaming of Carmen, and instincts always took over. I could be up and ready to shoot or run within seconds.

Obviously I was going to pass it off as military training if it ever came up, but she would want to know how else I was going to protect her and that's where the guns would come in. Time to confess to her that I had a bit of a gun fetish. I didn't need to hide that anymore.

I opened the door to the wardrobe and lifted the wooden bottom off the base. I had pried it off when I first checked in and hid all my guns and weaponry in the hollow base. With the bottom back in place, it looked like an empty wardrobe.

I decided to still hide them there – you never knew what the maids were going to think if they stumbled across them – but I would give Alana a little show of them. It sounded like she could handle it. If I were her, I would have invested in a gun a long time ago.

As for the silencers, the Ace bandages that kept the guns

tucked to my waist, the knives, the rope, the CF explosives, the tracking devices, the GHB capsules, the duct tape, blind-folds, and handcuffs – well I wasn't sure if she would buy it if I told her I was into some pretty kinky stuff.

I took out everything but the guns, a four-inch silencer for my .22, and the Ace bandage. I carefully placed them in a small Ziploc bag, and brought them into the washroom. With a small motorized saw I always had with me, I cut away the base of the cabinet underneath the sink and stuck them in there. I placed the bottom over the top of it then rearranged towels and extra rolls of toilet paper on top so it wouldn't attract any attention. I cut clean, and any leftover sawdust was cleaned up and flushed away, but even so I had to be meticulous. Guns I could explain. Everything else took me to a psychopathic level.

CHAPTER NINE

Alana

"Y" ou've lost your fucking mind, woman," Luz swore at me over the phone.

I was sitting on the balcony of the hotel room, watching the waves roll in. "You've been saying that for ten days now."

"And I'm going to keep saying it until you come back home."

"Do you miss me?"

She sighed. "I just saw you last night."

"Yeah, exactly," I told her. In the distance, over the rippling blue line of the Pacific, I saw a parasailer gliding down toward the boat. Everything was so bright and glittery and carefree in this part of town. I couldn't get enough of it. Staying with Derrin seriously made me consider selling my apartment and buying a place on the shore. Unfortunately, my apartment was owned and paid for by Javier, and I was pretty sure I couldn't do anything without asking him for permission. Sometimes I hated that he treated me more like a delinquent kid than his sister, but I guess it was better than nothing.

"You saw me last night," I repeated to Luz, smearing coconut and lime scented sunscreen on my arms. Though my wrist was pretty much healed, I had a bandage in place, and I was determined not to get any crazy tan lines. "You saw that I was fine. Better than fine. Great."

"That's only because of all the sex."

"You'd be great too if you were getting laid by a soldier."

"Shut up," she told me. "I'm still allowed to worry about you. And I still don't trust him."

I sighed. "I know you don't." I didn't blame Luz. Ever since I'd told her that I was temporarily moving in with Derrin, she was the one who was acting like they'd lost their mind. She told me all the things I already knew myself – that I didn't know him, we'd only just met, I was still vulnerable, etc. But the thing was, I trusted Derrin. I don't know why I did, but I did. He had promised to protect me and I believed him. And then later, when I saw his guns, I believed him even more. He had all the skills he picked up in the war, the affinity and passion for firearms, and the courage and determination unlike anyone I'd met. If anyone was going to get me through this, it would be him.

There was nothing to get through, however. As the days passed and the two of us settled into a routine of drinking, food, and sex (rinse and repeat), and our bond grew stronger and my bones healed, there was nobody out there coming to get me.

We were cautious too. Derrin always had his eyes on me, like he was born to have this role. But no one approached us. No one was following us. No one was waiting.

Some days I went down to the pool and had daiquiris, other days I went to the beach, all while Derrin stayed on the balcony watching me. I was right out there in the open, just ripe for the taking. And though the experience had been a bit nerve-wracking, time and time again the only people who bugged me were the hustlers selling their cheap trinkets on the beach. Damn, they were annoying. I'd have thought they'd leave their fellow Mexicans alone but they still seemed to think I needed god-awful cornrows weaved into my head.

A few nights a week I met up with Luz, and sometimes Dominga. Because Dominga worked for a sister chain, she had a few friends working at our hotel, and she told me they were keeping an eye on me too. It was sweet of her; I knew both of my friends were so nervous. But as time ticked on, I was becoming more and more convinced that no one was after me. It was an accident. It was vigilante justice.

Sometimes I almost wished they'd try.

Meanwhile, when I wasn't pondering my potential death, I was falling deeper and deeper for this steely-eyed man with a heart of gold.

It was wrong. I knew it was. I didn't fall for men, and I never fell in love. It's not that I didn't want it but it was never anything I pursued.

But I was falling for Derrin. I wasn't quite there yet, but I was well on my way. That feeling that borders on obsession, where your thoughts and body and heart crave him like water. You're in a blissful, warm haze when he's there and suffering in a dark hollow when he's not. It was made even worse because I knew he was leaving. He wasn't Mexican. He didn't have a job here or a life. He was a visitor on these shores. There was something so incredibly romantic and dramatic about that, the whole affair with a timeline, the impending goodbyes and heartache.

Thankfully I didn't dwell on it too much. I wanted to enjoy the present. The past was brutal and the future was unclear, but the present was brilliant. The present was in the shape of a strong, sexy man.

"I still think you should move back," Luz told me, bringing my focus off the ocean. "You're well on your way to recovery now. I say move back to your place and get a cat for company."

I scrunched up my nose. "Listen, you're the cat lady in our friendship here, not me."

She sighed loudly. "Fine. But I'm still going to call you every day and see if I can change your mind."

"And I'm going to keep having hot, wild sex with my soldier," I told her. "Looks like I got the better deal out of this."

She grumbled something and hung up.

"Did you just call me your soldier?"

I jumped in my seat, the sunscreen falling to the floor, and looked to the door where Derrin was standing there with a cocky grin on his face.

"Jesus," I said, hand to my chest. "How long have you been standing there?"

"The whole time."

"How did I not hear you?"

"I can be quiet when it suits me." He stepped onto the balcony and bent down to kiss me, soft and slow. He sat down in the other chair. I knew he wouldn't be there for long. I guess I could blame my injuries, but I've always been the kind of person who could just sit for hours and hours and not move a muscle. Maybe it was to make up for the fact that when I was flying I was on my feet all day.

Derrin, on the other hand, had a real problem sitting still. He was always moving. Sometimes I told him to chill out and forced him to sit down with a beer, but twenty minutes seemed to be his absolute max before he was up and doing stuff. The man just had too much energy, though I was happy he was absolutely tireless in bed. The other day we'd fucked six times, including a blow-job in the bathroom of the restaurant where we ate dinner. I couldn't get enough of him and he never seemed to tire. We made quite the team.

"So, Luz still hates me, huh?" he asked.

I gave him a sympathetic look. "She doesn't hate you. She just doesn't know you."

"Well, I tried to get to know her last night."

"It doesn't really help that you don't talk much."

"I do with you."

"Only because I talk your ear off and you're forced to keep up."

He clasped his hands together, leaning forward on his elbow, his hands trailing over the gleaming skin of my legs. "So what do you want to do?"

"About Luz?"

"Today. What do you want to do today?"

There were a bunch of things I wanted to do. Most of them involved his dick. I think he knew this.

"Aside from the usual?"

He nodded and tried to wipe the grin off his face. "Yeah. Want to go check out the market in old town?"

"The one that goes over the bridge? You planning on buying overpriced crap?"

He shrugged. "I'm a tourist, aren't I?"

Don't remind me, I thought.

An hour later we were getting out of a cab on the congested cobblestone streets of old town. We would have taken the rental car – he had gotten a super sexy Mustang – but parking in that area of the city was a total bitch.

Today was no exception. It seemed every tourist, expat, gay lover on vacation, and local was out and about. It gave me a sense of purpose and vitality. I had slipped on a light batik-print sundress for the outing, and even though I now had a walking cast on my leg, at least the doctor had been able to put a black one on so it looked a bit sleeker. Okay, it probably didn't, but it made me feel better. Plus it made it much easier to get around. I didn't have to use crutches or lean on Derrin as I had been doing.

Despite that though, he still grabbed my hand. The intimacy of it all surprised me. It sounded absurd after ten days of fucking and sleeping tangled together and cuddling and kissing, and all of that wonderful stuff. But this simplest gesture was so pure and so proud. As he led me through the crowd to the market stalls, I felt like he was showing me off to the world.

How pathetic was I that this was the first time I'd felt that? That I felt someone was proud to be with me?

I blinked back the hot, sentimental tears that wanted to fall down my face. I didn't want him to know how he was affecting me. He was starting fires in my soul with kindling I thought would never burn.

We walked along for a bit, and I couldn't remember the last time I had felt this happy – if I had ever felt this happy. It was like everything before this moment was a blank slate.

Even all the bad, the horrible, the sorrowful things, I felt like they couldn't hurt me anymore. There was just me and Derrin, walking on a hot day through the old town of Puerto Vallarta, taking in the smells of fried tortillas and salty ocean breezes. Mariachi music drifted in from restaurants where tourists were smiling awkwardly, trying to get them to go away.

Eventually we found ourselves in one of them, ordering half-priced margaritas. We dipped warm from the oven chips into fresh green salsa and ate them with juice running down our chins.

With a bit of a day buzz going on, we decided to try and walk back to the hotel. We'd cut through the town on the Malecon then walk north along the beach. If we got tired, we'd walk two steps to the nearest hotel and get a drink. It had all the markings of a perfect day. It *was* the perfect day.

We were walking through the town square, past the iconic church tower, when he squeezed my hand and said, "You know what, Alana?"

"What?" I loved the way his raspy accented voice said my name.

"Back in Minnesota, we have a saying that's pretty applicable right now."

I frowned, puzzled. "Minnesota? Isn't that in the states?"

He blinked then said, "Yes. I played hockey there for a bit. Big hockey state. Lot of Canadians go down there to play."

Made sense. "What is it?"

"I'm sweet on you."

I bit my lip to keep from laughing. "I think that's what

Americans in the movies say. Not ex-soldier, hockey-playing Canadians."

He shrugged. "It's true, though."

"Well, I guess I'm sweet on you too," I told him. "You know in Mexico, we have our own saying."

"Go on then," he said with a grin and wrapped his arm around my waist, pulling me toward him. I stepped forward, careful not to put my cast on his toes, and pressed against his chest.

A deafening crack rang out.

I felt wind at my back and something solid hit my cast.

Someone somewhere was screaming. It might have been me.

"Run," Derrin said through gritted teeth, staring up and over my shoulder, his grip on me like a vice.

I turned and followed his line of sight. There was quick movement at the top of the bell tower, then it was gone. I looked down at the space behind me where the ground was split open from a bullet. Pieces of concrete had hit the back of my cast.

I was standing there a second ago.

That bullet was meant for me.

I couldn't even process it. Derrin was pulling me along the square, racing for the cover of trees, while people screamed and scattered in all directions. I tried to run as fast as I could with my cast, but I wasn't cutting it.

Derrin knew that, but did what he could to keep me going. Pigeons took flight as we made our way past the gazebo, where a band had paused and was looking around in horror, and we scampered toward the road.

Another shot rang out, hitting one of the gazebo poles and ricocheting off of it. I would have screamed again if I had any breath left in me.

"We're not going to make it on foot!" he yelled at me. He yanked me behind a tree, leaving me there to tremble like a dog, while he leaped out into the road. A small motorbike was puttering past and he quickly knocked the man off. He fell, crying out as he hit the road, narrowly avoiding being hit by an oncoming car. Derrin hopped on the bike, wheeled it around, and drove up the curb beside me.

This all took place in the space of five seconds.

"Get on!" he yelled at me, his eyes blazing. But they weren't afraid. They were determined.

I did as he said, leaning on him and awkwardly trying to get my leg over the back of the bike. The man who owned the bike was getting to his feet, yelling his head off, while another bullet hit the sidewalk. I whipped my head to the square to see two men running for us, guns drawn.

This can't be real. This can't be real.

But it was. Derrin gunned the bike forward, and I quickly wrapped my arms around his waist, holding on for dear life.

Who was that? Who was that? Who was that? I kept wanting to ask, to yell, to scream, but I couldn't. I could only hold on and try to catch my breath. My heart was playing drums in my chest and the city I knew and loved was zipping past me in a blur. In seconds it had turned from a warm safe place to one that wanted me dead.

Why?

We zipped along the street, Derrin handling the bike like it was second nature, dodging pedestrians, overtaking cars, hopping on and off the sidewalk when we had to. All I could do was grip him and try not to fall off. Fear was in every part of me, begging me to pay attention to it, but I couldn't. Once I did, that would be the end of me.

I put fear in a box and managed to look over my shoulder. I thought after all of Derrin's fancy maneuvering that we would have lost whomever it was, but there in the distance I could see two motorbikes. They looked bigger. Faster. And they were gaining ground.

"Shit!" I screamed, finding my voice. It practically tore itself out of my throat.

Derrin quickly looked over his shoulder and only raised an eyebrow at the discovery. The bike went a little bit faster, but only a little.

We swerved to the right, heading down a narrow lane, nearly taking out the patio seating area for a restaurant, while people shouted and yelled at us. The sound of the bike's engine was deafening as it bounced off the close walls then multiplied.

I dared to look behind me again. Through the tangles of hair blowing across my face, I saw the two bikes enter the end of the lane, gunning toward us.

"Faster!" I yelled at Derrin. "They're coming."

"I'm trying!" he growled. "Hold on, put your head down!"

He rounded the corner then jumped the bike up onto the sidewalk where we proceeded to head right through a restaurant. We crashed through a table that went flying to the side, then zig zagged around people, waiters, and tables. Broken glass and dishes soared through the air. I kept my head lowered, pressed against his shoulder blades, my eyes shut tight. I didn't want to see any of this.

Derrin swiftly maneuvered the bike back and forth, and then we were in what sounded like a kitchen and then we were airborne, weightless, and I had no idea where we were going to land. I opened my eyes just after we hit the ground with a jolt, biting down on my tongue by accident. My mouth filled with the taste of pennies.

We had soared over the kitchen's back steps and were now twisting right onto a different road, Calle Santa Barbara, heading up the hill that led to most of the tourist apartments at the south end of town. We had a bit more distance behind us now, but the bike wasn't built for two, especially not someone as heavy as Derrin, and it wasn't made for hills, either.

It sputtered, the air filling with the strong smell of an overworked engine.

"I don't think we're going to make it," I cried into Derrin's neck.

He didn't say anything. We kept driving up the curving road, wheels bouncing over rough cobblestones, then a shot rang out. Then another. They hit the stones beneath us. Derrin jerked the bike to the left and another bullet hit a parked car. They were gaining.

"Keep your head down," he said.

I did as he asked and felt him reach into his shirt. He pulled out a small gun then twisted at the waist. I twisted with him, leaning out of the way. He quickly pulled the trigger and fired two shots, hitting one of the guys. He went flying off the bike and the bike fell to the side, just in time for the other assailant to crash into it.

One bullet hit, two down.

Despite being scared to fucking death and my adrenaline feasting on my veins, I was in awe.

I swallowed hard, trying to think of something to say to him.

"*Buen disparo.*" Nice shot.

His eyes smiled at me before looking to the road in front of us. "I like it when you speak Spanish, babe." Then he looked back again, and his eyes were cold.

I turned my head to look. A black SUV was thundering up the road toward us. It wasn't full of tourists out for a Sunday drive.

"Fuck," he swore. "Are you ready to get a little wet?"

I stared at him blankly. "What?"

He whipped the bike to the right, and we went thumping down flights of cement stairs, nearly knocking over an elderly couple climbing them.

"*Lo Siento!*" I yelled at them before I bit my tongue again. At the top of the stairs, the SUV paused then drove off. I knew the road curved down and met with the one we were about to land on. Sure enough, as soon as we hit the road, the SUV appeared at the end of it, turning toward us. Derrin yanked the bike into a condominium driveway then down a brick path that traced the edge of the building. Trees and bushes reached out for us, snagging our clothes and hair as we whipped through them.

Suddenly it seemed like it was the end of the line. There was a pool, and beyond the pool there was blue sky.

"Hold on!" he yelled back at me.

I couldn't hold on any tighter. I let out a cry as the bike

lifted off the ground, bounced on a lawn chair, and then drove off the edge of the patio.

We were flying. I kept my head down but my eyes were open.

A sandy beach passed underneath our feet.

Then next thing I knew we had hit something hard and cold, and my arms were ripped from Derrin's waist. Salt water burned my eyes, filling my lungs and nose, and I tried to breathe, to swim, but I was sinking, drowning. The cast was weighing me down.

Suddenly a strong arm wrapped around me and my head broke the surface.

"Breathe, it's okay," Derrin said, gasping for breath just as I was. "Try and swim, I've got you."

I tried to nod but couldn't. I focused on my breathing and moved my arms and legs as much as possible, but he was doing most of the work. When my eyes eventually stopped burning, I was able to see where we were.

We were in the ocean, a few meters offshore. The handles of the motorcycle were just beginning to disappear into the waves, sinking. Beyond that, sunbathers on the beach gawked while people ran to the edge of the condo's pool area to see where we had fallen. On either side of us there were outcrops of stone and rock where the waves gently crashed. We'd been lucky. We could have landed on those instead, and neither of us would be alive.

"Right here," Derrin said as he hauled me up to something. I floated around and saw that we had reached a jet-ski that was bobbing in the shallows, clipped to a buoy. I could barely process it.

He swam around me and tried to hoist me onto the edge of the jet-ski. I don't know how he was able to do it while swimming and unable to touch the bottom, but he was. I grasped for the seat, trying to pull myself up as far as I could without hurting my wrist. The shouts from the shore were softening; there were some splashes and a few people coming into the water, maybe to help us.

I don't know if the fall had knocked something loose in my head or I took in too much salt water, but I had a hard time focusing. All I knew was that Derrin was getting on the jet-ski. He pulled me up so I was in his lap and then he stabbed something metallic, like a small knife, into the ignition switch before hitting the button. The jet-ski roared to life, and he quickly unclipped it from the anchor before we peeled away from the shore.

I was staring blankly up at the patio where the crowd had gathered when I saw what looked like one of the men who had been chasing us – the guy on the motorbike who had crashed into the one who got shot. He was wearing dark aviator shades, but the length of his mustache was memorable. But when I blinked, trying to get my eyes to focus as we moved further away, the man was gone.

"I think I saw one of the guys," I managed to say before having a coughing fit.

"I know," he said. "Keep holding on."

"Where are we going? How did you start this without a key?"

How did you shoot someone while driving a motorcycle?

Holy fucking shit. He just killed someone back there. It was in self-defense, and I'm glad he did it, but oh my god.

Oh my god.

What was happening?

My breathing was becoming shorter, and it felt like I couldn't breathe.

"Hey, hey," he said, taking his hand off the bar and tilting my head gently so he could look at me. "We're okay. You're okay. We're going to drive this back to the hotel. It's faster than they are, and we have no reason to think they know where we are staying, okay?"

"How do you know that?"

"They would have killed us earlier."

"They would have killed me. They're after me."

He nodded. "And now they're after me because I shot one of their men. It doesn't matter. We'll go back to the hotel, get in the car, and we're out of here."

"We can't just leave the city!"

"Alana," he warned just as we passed over a large wave, landing hard on the other side. My whole body was starting to ache. I was so battered as it was. "If you want to live, you'll do as I say. And you'll answer my questions honestly, okay?"

If you want to live, you'll do as I say.

"Who are you?" I asked incredulously. He sounded like an action hero. My life had just turned into an action film. None of this could be real. This couldn't be real.

But I had said the same thing about my parents, Violetta, and Beatriz, too.

"An ex-soldier. And I want answers from you."

"What answers? Derrin, I told you everything I know. I don't know who those men were. I've never seen them before. I don't know why they want to kill me."

"How did your sisters die?"

I felt sick. "Oh, come on." I rattled off a few swear words in Spanish.

"Tell me how they died. Tell me exactly how they died."

He suddenly switched off the engine, and we came to a stop, bobbing up and down in the waves. There was no one behind us, and the only thing in front of us were banana boats. I could see our hotel from here, maybe just another two minutes of boating and we'd be on the sand. It didn't feel safe enough, and Derrin knew that.

"I will start the engine when I know the truth."

"Why do you want to know?"

"Because the truth could save us," he said, exasperated, and his jaw began to twitch. I had never seen him so bothered before. Part of me wanted to savor the fact that for once he wasn't being so cool and calm, but that stoic demeanor of his was probably the thing that kept us alive.

I tried to look over his shoulder, to see if anyone was following us again, but his fingers under my jaw kept me in place.

"How?"

I swallowed hard then coughed up a bit of seawater. I spit it into the ocean and realized there was no use pretending to be a lady around him anymore. Finally I seemed to catch my breath, and I willed myself to feel numb. Luckily, after what had just happened, I was halfway there.

"Violetta died in a car bomb," I said simply. "It exploded with her in it."

"Was it meant for her?"

I bit my lip and looked forward, trying to concentrate on

the white sand. So close, so close. "From what I understand, it was meant for a few people, maybe not her at all. Wrong place at the wrong time. But she was definitely with the wrong people."

"And Beatriz?"

"She was . . . it was on the news. She was beheaded. So was her husband. And my niece and . . ." I sucked in air, trying not to cry. "Nephew. Their bodies were burned, their heads displayed in public."

Derrin squeezed his arms around me tighter but didn't say anything. He didn't have to.

When he finally spoke, though, his voice was a bit cracked. "Who is your brother? Who is he really? Is his name really Juan Bardem?"

"No," I said. "His name is Javier Bernal."

He immediately stiffened. I craned my neck to look at him. He was slack-jawed.

"You've heard of him, haven't you? Of course, everyone here has."

"Yes," he said slowly. "I've heard of him."

"So that's the whole story. Violetta died from a bomb I think was meant for him. Beatriz and her family were tortured and killed and publicly shamed by Travis Raines, some sick fuck drug lord who is now dead himself, courtesy of my brother."

Derrin was staring at me with the most rigid, unblinking eyes, like he couldn't quite process this information. Wheels in his head were spinning.

I knew what was going to happen. He was going to take me to the beach. Then he was going to get the fuck out of there, leaving me to fend for myself. I was more trouble than I was worth. He was probably going to do that already, but telling him that my brother's enemies were probably my enemies really cemented the deal.

I was pretty much a walking dead woman.

And I could barely walk at that.

CHAPTER TEN

Derek

I felt like I'd been slugged in the face.

One sharp blow, blinding light, and then a million little pieces all falling into place like nerves returning home.

Javier Bernal.

I should have seen it coming. Bernal is just such a common last name, I didn't think anything of it. In America it would be like the name Smith. When I Googled Alana for research, I certainly never saw a single article or anything linking her to her brother. But it didn't really matter what I thought because this was the truth and it was hitting me hard. Of all the drug lords I'd worked with over the years, I knew Javier the best. The only admirable thing about him was his tenacity. And his payment. He spared no expense on hiring the best.

I'd seen him rise up the ranks of Travis Raines' cartel, break off on his own, and then take over Travis' cartel in the end, like salmon coming back to spawn.

But Alana was wrong about one thing. It wasn't Javier that killed Travis Raines. I was the one who put the bullet in his head. It was a well-placed sniper shot from the roof that took him out, saved the life of Javier's ex-lover, the con artist Ellie Watt, and put Javier in the driver's seat.

For some sad, sick reason I felt compelled to share this information with Alana. I wanted her to know that the man who tortured her sister – and I did know all the grisly details about that death – was killed by my own hands. I wanted her to know that I had helped get her vengeance, whether I knew it or not.

But it was the only way I had helped.

I had been hired to kill her and I hadn't.

Which cartel had done it?

I kept my mouth shut. I started the jet-ski up again and drove it to shore. I was wasting precious time trying to figure it all out here. I needed to get in our room and get us packed and on the road in five minutes. That is, of course, if they hadn't already discovered where we were staying. I looked up. No helicopters or small planes in the sky. Behind us there were no boats. Wherever the SUV was, it would be fighting traffic coming down Highway 200. If they didn't know, then we had time.

She was silent the rest of the way back to the beach. I felt a bit bad for making her talk about it after everything we had just gone through – there was no way she'd be able to process that so quickly, either – not a civilian like her.

Then again, she wasn't quite a civilian.

I beached the jet-ski and left it there to the amusement of a few beach bums. They could try and take it if they wanted, but I'd taken my makeshift skeleton key with me. There were few things that it couldn't start.

We quickly hobbled past the pool and into the lobby. I made sure my gun was hidden, tucked away in the bandage against my abs, but I knew I could whip it out at a moment's notice if needed.

A moment's notice would be if we were lucky. It's usually less than that.

After I did a quick sweep of the area and didn't see anyone unusual, I led her over to the elevators, one hand firmly gripped around her arm, the other hand hovering above the hidden gun. I pressed the button then kept her off to the side when the doors opened.

The elevator was empty.

Then I brought her inside and pressed the button for the sixteenth floor.

We stared at ourselves in the mirrors that lined the elevator. Both of us were soaking wet, and though you couldn't tell I had a gun on me, you could tell there was something funny going on underneath my shirt. Her hair was tangled all over her face, dripping down her back, and her dress was clinging to every curve. She might as well be naked. I hated the fact that I was so fucking turned on right now. That was the problem with this job. I was used to the guns, the chases, the violence. It didn't damper anything for me. Sometimes the excitement only fueled desire, except I usually got off by shooting a different gun. She wasn't used to it at all.

When the doors opened, I decided to take said gun out. Her eyes widened at the sight of it, even though she knew it had been there, she had felt it when she was holding on to me, when she saw me kill that man.

I wanted her to feel safe, and I wasn't sure what it was going to take for that to happen. It wasn't the sight of a gun.

We moved silently and swiftly down the hall to the room.

I immediately plugged up the peephole with my thumb and knocked quickly. I gripped the gun and waited, motioning for her to move back against the wall and out of the way before I put my head against the door.

There was no answer, no sound. I looked down, and knowing I had left the curtains open, I saw no shadow passing by the light coming from under the door. I hadn't expected there to be.

I quickly slipped the keycard out of my pocket and jammed it into the slot. When the lock turned green and the mechanical locks whirred open, I opened the door, crouching down as I followed through, my gun drawn and ready to shoot.

The room was empty.

I stood up then motioned for Alana to come in. She did so like she was walking on eggshells, her arms held stiffly against herself. She seemed to be going into shock.

I told her to stay put then did a quick search of the room. My guns were there, my other stuff was there, and nothing had been searched or tampered with. They hadn't found us. We still had time.

Just not much of it.

"Alana," I said to her, but she didn't look at me. I went over and placed my palms over her upper arms, holding her as I stared at her frozen face. "Alana Bernal." She finally looked up. "Listen to me, Alana," I said, knowing it was best to keep calling her name. "We're safe for the time being, but we have to leave. I'm giving us a ten minute window and then we're out of here. I'm pretty much already packed – you know I travel light. I'm going to pack up your stuff while you take a shower, okay Alana. Hold on."

I went into the bathroom and brought the gym bag out from underneath the sink. Her blank eyes followed it as I placed it on the couch. Then I took hold of her arm and led her into the bathroom. I ran a hot shower, stripped her dress up over her head until she was just in her bra and underwear, and then I took those off too. She may have turned me on in the elevator, but now it was apparent she was frightened to death – a scared, lost little girl, and that made my protective instincts go into overdrive.

I was going to get her far away from here. Then we were going to solve this.

CHAPTER ELEVEN

Alana

I think it must have been late when I finally stepped out of the fog. That's what I called it, the fog. I guess some might call it shock, but when I looked back at that day, the events between being shot at from the Puerto Vallarta bell tower and being in Derrin's newly rented Camry while he handed me a Coke from the gas station, it was all just a fog, like a grey, hazy mist that never really cleared.

Sometimes I wondered if it really all happened, or if it had been a dream. But my body ached and my limbs were covered with scratches from trees whipping us, and my eyes still burned from the salt.

It had happened. Someone tried to kill me. Actually, a bunch of people tried to kill me, but I had no doubt they were all hired by the same person.

Now Derrin knew the truth, and because he was with me, taking care of me and making sure we were taking all the right steps, I didn't mind that he knew. He was one of the few people on earth now that did. He knew the truth about my sisters, about Javier. And he was still with me. In fact, I think he was the only thing keeping me alive.

"How are you feeling?" he asked gently as he got in the car. "You're looking better."

I took a timid sip of Coke. It wasn't very cold but it was fizzy enough. "I think I'm finally, um, here."

"Good. I missed you."

I eyed him, caught off guard by the sincerity in his voice. I swallowed the drink down, my throat buzzing.

"Where are we?"

Now I was really looking at my surroundings. We were in the parking lot of a gas station beside a highway. It didn't look to be an overly busy one, so I didn't think it was the one that connected Puerto Vallarta to the coastal cities. Though it was dark out, there was a line of orange and purple to the left of us, burning the tops of some mountains. We weren't near the ocean either.

He tapped the GPS. "This thing is telling me we're outside Tulepe, two hours east of Mazatlan."

"I miss the Mustang."

"And I missed that attitude," he said. "But you know we had to take it back. These people have connections everywhere. If there was any chance they might've stumbled across the hotel, our identities would be really easy to find, the valet would fess up, and they'd be looking for the black Mustang everywhere. No one looks twice at a Camry."

"And how are we supposed to get away in a hurry?"

"We won't be doing that in a hurry," he said. "We're being extra cautious, extra safe, and staying one step ahead. At this point, they've lost us. If they had found us, we'd be dead. Now we figure out what our next moves are."

"You're awfully good at this."

"I watch a lot of spy movies."

"I don't believe you."

"I was in the army."

"That I know," I said, and went back to sucking on the straw, feeling like a confused little child. Derrin did know a lot, about everything, it seemed. More than the average person should, and he definitely wasn't average. But no matter what he really did for a living or what he knew, he was saving my life and I trusted him more than anything.

"Can I call Luz and Dominga?" I asked hopefully.

He shook his head. "No," he said. "Not yet."

"Not ever?"

He sighed and rubbed his hand over his eyes. "I'm tired. Let's get a hotel room."

"Do you think that's safe?"

"For now it is. They don't know who I am."

"How do you know?"

"I just do." He shrugged and thumped his fist against the steering wheel. "You're the bigger problem. But don't worry about that. I know a lot of people here who can get us fake IDs. They don't ask questions, and they don't talk."

"Do any of these people work for the cartels?" I asked suspiciously.

He gave me a look. "Everyone in Mexico works for the cartels in one way or another." He paused. "Isn't that right?"

"No," I told him. "There are a lot of honest people in this country making an honest living." I paused. "In the morning, I want you to take me to see my brother."

He wiggled his jaw uneasily. "That wouldn't be wise."

"Are you scared?" I had a hard time imagining he was scared of anything.

"I'm not scared, but it wouldn't be good. People can't just meet drug lords. It doesn't work that way."

"I'm his sister."

His face turned grave. "You are. And he had more sisters. I'm sorry, but I have no reason to believe that Javier is going to protect you."

That stung even though it was the truth. "He's all I have."

"You have me."

"I don't even really know you." *It just feels like I do. It just feels like I don't need to.*

"And yet I'm still here, saving your tight little ass today. Where was your brother when you were in the hospital? Did he ever come to visit? What about after? Do you think he'll be here for you now?"

The lashes kept coming. My nose felt hot, and I blinked a few times, trying to hide the disappointment. "This time it's his fault," I said.

"It's always been his fault, Alana. You never asked for this."

"It was my father's fault before then."

"And still, you never asked for this. Your father is dead. Your brother is not. You're alive and I'm here with you."

"I need to see Javier."

"Then get him to meet you somewhere. I'm not taking you there, wherever he lives. That's like walking into the lion's den. A gringo like me . . . he'd never let me out of there alive."

I glared at him. "Oh, he's not that bad."

"I know what he did to Salvador Reyes and his men. I know the way he took over the Sinaloa Cartel, the same way he did with Travis Raines. That made the news back in

Canada too. I'm not taking any chances. Tomorrow, you call him from a payphone – I'm sure there's one somewhere – and you tell him what happened, and you tell him to meet you there, where you call him from. Tell him to bring his wife too."

"Luisa?"

He nodded. "Yes. From what I've heard, she keeps things civil."

"I think you've heard wrong. You can't believe everything you read on the internet."

He went on, not hearing me. "I'll be waiting with a gun trained on his head just in case anything goes wrong."

I slapped his leg in protest. "No you won't! Jesus, Derrin, he's my brother. He's not out to get me. He's not the one who ordered the hit. For all I know, he might be behind the vigilante killing."

He shook his head ever so slightly and stared out at the fluorescent lights of the parking lot. In the distance, the sky was completely black now. Only the lone headlights blinded our eyes as they passed.

This was a lonely, lonely place and I was suddenly aware of how alone I was.

But I wasn't, was I?

I stared at Derrin's profile, at the strong, hard features of his face, the way his chin dimple was only visible in a certain light, like now, the way his hair was starting to grow in more, a light brown color. He still had the perfect head. He had the perfect everything.

"Okay," I conceded. "I'll do as you say. But please, don't do anything stupid. None of this forgotten army stuff. If you're suffering from PTSD, and I'm pretty sure you are suffering from a lot of things I might add, this won't be the time to sort it out."

He turned his head and held my gaze. "I'm not going to shoot your brother. Or your sister-in-law. Or you. I just want to keep you safe. And I will, at any cost."

I frowned, studying him further but not finding any other layers beneath his handsome features. "Why are you doing this for me?"

He smiled sadly. "Because I can." He sighed then started the car. "Let's go find ourselves a hotel, drink some beer, and see if we can fuck each other to sleep."

Twenty minutes later we were staying in a rustic but fairly clean motel. No one was drinking. No one was fucking. We were asleep the minute we hit the pillows.

The next morning I woke up feeling wooden. My tongue was swollen from where I kept chomping down on it during the motorcycle chase, and every part of me hurt.

But I was alive when I shouldn't be, and I couldn't complain. I'd cheated death more than once. Hell, I'd given it the finger.

Derrin was already up, shirtless with his back to me, staring out the crack of light in the drawn curtains and fiddling with something in his hands.

My god he was a fine man. Even now, or maybe even more so, he was everything I'd ever wanted. Each sculpted muscle in his back, from the dimples near his waistband to the ripples that planed off his spine, spoke of what a tireless, tough, well-oiled machine he was. He was so big and strong, my protector. But it never made the fear go completely away, because when it came down to it, he was an ex-soldier. He wasn't Rambo. He wasn't even David Caruso. He was a Canadian with some muscles, a bit of training, and I suppose a lot of luck. He had determination, and he was much, much smarter than his appearance led you to believe. But he wasn't part of the cartels. He didn't know this game or the way things worked as much as he thought he did.

He was so confident he knew how things were going to go that I started to believe him too. But unless there was something about him that I didn't know (and that wouldn't be surprising) I had to keep my guard up. I couldn't rely on him for everything. I had to go on what I knew.

He didn't know my brother at all, just from what he had heard on the news. And while drug lords usually couldn't be trusted, it didn't mean they were all bad people. Javier *was* bad – he didn't get to where he was without being so – but he wasn't as bad as people thought. He'd certainly never hurt me, let alone purposely put me in jeopardy. Marguerite and I were all he had left, and though I hadn't talked to him a lot lately – he seemed to be increasingly busy, which I understood, considering – we had a good relationship. I helped him out when he needed it, and he helped me financially when I did.

And now I had no doubt he would come through when my life was on the line.

I was thinking that and blinking the fuzzy sleep out of my eyes while Derrin took what was in his hands, the Ace bandage, and began to wrap it around his stomach. After the third pass around, he slipped a small handgun in there then wrapped it again, securing it tightly.

When he turned around he wasn't surprised to see me staring at him. I was starting to think he had eyes in the back of his head.

"What's the plan?" I asked, not wanting to mention the gun. That gun had come in handy.

He slipped on a t-shirt, poured a cup of tarlike coffee in a styrofoam cup, and handed it to me before sitting on the side of the bed. I drew my knees up to my chest and took a sip.

Disgusting. I loved coffee but I wasn't about to drink motor oil. I made a face and handed it back to him.

He held the cup in his hands but didn't drink it, looking ahead at a spot on the wall, totally focused.

"We'll check out of here and go up the road for a bit. Find a big public area, like a mall. Find a payphone there and tell him that you need to meet him right where you are at a certain time. Where does he live?"

"About three hours from here. It's remote but he can get here faster than that. I think he has a helicopter now."

He took in this information. "Okay. We'll give him three hours. Then we find another hotel. Check in, under my name only again, and wait there. With two hours left, we split up. I'll be watching you the whole time."

I rubbed my lips together, feeling so damn nervous. "Then what?"

"What do you mean?"

"What happens to me?"

"I don't know. I guess that depends what you're going to ask of him. Do you want to walk off with him, to his compound? Do you seriously believe you'll be safe there?"

"Of course I'll be safe there. I'd have to be. *He*'s safe there."

"Yes," he said with a nod. "It would seem."

"He has people everywhere protecting him, the whole state is behind him. Most of the other states too. He practically owns half the country. I'll be safe with him."

Derrin didn't look convinced and sighed. "You're a free woman. I'll do whatever you want me to do as long as you're certain it needs to be done. But the question is, do you *want* to go with him?"

I pursed my lips and reached for the coffee. Maybe I did need a hit of that stuff.

Twenty minutes later we were on the road and looking for the perfect meeting place. I felt somewhat safe. No one was following us; in reality, how could they be? We had been so careful. Not only did Derrin have the gun strapped to his waist, he also had a knife in his boot and another gun strapped around his leg in a holster.

Yet for all his guns, he didn't seem to be enjoying himself. This wasn't a cops and robbers game to him. It wasn't a game at all. He took this all very, very seriously. As I guess one should when you were being trailed by Mexican assassins. Again I had that feeling that there was far more to Derrin's story than I knew, and I wondered if the truth would ever come out. I wondered if I wanted it to.

While we searched for big, public spaces throughout the dry countryside and graveyards of empty roadside stores, I thought about what I would do. If Javier offered me protection, I would have to go. But that didn't mean I wanted to. To be honest, I didn't at all. Being at his compound wouldn't make me feel safe, even if I was safe. All those bad, bad men walking around, owning the place. I'm sure they would treat me with faux respect, but I'd be the first one thrown under the bus. I could never sleep knowing who those men were, what they orchestrated. Though I'd never been to Javier's place, I had heard the rumors, of the twisted doctor and the torture shed in the back. Prostitutes that were killed in the house after sex, or shot for fun.

Now Javier was married – a quick ceremony somewhere that I hadn't been invited to – but I wasn't too sure that having a woman around was changing him for the better. If anything, I think he was making *her* worse.

I guess I'd find out soon, if Javier wanted anything to do with me at all.

And, of course, at the heart of it, I didn't want to leave Derrin behind. Who knows how long I'd have to hide out, and the direction that my life would take. I wanted my life to go in whatever direction Derrin was heading in.

I was falling in love with this man. Fast and hard, just the way he lived and fucked. I wondered if he would love the same way too.

I wanted to be the woman that healed him.

"Bingo," Derrin said, smacking the dashboard.

I looked to the left and saw a giant, brand new Wal-Mart on the side of the road. The parking lot was packed, and there were a few half-finished office buildings and shops flanking it.

"Wal-Mart?" I said incredulously. "You think Javier is going to come meet me at a Wal-Mart?"

Derrin grinned beautifully. "He'll have no choice."

Soon I was at a payphone located just outside the washrooms. Wal-Mart was a living hell full of bad lighting, sad faces, and screaming children. We had only started getting them everywhere in Mexico a few years ago, but it was like all the American stereotypes followed them down here. This was one of the supercenters that had a McDonald's in it and a produce section that pissed off all our farmers. It reeked of everything I hated.

I dialed Javier's number, not knowing if he would pick up. He wouldn't recognize the number, and my own phone had been in my bag when we drove into the ocean. It was now lost at sea.

"Hello?" someone answered. It wasn't Javier. Could I have gotten the wrong number? He always answered his cell. Unless he had his number changed recently, which was possible.

"Uh, hello. Is Javier there?"

"Who is this?" asked the voice, amused. It didn't seem familiar to me.

I didn't want to tell him anything yet. "Is he there? Is this his phone?"

"I'll tell you what you want to know once you tell me who you are."

"If Javier is there just tell him it's his sister."

Silence. Was it possible this person didn't know he had sisters?

"Hello?" I repeated.

"What's your name?" he asked slowly.

"Alana Bernal."

"I see. And you say you're his sister, hey?"

"Last I checked," I said, getting annoyed now.

"Interesting. Can you hold on a moment?"

"What's your name?" I quickly asked.

"Please hold." I could hear muffled speaking like a hand over a receiver.

After a long minute, Javier answered. "Alana?"

I breathed out a sigh of relief and put my hand against my forehead. "Javier. Thank god."

"Where are you calling from? This isn't your number." He sounded ruffled. He usually sounded as cool as a cucumber.

"Sorry," I told him. "I didn't have a choice. My phone is gone. I'm calling from a payphone."

"Where?" he asked.

"I don't know," I said. "Outside of Durango, I think."

"What the hell are you doing there?"

"I'm in trouble."

For a moment I thought he was going to ask me what I did, maybe scold me for some money problem. "I saw something in the news," he said carefully. "Gunshots in Puerto Vallarta."

I took in a deep breath. "The gunshots were for me."

I heard him inhale sharply. "Are you sure?"

"Yes. We were walking through the square—"

"Who is we?"

"Me and my boyfriend," I said on the spot. I didn't know what else to call Derrin, and I knew if I made him sound more casual than that, Javier would grill me about it.

"Boyfriend? What boyfriend? What's his name?"

"Derrin."

"What the hell kind of name is that?"

"He's Canadian."

"Oh, that figures. Go on."

"We were walking through the square. Someone in the clock tower took a shot at me. We ran, got on a motorbike, and ended up outrunning them."

He didn't say anything for a moment. "Alana, Alana, Alana . . . if what you're saying is true, you don't just outrun someone who is trying to kill you. Not here. Not you. That's impossible."

"We outran them," I said, raising my voice. "Look, we got away."

"Just like that?"

"Yes. We got back to the hotel room, packed up our shit, and fled."

I heard him groan to himself.

"What?" I asked. "What is it? What do I do?"

"What do you do?"

"Javier . . . people are after me. Probably the same people who murdered Beatriz."

His voice grew cold. "That was Travis Raines. He is dead."

"And there are others just like him trying to teach you the same lesson. I wasn't hit by a car by accident – that had to be on purpose. And now there were actual bullets aimed at my head."

"Are you sure they weren't for the Canadian? He does have a stupid name."

"Javier, please," I begged him, my voice cracking. "Help me."

He exhaled hard. "Fine. Where should I meet you?"

"I'm at a Wal-Mart."

"Wal-Mart?" he asked incredulously.

"Yes."

He sounded like he'd choked on something. "You can't be serious."

I could feel my face going red. I was fed up. I didn't care who he was, he was still my brother.

"I am serious. Come to the Wal-Mart outside of Durango, or wherever you manage to trace this call to. I'll be sitting on the corner of a water fountain between Wal-Mart and an office building. Bring Luisa."

"Luisa, why?"

"I want to talk to her, too."

I hung up the phone before he could protest anymore then left the madness of the store. As I took the stairs down to the parking garage underneath the main lot, I grumbled to myself. After everything that had happened – the accident, the fact that he heard about the gunshots on the news – he still wasn't acting like this was a big deal. I had almost died several times. Why was that so hard for him to believe? Why didn't he care?

I walked through the garage, which was only half-filled with cars since most people had parked up top, and found the Camry. Derrin was in the driver's seat, his face taut. His eyes quickly flew to me, and he leaned over to open the passenger door.

"How did it go?" he asked as I sat down and closed the door after me.

"It could have gone better," I said, trying not to sound as resentful as I felt. In a petty way, I didn't want Derrin to think he was right about him.

He was watching me, his eyes unreadable yet they seemed to be reading me. "Tell me what he said."

"Well, first of all, he didn't answer. It was some other guy.

From the way he questioned me, it was like he didn't know I existed."

This piqued Derrin's interest. "Is that so? Did you get his name?"

"He wouldn't say."

"But he got yours."

"Yes."

"Javier was probably trying to protect you and Marguerite, keep you a secret."

"Well, I kind of went and messed that all up, didn't I?" I scratched angrily at the skin around the top of my cast. I wanted this fucking thing off. "Anyway, Javier told me he heard about the shootings on the news, but obviously he didn't know I was involved. In fact . . . it really sounded like he didn't believe me."

Derrin only grunted.

"I told him where I was. He wanted me to go meet him somewhere else, but I told him no."

"Good girl."

I managed a smile. "It didn't feel right otherwise."

"Did you mention me?"

I paused. "Yes."

He cocked his head. "And what did you tell him?"

"I told him I had a Canadian boyfriend named Derrin."

"Really? And what did he say to that?"

"Well, he was surprised because I never really have boyfriends. And he thinks you have a stupid name."

"Charming brother you have there."

I shrugged.

"So is that what I am?" he asked, leaning closer to me. His

fingers traced the skin on my shoulder and a subtle shiver shot down my spine.

"If you want to be," I said quietly, suddenly feeling shy. So not like myself. What was I, twelve?

He reached out and cupped my face in his hand, his sky blue eyes searching mine, trying to overturn every buried stone. "I want to be. If you'll have me around."

"I've kept you around so far," I joked.

His brow furrowed. "I want to be important to you."

I knew he was being serious – when wasn't Derrin being serious? But my default reaction was always to make a joke when things got too heavy. I had to rein that in, swallow it down, even though I was too afraid to take what he was saying as truth. At some point, Derrin and I would part ways. It would have to be that way. He was just a tourist here in a foreign land. He couldn't live in Mexico forever. Why would he even want to?

"Alana," he said. "No matter what happens with your brother, you have someone here that has your back, all the way to the end."

"To what end?"

"To the end of it all," he said, his voice grave. "And I'm not going to let you go so easily. I want you to figure it out with Javier, see what he knows, see if he can help. But if he has no ideas, if he doesn't seem to care, you'll be better off with me."

"How can you say that?"

"Trust me."

"I want to," I automatically said. I corrected myself. "I *do* trust you."

"You don't. And I don't blame you. But if you stay with me, I can make a better life for you. It doesn't have to be with me, but I can get you out of here."

"How?"

"Come up north with me."

I curled my lip. "Too cold."

"The west coast isn't cold at all, you'd love it," he said. "But if not, then Europe. Some small island in the Caribbean. South America."

It sounded tempting. But the whole thing was absurd. "I barely know you."

"I know. And I barely know you. But this is what's going to keep you alive." Now he was cupping my face with both hands. "Alana, unless the men who are after you are killed, unless the person who wants you dead is found out then taken out, this isn't going to stop. There is a lot of money on your head."

I frowned, feeling icky at that assumption. "How do you know that?"

"I just do."

"Like you know how to kill a person and ride a motorbike at the same time?"

"Yes." His grip tightened, his gaze more intense. I felt like he was going to devour me. "Your life as you've known it is now over."

I swallowed the lump in my throat. "You said that I could talk to Luz—"

"I did say that. And I meant it. But I also said not now. They'll be in danger, too, if they talk to you, so leave them out of it. Send them a postcard from a random place. Alana, you're going to need to say goodbye to the person you were. Alana Bernal ended when she was hit by a car."

I felt like a force field went up around me. I wasn't feeling any of this. It wasn't sinking in. No. This wasn't the way. My brother would fix everything.

I looked away and pulled out of Derrin's grasp. "I need to talk to Javier."

"And you're going to. And I'm going to watch the whole thing," he said, straightening up. He started the car. "Let's go find us a place to stay for the night before he gets here and everything changes."

CHAPTER TWELVE

Derek

B eing Derrin Calway was becoming harder and harder. I had messed up once, telling her about Minnesota when I should have said Winnipeg, but I don't think she thought anything of it. Still, it was getting increasingly hard to pretend I was just an ex-soldier. She knew I was something more, and I knew in the future I was going to have to tell her the truth.

The question was, how much truth. It's one thing to say you have experience in "getting shit done" for people. It's another to say you're a professional assassin, one that put a bullet in Travis Raines' head at the request of her brother. And it's another to say you were the vigilante who shot the driver in the head, only after you failed to kill her to begin with.

Where did the truth end and where did I begin?

I'm not sure I'd ever figure it out and not come out more of a shell than I was going in.

I didn't trust her brother at all. I knew Javier enough to know that she did mean something to him, but a man changes when he comes into power and I'd seen him change a lot. I wasn't even expecting him to show up to meet her. He was the man in charge of the seedy underbelly of half the country, he wouldn't want to risk anything by going after his sister.

Then again, there was the chance that his marriage had softened him. That's why I wanted Luisa to be there. Alana would be able to get a better read off of her. She wanted to believe the best of Javier a little too much.

While we drove around looking for a cheap, simple motel that I could pay for in cash, I wondered if Javier could be behind any of this. The man who had called me and ordered her hit definitely hadn't been him. Javier's voice and mannerisms were far too distinctive. But could it have been someone working on his behalf? Perhaps it was the man Alana had talked to on the phone, even though he'd pretended not to know who she was.

Who was Javier's right-hand man these days? Esteban Mendoza. Could it have been him on the phone? I wasn't sure. I never paid too much attention to Este back then because he was a bit of a chump, a surfer dude who didn't do shit but wanted to weasel up the ranks. He was proficient in surveillance and electronics – we were able to do the raid on Raines' house all because of him. But Este didn't seem to have the chops for much more than that.

Then again, being second to Javier meant doing a lot of dirty work. An order was an order. But why would Javier want his own sister assassinated? That's what didn't make any sense at all. I didn't trust him, and with good reason, and I thought if she went off with him it would do her far more harm than good. But I didn't know if he'd want to kill her.

I started thinking that even if she did go off with him, maybe I could put myself back in the picture somehow. Ever since I defected from him after the Raines' takeover years ago and helped Ellie Watt out of Honduras to rescue her father – for a price higher than Javier's of course – I'd never seen Javier again. I couldn't just stroll up to him and ask if he needed any help. Javier held grudges like nobody's business, especially those that concerned his ex-lover, and he'd shoot me on the spot.

I guess the problem now was how far I was willing to go for Alana. She'd said again and again how much we didn't know each other, and she was right every time. But even then, I couldn't stay away. I couldn't from the moment I saw her in the airport parking lot. Just one real look at her and she'd done something to me, stirred something that had been dormant for so long.

I couldn't leave her. I just didn't know how to get her to stay with me.

Eventually we found a nice enough hotel. We had an hour to kill before I drove us back to the Wal-Mart and I wished we had more. On the off chance she left with her brother and I never saw her again, I wanted to remember exactly how she felt to touch, to hold, to kiss, to be deep inside of.

Once we got inside the room, I locked the door, drew the shades, and then pulled her into my arms.

The need to drive my cock inside her suddenly overpowered me, and I grabbed her face, kissing her hard, my hands moving down into her hair, down her back to her ass where I squeezed hard. She let out a cry of pain, but it was good pain from the way she attacked me, hands, lips, teeth everywhere.

I'd never felt so hungry for her. Apparently she felt the

same. So much adrenaline, emotion and futility hung in the air, throttling our bones, stirring our blood, making us starved, wild animals.

Death made sex feel much more alive.

I quickly pulled off her shorts and thong and spun her around. I pinned her up against the wall. The bed wouldn't do this time. It was too soft, too comforting, too forgiving. I wanted her raw and real. I wanted to feel the pain with the beauty, the harshness of it all. I wanted to feel all of her.

She wrapped one leg around my waist, her cast on the other hooked around my thigh, and held me close to her as I fumbled with my zipper. Once my dick was free, my pants dropping to my ankles, I wasted no time in guiding the tip into her, just teasing her cleft with her own slickness.

"I need to feel you," she cried, her head back, her hips trying to thrust closer, to get purchase. Her nails dug into my back.

"You'll feel every inch, babe," I groaned, feeling her expanding for my tip, so greedy and hungry, just like me.

"Now, Derrin, *por favor.*"

Her cries were my undoing. I thrust into her, so wet, so tight, so damn beautiful. I was meant to be this deep inside of her, pushed in to the hilt, like I could stay here forever, like I was supposed to.

I caught my breath, nearly losing it, and pulled out slowly, relaxing into a rhythm, trying to hold myself in check. She felt so good and I started rubbing her clit with tiny, circular strokes. She started panting, squirming, wanting more.

"Harder," she pleaded. "Keep going."

I bit at her neck and sucked beneath her ear, loving how

pushy she was. I kept at it, slow and steady, not ready to give her everything just yet.

"Do you like that?" I whispered, delighting in the primal lust that was spilling out of her mouth in load groans.

I thrust into her deeper, faster, torn between wanting to come and wanting this to go on forever. She held me tighter, her nails sharp and drawing blood as I pounded her, keeping my fingers on her wet clit quick and steady. Her grip around me began to loosen as she came close to the edge.

"Alana," I cried out breathlessly as the pressure reached the breaking point. Everything tightened, from my balls to my abs, before I came hard and poured into her. This was so raw, beautiful, that I could barely hold her up anymore. I felt as my seed spilled into her, something was spilling into me and filling up all the caverns deep inside, the dark and hollow places. They felt brighter now. Warm. Real.

She cried out as she came, loud enough for the room next door to hear. But I didn't care. I didn't care about anything except her. My heart simmered.

I breathed into the hollow of her neck, drowning in her smell, the feel of her as she pulsed around me, the sound of her breathless noises she probably didn't know she was making. I'd never been in so deep. I knew I wouldn't walk away from this woman unscarred.

"Shit," she said, smiling and catching her breath. Her legs began to shake around me, worn from the strain, and I grabbed a hold of her, gently lowering her to the ground. She wiped the sweat from her brow and frowned at the marks her finger-nails had made on my shoulder.

"I'm sorry," she said, nodding at them.

"Don't you ever," I told her, brushing her wet hair off her face. Everything about her glowed, so hot, so warm, so larger than life.

"You know what you are?" I asked her, leaning in until my lips grazed the rim of her ear.

"What?"

"Sunshine."

Redemption.

Even after the sex and intimacy, the ride back to Wal-Mart was strained. Both of us were locked in our own heads, being eaten by our own fear. My fear – the first real fear I had felt in some time – was that I would never see her again. If I never saw her again, I couldn't protect her. If I couldn't protect her, she would end up dead.

Her fear . . . well, I could only imagine. I just hoped it was enough to keep her on her toes but not too much that she would panic. Fear can only work for you if you know how to recognize it and use it.

Our plan was relatively simple, yet as we sat back in the parking garage, now a bit more full thanks to after work shoppers pushing their carts back and forth, it seemed daunting. There was a mild sense of chaos here, which usually helped me think but today it wasn't cutting it.

I had my sniper rifle and silencer with me, as well as my .22. I would go up first by the doors at the far end of the parking garage, ones that led up to an empty office building. The doors would be locked but that was never a problem for me. I would then secure a spot in an office on the highest floor. I wouldn't be right at the window overlooking the fountain – that was too obvious – but I'd try to find one further back with a clear shot. Then I would wait. The moment Alana looked like she was in trouble or being taken against her will was the moment I would pull the trigger.

In some ways, it was phenomenally easy to kill Javier this way. He would know that too. But what enemies he had I'm sure were masquerading as his friends. In fact, I knew for certain he had no friends. I assumed he knew that too.

And Javier would probably travel without telling anyone. Maybe Esteban. No one would expect to see him here, so he would be safe. In Culiacán, where he lived, that was a different story. People would expect him there. But here, even though he probably felt inconvenienced by the travel, he was actually fairly safe.

But *I* was here.

"So," Alana started, scratching at the top of her cast nervously.

"So. Are you ready?"

She shook her head, her eyes wide and searching. "What happens if I go with him? If he promises me safety. What happens to us?"

I tried to smile but failed. "I'll be here whenever you need me."

"You'll stay in Mexico?"

"Of course."

"Don't you have to go home?"

"I don't have to go anywhere, Alana."

"What if I want to see you again?"

"You can email me." Even though it was the best way to

get a hold of me, it still felt so cold, so wrong, to have our contact with each other go from skin to skin to email.

"Not call?"

"I'll probably get a new phone and number to be safe."

"Oh," she said, looking panicked.

I put my hand on her leg, relishing in the warmth of her skin. "When I get a new phone, I'll email you the number. Any time you want to leave, I'll come and get you. Your brother won't hold you there. Remember, this all has to be your choice and your choice alone."

"But if I choose to go, this is it? I mean, I won't get to see you before?"

I wiggled my jaw back and forth and breathed out through my nose. "It wouldn't be safe for him to see me. I'd rather not, you know, be exposed to a notorious drug lord if I can help it."

She nodded. "I get it. Well, I guess you should probably go take your place."

Something in me seized, but I did what I could to ignore it. "All right. If you don't go with him, if anything, anything at all seems the slightest bit wrong, change your mind. Just get advice. See what your options are. And come back here to the car. I'll meet you and we'll be on our way."

"Derrin," she said, adjusting in her seat to face me. She looked so soulful in that moment that I wished to god she was calling me Derek instead. It would only feel real when she used my real name, knew the real me, everything I was, and still stayed.

But she wasn't staying.

Before I could say anything stupid, I quickly leaned over

and grabbed her face in my hands, kissing her hard like I was trying to create an impression on my lips, like she could seep into my skin and stay a permanent reminder. She tasted sweet and felt soft, and that fire inside me was burning away. No matter what, I would protect her.

I pulled away, breathless and surprised to see the moisture in her eyes, tears threatening to overflow. I quickly grabbed the gym bag from the back seat that had the sniper rifle in it, and then left the car, shutting the door behind me. The sound echoed through the garage, lonely and cold.

I didn't look back, but I would see her again. I was on my way to protect her.

CHAPTER THIRTEEN

Alana

I'd never felt so unsafe, so alone, until I watched Derrin walk away from the car and disappear into a stairwell. I don't even know how he managed to break the locked door so seamlessly, so naturally, without causing any attention, but he did. Now I was sitting in the Camry wishing I could keep an eye on the time. A watch would have been nice. A new phone would have been nice.

Sometimes I was hit with the overwhelming reality that my life would never be the same again. Something as simple as losing my phone, all my pictures, my useless contacts, my apps – something so normal as that and I felt like I'd never be able to have a good life again. Just the idea that Luz and Dominga were probably calling it nonstop, calling the hotel, checking up on me, was a wrench in my heart. Dominga's maid friend was probably searching the room on her behalf, panicked at our disappearance.

Provided someone else didn't get to the room first. I could finally see why Derrin didn't want me in contact with them at all. I hated that they had to worry, but they would be the first people my enemies would go after for information. If I knew anything, it was how much they loved to extract the truth from their victims. And when the victims didn't know anything, that made it even worse.

I didn't wipe the tear that rolled down my cheek, but I told myself it would be the last time I cried. It had to be. Javier was meeting me here, at least I hoped, and he would fix everything. He would get me out of this mess.

When I figured I'd spent about an hour in the car, I took in a few deep breaths and finally got up. I walked over to the stairs that led up to the Wal-Mart, my cast echoing as I walked. I was less and less awkward, but the damn cast was a reminder that I was always at a disadvantage, and if I really concentrated I'd realize my ankle was throbbing painfully. All that running yesterday had done a number on it and yet pain was the last thing my brain was processing. It was all fear now.

Once up top, the sun hit my face and cleared a bit of the darkness away. Wal-Mart was busy, full of people living their normal lives, going to their cars with bags full of useless crap. I envied them, the blissful ways they could just continue living in ignorance. None of them could have appreciated how easy they had it. I sure as hell hadn't appreciated it two weeks ago.

I walked past the front of the store, past the vending machines stocked with tamarind and pineapple sodas, past robotic horses that children could ride, and gumball machines. I headed over to the fountain.

It was large and circular, made up of terracotta tile with water flowing into a blue-hued pool with only a few pesos at the bottom. There was a bench in the shade where an old man was dozing, a newspaper and a sandwich beside him, but other than that the place was empty.

I tried to look up at the windows of the office building next door, but knew the sun would be in my eyes if I did – it was late afternoon and close to setting behind it – and if anyone was watching me, they might get suspicious. I just had to believe that Derrin was up there, watching over me.

But what if he wasn't? What if he'd skipped town? It was so hard to know, to trust.

It was possible. Anything was possible. But I had to have faith in him. There were few things left that I could believe in.

I took a seat at the edge of the fountain and waited. I wished I had a book or something to make myself look less obvious, but since I was waiting for someone, it didn't really matter. I stared at the tiny birds that hopped around at my feet, chirping, looking for a handout, then watched the highway beyond the store as it piled up thicker and thicker with traffic heading out of Durango, moving like syrup.

Finally a figure caught my eye. She was short, maybe 5'2", and dressed in a strapless yellow sundress, wearing wedge heels, and holding a Chanel bag under her arm. Long dark hair flowed behind her. Even though she was wearing the world's biggest sunglasses, I could still tell it was Luisa. She had this way about her that made her stand out among the masses, and it wasn't just her beauty, nor the fact that she now dressed impeccably well, like a patron's wife.

Unfortunately, Javier was nowhere to be found. When I first met Luisa, I was witness to the warmth and soul she had as she was reunited with her parents in my apartment, but every other time it was a little less and less. I didn't think she was a bad woman by any means, but there had been a hardness creeping into her heart. I suppose that would naturally happen if you were married to someone like Javier.

She stopped right in front of me and I caught a whiff of honeysuckle perfume. She didn't take off her glasses, and she didn't smile. Instead, she looked around her in all directions, checking out everything, including the empty office building, until it seemed she was satisfied.

"Alana," she finally said and only then did she push her sunglasses on top of her head. She looked beautiful but tired. Her eyes, thankfully, were kind, especially as they focused on my bandaged wrist and cast. "Is that from the car accident?" she asked softly.

I nodded. "Yeah. But I'm almost fully healed. Doesn't hurt at all," I lied.

She smiled stiffly and looked around her again.

"Where is Javier?" I asked.

"Are you alone?"

"Of course."

"Where is your boyfriend?"

"Not here," I told her, then quickly added, "In the car."

"We're not going to get to meet him?"

"Then Javier is here," I said.

She nodded. "He is."

I frowned. "But you were sent to make sure the coast was clear?"

"I wasn't sent." She smiled at me. "He didn't have much say. I wasn't about to let him just waltz out here, and he wasn't going to let me either. But marriage takes compromise." Her smile twisted slightly.

"You don't trust me?"

She cocked her head. "I want to trust you, Alana. But this whole thing is so bizarre. It doesn't sound right. You must understand that."

"You think I'm trying to set Javier up?" I asked, feeling hot and indignant. "He's my brother."

"I know that. And you are part of what little family he has left. But if what you are saying is true, then you could have been followed yourself. The only reason anyone is after you, I'm assuming, of course, is because they are after him in some way. Or it could be someone right in front of your eyes. We would be stupid not to take due diligence on this and we are not stupid."

Wow. She was sounding less like a wife and more like a member of his team.

"So where is he?" I asked, scanning the parking lot.

She slipped her sunglasses back on. "He wants you to come meet him. On his terms."

I stared at her blankly. I couldn't leave this spot, not with Derrin watching.

She held out her hand for me and the diamonds on her rings blazed in the sunshine. "Come along, I'll take you there."

"Where?" I didn't want to take her hand.

"Not here," she said. "You're not afraid of your own brother, are you?"

"Is he afraid of his own sister?"

She raised her brow for a second then jerked her chin in the direction of Wal-Mart. "Come."

I sighed, feeling horrible about this. I wasn't afraid of

Javier, but being out of Derrin's watch felt wrong and I knew he was probably freaking out – well, as much as Derrin could freak out – up in the office building. I just hoped he didn't try and take Luisa out.

I grabbed her hand and she helped me to my feet. Once I was up, her grip was surprisingly firm which didn't really sit well with me. It was almost as if I were being escorted somewhere.

Somehow I resisted the urge to look over my shoulder in Derrin's direction and kept walking. Even though Luisa had shorter legs, I still had to hustle to keep pace with the cast on.

"That can't be much fun," she noted as she eyed me again. Her voice was softer now, like she was finally being herself and not the wife of Javier.

"None of this is fun," I told her.

She made an agreeable sound then led me toward the Wal-Mart doors.

"He's in there?"

She nodded as the automatic doors opened for us and we entered the world of mayhem again. I was getting really sick of this store.

"This is as safe a place as any," she said, her voice lowered now.

"How is that possible?"

"Who would ever suspect Javier Bernal would be in a Wal-Mart? No one would even recognize him in here because they wouldn't expect to see him. Hiding in a big SUV? Yes. In here, no."

"So he's unprotected."

She led me down the aisles. "No, he's never unprotected. He's never alone. But take a look around and I bet you could never pick any of our men out."

I briefly glanced around. I saw women pushing strollers, slobby looking men with giant beer bellies and trucker hats, short men wearing cheap dress shirts tucked into high-waisted jeans, a guy who looked like he just got back from surfing, store employees in starchy uniforms. They could be anyone. Or she could be bluffing. I would never know. Neither made me feel safe.

In fact, I didn't even recognize my own brother until we were halfway down the canned food aisle. His back was to me and it looked like he was examining a can of beans or something. But of course as I got closer, I knew it was him without a doubt.

Even from behind, he dressed impeccably. His hair was a bit shorter now and not so shaggy at the back. I think last time I teased him that he was close to having a mullet like the redneck Americans do. He must have taken it to heart. Aside from his hair, he was wearing a crisp suit jacket, dark blue with black pants. He wasn't the tallest man in the world, but he had a way of holding his body that could fool you into thinking he was.

We stopped a few feet behind him, and even though I wanted to say something, I knew Luisa was the one who should.

"I've got her," she said.

Got her? And with those words, the blood in my veins took on an icy touch, like I was hooked up to one of the IVs again.

Javier slowly turned his head to look at me, staring at me inquisitively for a moment. He didn't smile, he didn't say anything, he just studied me like I was some sort of imposter. His eyes were burning with that amber intensity they got when he, well, they were always like that.

Finally he looked down at my cast and up again to my face, tilting his head. "You look like you got hit by a truck."

"It was a car," I reminded him.

He raised his brow then idly checked the gold watch on his wrist. "All right, let's make this quick."

I was a bit stunned. I wasn't sure how I could make any of this quick. I wasn't even sure what was supposed to take place.

"Do you want me to explain again what happened?" I asked. Luisa took her hand out of mine but now was holding my arm by the bicep. I looked at her, slightly aghast, but her attention was on her husband.

"Yes," he said simply. He put the can back on the shelf and slipped his hands into his pockets. "From the start. From when you were hit by the car."

Jesus, this was going to take forever, especially since he already knew most of this. But I knew what he was doing. Javier had a way of sucking the truth out of you just by looking at you. He was discerning once and for all whether I was telling the truth or not. It bothered me that he didn't fully believe me yet, but then again I guess he hadn't survived this long by trusting everyone, including family.

I wondered if I would have to start doing the same thing.

But as I told him everything from the beginning, I could

see a softening coming into his eyes. He believed me. He could see the truth.

"So you were walking through the town square when the shots happened?"

I nodded. "Yeah. Obviously we didn't notice them."

His eyes narrowed slightly and he exchanged a look with Luisa. "But if these are trained assassins as they seemed to be, how did you not get hit?"

I shrugged. "I don't know. Derrin pulled me in for a hug or something. The ground behind me exploded. Near miss. Then we ran."

"And how well do you know this Derrin? Not at all, right?"

"I know him enough. He saved my life."

Javier smiled, almost smug. For some reason it reminded me of a snake. "So it would seem he did."

I chose to ignore that. "So what do I do now? They're after me because of you."

His eyes turned cold. "So this is my fault, is it?"

"You know what I mean."

"Oh, I know what you mean," he said coolly. "I have no doubt these people want to send me a message. But more than that, I think they mean to deliver the message themselves."

"What does that mean?" I tried to fold my arms but Luisa held tight.

He tapped his long fingers along the cans on the shelf. Somehow they were always so manicured. He must never have to do any dirty work these days.

"It means that it sounds like whatever has happened to you has been part of a more elaborate scheme, to bring someone you don't know into your life. To make you trust them. To make it seem like your life is in danger."

"It is in danger!" I yelled at him. A shopper passing by gave me a quick look before hurrying away.

"Keep your voice down," Luisa warned me.

"Get your hand off me," I growled right back, ripping my arm out of her grasp.

She took a step back, hands in the air, looking to Javier for his orders. He shook his head slightly then turned his eyes back to me.

"Your life may be, but I have no reason to believe that bullet was ever meant to hit you. Same with the car. Same with the motorcycle chase. These people are fake. They are only making it look like they're after you. How else could you explain that you got away?"

Because Derrin is way more than you think he is, I thought to myself. *Even I don't know what he's capable of.*

At that thought I had to wonder where he was right now. Surely he would have come out of the office and trailed me. He had to be watching, but I was too nervous to look around and see.

"So what," I said, "you think that this is all a ruse for me to trust him."

He nodded sharply.

"And then what? Wait to kill me?"

"Oh, I'm sure he's going to wait to kill you," he said, so casually that it got under my skin. "But that's not a promise. He's waiting for you to come to me. Like you just have. He wants me to take you in."

I shook my head. "No. No, he's the one who didn't like

this idea. He wants me to stay with him, he told me it's not safe for me to go off with you."

He tilted his head, considering. "Well, that may be true. My place is no place for a lady."

Luisa cleared her throat in annoyance. He flashed a disarming smile at her. "Luisa, love, you are no longer a lady. You're a queen."

I wrinkled my nose. "Ugh. Cheesy."

He looked to me, not amused. "Whatever would I do without my sister acting like a brat?"

My mouth dropped open. "I am not acting like a brat! I'm scared, Javier. I thought you would help me." I looked to Luisa. "Or at least you. I saved your parents' life, remember? I held on to them for weeks. Do you think that was easy? We were all scared shitless."

Luisa's face momentarily crumpled. There was still a good, kind woman in there somewhere. She was just getting buried by Javier.

She glanced at him. "We should take her in."

"No," Javier said adamantly. "No. This is very clearly a trap. We would take her with us and he would follow. I have no doubt, Alana, that this man is not who he says he is. He is using you to get to me, to who he really wants."

I placed my face in my hands in frustration before throwing them out to the sides. "So then what? You're going to assume something you know nothing about and you're just going to leave me here? With someone you think aims to hurt you, hurt me?"

He frowned and ran a hand through his hair with a sigh.

"Don't be so dramatic, Alana. Of course not. I'm just telling you you're not coming with us. I'll make sure you're safe."

"How?"

He took a step closer to me, eyes boring into mine. He could sure be intimidating, I'd give him that. He slipped his hand into his front pocket and pulled out a business card with his first two fingers. He flicked it out to me.

"This is the number I want you to call from the payphone you used earlier. There will be instructions. Call the moment you see us leave. Then go into the women's washroom and wait. Do not leave for anything."

"But Derrin . . ." I started.

He gave me a caustic smile. "Obviously he will not know of this. Did you not hear what I just said? He is not your boyfriend, Alana. He is not your friend. He is my enemy. He is your enemy."

"Who is he?" I asked, my voice coming out in a whisper.

"I have no idea," he admitted. "But it doesn't matter, does it?"

But it did. It did so much. And at the heart of it all, I knew Javier was wrong.

Wasn't he?

"We'll be in touch," he said, forcing the business card in my hand. When I made a fist around it, he put his hand on my shoulder. He gave it a squeeze and stared at me intently. "I will take care of you, you got that? The only way I know how."

Before I could be touched by this rare show of affection, his gaze slid to Luisa and he straightened up. "Let's go," he said to her.

She nodded, gave me a small smile, and then the two of them walked quickly down the aisle of canned goods, the king and queen of Mexico.

I watched until they disappeared around the corner and into the mass of shoppers.

I felt like collapsing to the ground. The business card in my hand felt like lead, a choice I had to take.

Unless I took none at all.

I slipped it into my pocket.

I didn't want to believe what he said of Derrin, even though some of it made sense. But of course Javier had never met him. He didn't know him. Neither did I, but I at least felt like I knew something about him. I knew he was sincere, and while he might be lying about some things about his past or who he was, I knew that when he was holding me, kissing me, fucking me, that was all real.

He did care about me. I had to trust that.

The question was, could I trust that more than I could trust my own brother?

I slowly walked down the aisle in a daze. Once I got to the doors, I had the option of going to the payphone or of going downstairs to the Camry to see Derrin. Maybe I even had the option of both.

I was almost at the end of the aisle when I bumped into someone with a small basket full of groceries.

"Sorry," I mumbled, and looked up.

It was the surfer-looking guy I had seen earlier. He had a baseball cap pulled down low over his light brown shoulder-length hair, but when he looked down at me I could see his eyes were a very clear hazel, more green than brown. He might have been handsome if it weren't for an ugly scar on the left side of his face.

I immediately averted my eyes, not wanting to stare, and tried to move past.

"No, I'm sorry," he said.

The way he said it, so gravely, made my skin prickle. I paused and looked over my shoulder at him.

He was smiling at me in a way a stranger shouldn't. I was used to men leering at me, but this was different. Besides, it was creepy when men leered at a girl in a cast, like the fact that I was vulnerable and broken turned them on even more.

"Do I know you?" he asked, frowning insincerely.

I wasn't in the mood for pick-up lines, especially from weirdos.

"No," I said, glaring at him. Then I turned around.

"I think I do," he said quietly.

I swallowed hard. I wanted to keep walking. I needed to keep walking.

"Alana Bernal," he added.

Fuck. FUCK.

I should have run. I should have just run. But I slowly pivoted around to face him. There was a chance he was with Javier. Luisa said they were all over the store. This was probably one of his men.

"You know my name," I told him, trying to sound casual, hoping he couldn't hear my voice shake. "I should know your name then."

"You probably do," he said matter-of-factly. His grin widened. "I think many people do. If they don't, they will."

He wasn't going to give me his name.

"Do you work for my brother?"

"I work for no one but myself." He slowly reached into his basket of groceries. I didn't wait to see if he was going to pull out a banana. I knew it was a gun.

I turned and leaped to the left, knocking over a display of gravy powder with my cast, and got behind the end of the aisle before a gunshot went off.

It missed me, but brown gravy powder filled the air. I kept running, thankful that the whole store was erupting into extreme chaos. Everyone was suddenly screaming, shoving, crying, running. I was swept up in the mass of shoppers trying to exit, pushing their carts into everyone and everything.

Whoever the fuck that guy was, he definitely wasn't an assassin for hire. He did a pretty shitty job of trying to take me out. But he still tried to kill me all the same, and I had to get out of this fucking store while I could, if I wasn't trampled to death by the mass pandemonium.

There were no more shots, just screams, but even then I was frantically searching the stampede of people for Derrin, Javier, somebody to help me. I didn't know if the man was still behind me, if anyone saw him with the gun, if he was blending into the crowd or being arrested by store security. I didn't know and I couldn't know. There was no time.

I did what I could to get through the crowd and eventually just let the swarm push me to the bottleneck at the doors, everyone packed in tight. People kept stepping on my cast and swearing, but I didn't feel a thing.

Finally I was outside, and I immediately ran down the stairs as quickly as I could to the underground garage.

Down there, other people were running for their cars. It was just as crazy, people peeling out of spots, swiping parked cars, nearly hitting other shoppers. Then at the end I saw Derrin, running toward me.

My heart swelled with relief at the sight of him. This man would protect me. He would keep me safe.

My brother had to be wrong.

"Alana," he said, grabbing my face with his hands. His eyes looked wild. "What happened?"

"There's someone in the store, he looked like a surfer bum. He tried to talk to me, said my name. He knew who I was, Derrin! Then he pulled out a gun. I ran, he fired once and missed. I don't . . ." I paused to catch my breath, nearly collapsing into his arms, "I don't think he's an assassin, he didn't have the skill. But he still tried to kill me. No doubt."

"And your brother? Where is Javier?"

"Gone," I said just as the sound of screeching tires filled the air. The chaos was growing.

He grabbed my hand, and that alone filled me with strength. "Come on, let's get out of here while we can."

We ran to the car, Derrin literally sweeping me off my feet as a truck almost backed into me.

We made it into the Camry quickly as the doors were unlocked. It didn't really register as strange, just convenient since we didn't have to fiddle with the keys.

I jumped in and Derrin took the keys from me, sticking them in the ignition.

Suddenly proverbial bells started going off in my head.

A warning.

Instinct.

"No," I said just as Derrin turned the keys.

The car stuttered strangely with a loud grinding sound, refusing to start.

"Stop!" I screamed, and he immediately took his hand away, eyes wide as he looked at me.

"The doors were unlocked," I said quickly, barely able to breathe. "I know I locked the doors as I left."

I'd never seen him look so afraid as the realization dawned on him. If he had tried harder, even pushed the key over just a millimeter more, the car would have exploded.

Someone had put a car bomb inside for us.

Someone already knew we were here.

"We have to run," he said, a twinge of panic in his voice.

I'd never heard that panic before.

I nodded. Fear had a net above my head.

We both jumped out of the car and he ran over to me, grabbing my hand and leading me down the parking lane toward the stairs at the end, going against the flow of traffic and people who were leaving. I guess he figured the fastest way out of here was to just get above ground first.

We were almost at the end when the man appeared, the scarred surfer dude with the gun at the bottom of the stairwell, a throng of people on either side of him.

"Shit!" Derrin yelled, and at the same time I said, "That's him!"

The man smiled when he saw us and began to push people out of his way.

Derrin pulled me to the left, darting between cars and then down the lane on the other side in the opposite direction.

Suddenly a man appeared at the end, tall and formidable, a stiff face in a stiff suit. He had a gun at his side.

He wasn't here for Wal-Mart's savings.

He fired at us just as Derrin pulled me behind another car. We fell to the ground beside it, glass shattering around us as I covered my head, leaning back against the rear door.

"Stay here," Derrin commanded, pulling out his gun. He got up into a crouch, both hands on the gun. Even throughout all the violence and mayhem, I had to stare at him in awe for a minute. In his cargo pants and white t-shirt, with his buzz cut, steely eyes, and sheen of sweat on his muscles, he looked every inch the man who was going to get me out of here.

My man.

Then the window on the car beside us exploded, glass raining down on us, and I screamed, forced back into this deadly, and very real, game.

Still in a low crouch, Derrin pivoted around the corner of the back of the car and fired at the person behind us. There were two shots and then nothing. With all the noise around us, I couldn't tell if he had hit the guy.

Then there was another shot in the opposite direction, the bullet zinging off the fender of the car on the other side of us.

Derrin looked at me and jerked his head to the right. "Stay down low, hide behind the cars, and go as fast as you can to the exit ramp. The other guy is down, I'll take this guy."

And with that he suddenly sprang up and fired off a few rounds of carefully aimed shots. He swore, obviously having missed, and looked down at me. He was angry now. "Go, dammit! I've got this."

I shook my head, paralyzed by fear. "My cast, I can't crouch like that."

"Fuck," he swore. "I'm sorry."

Then he quickly fired off two more shots. "Reach for my other gun, it's strapped around my calf," he said.

I could at least do that. I quickly pulled up his pants' leg and took another handgun out of its holster. I held it up to him and he placed the one he was carrying in my hand.

"There are two bullets left, use them wisely," he told me.

The gun didn't feel as heavy as I expected it to, and my fingers wrapped around it like a lifeline. I had no idea how to shoot one of these but I wasn't afraid of it. I would gladly use it to protect our lives.

Derrin quickly dropped to a crouch beside me as he slid the hammer back on the other gun. "The scarface guy is still out there," he said, his voice rough and low. "He's hiding behind the concrete pillar. His aim isn't the best and that's what's saving us right now."

"I'm pretty sure you're what's saving us right now," I said breathlessly.

His lips twisted into a grim smile. "We'll see. We have to make a move or he won't come out and we'll be stuck here."

"Someone has to come and stop him. Security."

"I think security has run with everybody else."

"What about Javier?"

He sighed and quickly wiped the sweat from his brow. "If your brother is still here, he's hiding in his car behind bulletproof glass. I'm sorry, Alana, but he would not come back in here to get you."

I had a feeling that was true. It still hurt though.

"Are you ready?" he asked, leaning in closer. "Go left and left again. You run as low as you can and I'll stay up as your shield, all right? When I yell, we'll dart across the lane and keep going till the end. We'll hit the stairwell to the offices. I can open the door and lock it from the inside. The place is empty. It's our way out." He took in a deep breath. "Ready?"

I managed a nod, my grip tightening on the gun.

"Now," he said, and popped back up. Shots were fired in both directions, but I ran hunched down as low and quickly as possible with my injuries. I could feel Derrin right behind me as I turned left at the hood of the car, running flush along the lane. I couldn't help but scream every time a shot was fired off, whether it was from Derrin or scarface. Everything was so much louder down here, so much deadlier. I felt like a rat caught in a maze with several big cats on the loose.

"Head across!" Derrin yelled, now at my side, though in a second he was pivoting around again to take another shot. I darted across the lane, nearly getting hit by a car that suddenly had to slam on its brakes. The person honked, yelling, but the minute they saw Derrin with the gun, they shut up.

We slipped in between cars, ran across another lane, and then finally reached the door to the office stairwell. I was practically flat against it, Derrin pressing me against the door and shielding me as he quickly stuck a makeshift key into the lock with one hand while aiming his gun behind him with the other.

"Hurry." I couldn't help but whimper. The lock didn't seem as easy for him now as it was earlier. Then he dropped the key which clattered loudly on the concrete.

"Fuck," he swore. He gave me a look like he expected me to drop down and get it, but I couldn't do that quickly with my cast. So he rapidly ducked down, and it was at that moment that I saw scarface appear.

He was dead ahead of us, standing between two cars on the other side of the lane, gun raised and aimed right at me.

There was no time for Derrin to stand back up and protect us.

Before I knew what I was doing, I was aiming the gun at scarface, holding it with shaking hands.

Then I pulled the trigger.

The first shot had a bit of kickback and I missed, so as soon as I could, panic and adrenaline coursing through my veins, I pulled the trigger again just as he was about to pull his.

My gun fired, the last bullet sailing through the air, and suddenly scarface howled, tilting to the side. His own gun went off, but at an angle, the bullet hitting the roof above the lane then bouncing back down to the concrete.

I shot him in the fucking leg.

"We're in!" Derrin yelled, now at the lock again and turning the handle. I was too stunned at what I had done – I'd actually hit the guy! – that I couldn't help but be frozen in place, watching as scarface grabbed a hold of his leg, groaning in pain.

Derrin grabbed my arm and jerked me inside the stairwell, the door quickly closing behind us. He immediately locked it, then turned to look at me, the light dim from only one bulb near the top of the stairs.

"You're full of surprises," he said, looking joyous before kissing me quickly on the lips.

"Must run in the family," I said blankly.

He nodded and said, "Come on, we aren't in the clear yet. You got his leg, but that's only going to make him angry. Leg wounds are like that."

He grabbed my hand and we jogged up the stairs to the top. I held my breath as Derrin put his hand on the door-knob, but to my relief it opened into an empty marble-tiled office lobby. We ran to the front doors, and suddenly we were outside, bathed in the brilliant orange of a slowly setting sun, the sky periwinkle and sprinkled with early stars.

Derrin led me along the back of the building, away from Wal-Mart and the chaos, toward the back fences of residential properties. He opened a back gate and cut through someone's backyard before we found ourselves on a suburban road.

We stopped by a dark green 80s Nissan that was parked by some shrubs, and Derrin, with just a quick glance around to see if any neighbors were watching, opened the driver's side door. It wasn't even locked.

I guess we were stealing this car. I couldn't even protest at this point. I'd just shot somebody.

I got in, and it took two seconds for Derrin to quickly cross some wires underneath. The car started without a problem, and we were off, bolting down the road in a stolen car before pulling onto the highway and getting lost in a maze of traffic. We headed away from Wal-Mart, which was now covered in a sea of red and blue police lights, and in the direction of our hotel.

"You all right?" he asked me as the sun slipped below the horizon. The car reeked of cigarette smoke, which was giving me a headache. I rolled down my window. I wanted to puke.

"I don't know," I said, my eyes focused on the dying light in the sky. It was the truth. I didn't know if I was all right. I mean, I couldn't be. How could anyone be? But at the moment it was all very numb. My heart was still drumming along in my chest, my pulse and breath racing. I felt wired and alive, but dead at the same time, like everything had happened to someone else and I was just feeling the after effects.

I wasn't as stunned as I was the other day though.

"I'm not about to slip into a coma," I told him. "But I don't think I'm a hundred percent."

He nodded, his grip massaging the wheel. "You're doing good. You're doing real good. We're going to get ourselves to the hotel, get our stuff, and leave. We're going to hole up somewhere with a lot of people, maybe Mazatlán. Find a nice beach hotel and hunker down for a few days. We're going to work through what happened. We're going to fix this."

"I don't think we can fix anything," I said, almost to myself.

"We will," he said with pure confidence. "We've seen the enemy now."

"And he's seen us."

"Alana, he's always seen us."

He was right about that.

It wasn't long before we were at the small hotel, quickly packing up our stuff. We were in and out in minutes.

We threw our bags into the back of the Nissan and drove west.

CHAPTER FOURTEEN

Derek

Y ou can sweat, even in dreams. Always in my dreams.
It was a blindingly hot day, the kind that makes
you curse the country to the ground. The sun was so
strong, so merciless, that it made you wonder how anyone or
anything could survive here at all. It was like living on the
sun, and everywhere you looked, the glare burned right
through your eyes. On those kinds of days, everyone was
partially blind.

I had driven Carlos into town, knowing full well what was
going to happen. He was exchanging money with Matice
Marquez, one of the most powerful men in the Gulf cartel.
I knew the money wasn't real. I also knew the drugs Marquez
was passing over weren't real either.

Both sides were screwing each other and they knew it.
More than that, they welcomed it. This way, someone could
be taken out with good reason. Even though the cartels were
beyond the law, some of them still run on an odd set of
morals. There was a lot of pride and a lot of honor in the
way that transactions were handled, in the way businesses
were taken over, in the way people were killed. No one was
above a bit of torture, but there had to be a good reason for

the torture. They would tell themselves anything to make it seem like they were better than everyone else and still pure in the grace of God.

Bunch of delusional pussies, that's what I had thought at the time. It's what I still thought. But I still didn't think anything of it. If Carlos died, it didn't mean I was going to die with him, and it didn't mean he wouldn't have it coming. Carmen and I had discussed for a while now what we would do if I got out of Carlos' clutches. Originally when I had started working for him, I thought it would be easy to leave. But I got too close, and in getting close, he demanded my loyalty. I would only work for him, forever, or until he let me go. And since being let go usually ended with a bullet in the head, Carmen and I had to bide our time.

When I drove Carlos into town, I didn't expect to see so many people. Not just from the cartel, who were loitering very noticeably on the side of the road outside a barber shop, but all the townsfolk in general seemed to be out and about. I remembered something Carmen had said about some Mexican Saint Day earlier that morning, which seemed to explain why everyone seemed dressed up in their Sunday best, even though it was a Tuesday.

"Stay here," Carlos said without even looking at me. I had parked a few yards away from where this was taking place. There was a gun in the glove compartment that I could use if anything went wrong, but I knew he wanted me to be the getaway car.

I sat there, waiting and watching as more people gathered. They all looked the same – high-waisted pale jeans, cowboy or Timberland boots, pastel dress shirts. Some had hats. Some had lariat ties of skinny leather. Their wrists gleamed with gold watches, and their faces bore large aviator shades that reflected the killer sun.

Suddenly, Carlos and Marquez were meeting. I had only taken my eyes away for a second. The exchange went down in the middle of the street, like an old Western, and just like the damn Old West, guns were already drawn on either side. They weren't visible, but I could see them. I could see the blood in their eyes, even beneath their shades.

Usually at this part in the dream Carmen appeared, as she had done in real life. But this time something was wrong. I could see her from far away, walking over to Carlos. But her hair was different. It wasn't this long black mess of curls, but now this wavy, sun lightened hair. The dress wasn't red and white and long, but black and short.

This time it wasn't Carmen at all.

It was Alana.

And she was about to be gunned down.

Before I knew what I was doing, I was grabbing the gun from the glove compartment and running out of the car.

I screamed her name like a banshee and she froze, a deer in the headlights, all long legs and curves, watching as I ran toward her. Like Carmen, she had no idea what was about to happen. Neither Carlos nor I had ever told Carmen what was going on that day. We liked to keep her in the dark as much as possible. Carlos, I'm sure, because he didn't trust her, and me, well I wanted to protect her as best I could. But this time I couldn't. For reasons I'll never understand, Carmen was there that day. Sometimes I wonder if it was to show her a lesson. Sometimes I wonder if it was to show me a lesson.

In this dream, Alana was just as stunned until she realized what she was caught between. Like Carmen, she started to run toward me, when she should have run away from me. She was running toward me because I was her man, the one she loved, the one she wanted to have children with. I was her safety, her solid ground, and her light. I was supposed to protect her.

Alana ran toward me, arms outstretched, seeking my protection from the big bad world.

And as I failed Carmen, I failed her.

The gunfire erupted like fireworks.

Alana screamed as the bullets tore into her from all sides. And yet she wouldn't fall. She was stronger than that. She ran until there was barely anything left to her, skin hanging off in shreds, blood covering her bullet-ridden body from head to toe. Yet she was still beautiful. Still so beautiful, even in the hands of death.

She collapsed at my feet, clawing at my legs in a vain attempt to reach me, in a vain attempt to live.

I couldn't move. I could only stare at her as she looked at me one last time.

"*Te amo,*" she whispered, blood spilling from her mouth before she collapsed dead.

With a start, I woke up from the dream, covered in sweat. Alana was alive and in my bed in this dark, hot hotel room, sleeping soundly in my arms.

I love you too, I thought.

"I like this place," Alana said as she peered through her sunglasses at the hotel in front of us. We'd just arrived in

Mazatlán after staying the night at a far-flung roach hotel.
We had been driving around the beach hotels looking for
something simple yet popular. Not too fancy, not too shabby,
but some place where we could lay low for a week. People
were obviously looking for us, but now that I knew who was
doing the looking, we at least had a chance here.

He wasn't as powerful as I had originally thought. Not yet,
anyway. That was probably the whole point of it all.

"Then this is the place," I told her, taking the Nissan
down the street and around the corner where I found a
place to park. We were going to leave the car here, make
sure there was no trace of us inside, and then never see it
again. It was too risky. When it came time to leave, we'd
just take another car, though from where we were there
was always the possibility of taking the ferry across the Sea
of Cortez to La Paz, or even a boat. The more options, the
better.

We got out of the car with our stuff, and as she smoothed
a strand of hair off her delicate face, she said, "How are we
going to pay for this hotel? It looks like they'd only accept
credit cards."

"You let me worry about that," I told her. "Why don't you
go around back and hang out by the pool for a bit, and I'll
come get you when I have a room."

She nodded, though she didn't look too convinced, and
we crossed the street together.

I had told Alana that we needed to stop being Derrin and
Alana for a while, and that paying with plastic was the easiest
way to get traced. But whipping out another credit card, in
another name – Dean Curran – meant having to explain why

I had a fake credit card and ID to begin with. If only she knew how many I actually had.

To be fair though, it was pretty obvious that there was more to me than what I had told her. She knew it, she saw it with her own eyes. Yet she was still staying beside me, still trusting me even though I was living the largest lie. She believed I could protect her and save her, and so far I had.

But it wasn't without luck.

Yesterday when she met Javier, I thought I'd lost her. The moment she walked off with Luisa I was certain she would be put in a black SUV and I would never see her again. But to my surprise, they went into Wal-Mart, which was an unpredictable move on Javier's part. No one would have ever guessed a man like him would set foot in a place like that.

It wasn't easy getting a good look at their meeting. The place was crawling with Javier's men, some of whom I actually recognized and could have recognized me if they'd seen me. If that happened, that could have put Alana's life in more danger, and considering I knew now what Javier and she discussed, I had no doubt that's what would have happened.

So I had to stick to the outskirts and trust that she was going to be okay. I loitered around the outside of the store, the parking lot, the parking garage, trying not to pace, to seem suspicious. I was in the parking garage, about to head to the car to wait in there when I heard the screams and saw the stampede of people.

At first I didn't know what had happened to cause all of this, yet all I could think of was that Alana was dead. I had failed her and had failed myself. There would be no redemption here, no second chance at life or at love. There would be only cold, hard failure and a chain attaching me to a life I could never escape.

But then I saw her face, her beautiful, scared but strong face above the masses, and I knew we would get through this. She was better than I had thought – braver, harder.

She ended up proving it time and time again in that garage. We escaped because of her. Because she shot her killer. She shot the man who had hired me to kill her. She shot the man behind it all. The highest bidder.

Scarface was none other than Javier's right-hand man, Esteban Mendoza. It was something I should have seen coming. I had considered him, of course, but my mistake was in immediately dismissing him. I had greatly underestimated that man. Not necessarily his skill. The man was certainly no assassin. But I had underestimated his resolve and ambition. This was a man that wanted to destroy Javier one step at a time. He had patience and he had time, and he knew taking Alana out would accomplish that.

And, I was sure, if it didn't, there would be no harm, no foul. Este would try something else to move up the ranks. The man had always been a weasel and his driving force was pure old-fashioned jealousy. Funny how that's always what it comes down to, isn't it? The envy, the desire to have something – a life, a love, a car, a career – that someone else has, that they'll do anything to possess it. I had no doubt that Esteban meant to take over the cartel, not by murder or brute force, but by working the system and making Javier as vulnerable as possible.

My problem now was that Esteban knew I had seen him and recognized him. We had worked together a lot, so it was almost like seeing an old friend, albeit an old friend you never liked and thought was annoying as hell. He knew, as I am sure he did before, that I was helping Alana. I wasn't in it to kill her. He knew very well who he was up against and was going to play his cards accordingly.

The other problem I had was that I couldn't exactly tell Alana this. She didn't know who Esteban was and would have no explanation as to how I would know, unless I came clean. While Javier was a public figure of sorts, Esteban wasn't. He was behind the scenes and someone like "Derrin" would not have recognised him. Even Alana didn't. That was my only option. If I could somehow come clean and tell her most of the truth, it might be enough for her to call her brother and tell him. Javier would have Este's balls in a hog's mouth before the end of the day. He never took betrayal lightly. That was one of the few good things about him.

But then there was yet another problem. What if Este was acting on behalf of Javier? Then none of this would do any good and our plans to get out of the country had just gotten a whole lot more complicated. Este only had a certain amount of power on his own, but Javier practically owned the country.

"Have a nice stay, Mr. Curran," the front desk girl said to me with a big, gap-toothed smile. I snapped out of it, took the room key and credit card back from her, and went to find Alana.

"So, how *did* you manage to get this hotel room?"

We'd been staying at the hotel in Mazatlán for five days now, and this was the first time this had come up. I'd known it was coming. There was too much silence humming between us these last few days, too much tension and furtive looks. Sometimes I worried she was pulling away from me. Even the sex was feeling more distant when all I wanted was to feel closer to her.

These secrets and lies were becoming too much to ignore. I could only hope that the little slice of truth I was going to tell her would be enough to satisfy her and heal the rift. Once that was dealt with, we could fully concentrate on our next steps. Now, like we had done in the hotel in Puerto Vallarta, we were stuck in some kind of limbo. We were waiting for something, and I didn't know what. Perhaps this was it. Perhaps we were waiting on my honesty.

We were lying on the bed and she was flipping through the TV channels aimlessly. It was pouring rain outside, which was nice for a change, but it kept us inside instead of at the pool or on the private beach. We never went into the town. We stayed as close to the hotel as possible, not risking it.

"Do you really want to know?" I asked, my hand trailing up and down her thigh, pausing at her cast. I knew she needed to see a doctor soon to get this thing off, and something told me we needed it done sooner rather than later.

She nodded then looked over her shoulder at me. "Do you have a fake credit card?"

"Yup," I told her. "Fake ID, too. Driver's license, passport . . . you name it."

"Why?"

I shrugged, trying to sound casual. "I got into some bad things . . ."

"Drugs?"

I shook my head. "No. I made some mistakes with the wrong people, let's put it at that. I have some fake identities to use, depending on where I am."

"Where were the mistakes made?"

"Canada," I said, but it pained me to stick with the original lie.

"Are you a wanted criminal there?"

"You could say that," I told her, and her face fell a bit. "I was a bodyguard for some shady people."

"So that's how you know how to do all that stuff," she mused.

I nodded even though there'd never been a mere bodyguard who could do what I do.

"Anyway," I said quickly, "I wanted out and they wouldn't let me out. I stole some money and ran. I made it down to Mexico and here I am."

She pursed her lips. "This is making sense now. How long have you lived here for?"

"Two years," I told her. Again, lying through my teeth.

She straightened up, swinging her legs out so they were crossed over mine. "And that's the whole truth?" she asked, looking me dead in the eye. "You're Derrin Calway?"

Derek Conway. I'm Derek Conway and I'm a mercenary for hire, a trained assassin for the highest bidder. I was ordered to take you out by Esteban Mendoza, your brother's right-hand man, and I was going to, if only you hadn't been hit by that car.

But I only nodded, cool as ice.

"So all the stuff you have with you, the guns," she said. "And the other stuff."

"Other stuff?"

"I know about your other bag."

I guess I'd been sloppy with that. I tried not to look sheepish.

"Oh."

"So the other stuff and everything, are you hoping to become a bodyguard down here? Is that why you have it?"

"Yes," I said. "It's really the only thing I know how to do."

"Were you ever a personal trainer? A soldier?"

"Yes to both those things." Finally, something that wasn't a lie.

She seemed satisfied with that but sadness threaded her brow.

"What is it?" I asked.

"I guess I'm just trying to take it all in," she said. "I'm glad you told me the truth, but it adjusts some things, that's all."

"Please don't let it adjust the way you feel about me. Or the way you think I feel about you." I ran my fingers over her soft cheek. She closed her eyes to my touch as I brushed a strand of hair behind her ear.

"How do you feel about me?" she whispered.

"Like I'd do anything for you," I told her softly. "And I would."

"But what about here," she said, reaching forward and placing her hand on my heart. I swear I could feel it grow in size, hot like the sun, just from her touch. "Do you feel anything here? For me? For anyone?"

From the way she said anyone, I could tell she meant Carmen.

I took in a deep breath. "I do. For you. It's complicated."

She nodded, looking away. "I know it is. I can tell. You don't even know me."

"Stop saying that," I told her, grabbing her hand. "I know you. I *know* you, Alana. I've seen you at your worst and I've seen you at your best. And all I want is more. More you, more everything. I want a chance to have you where we can be free and be us and not have to look over our shoulder." I paused. "I'm just . . . this is new. It's different. It's beautiful."

"Even though we're on the lam and running for our lives?" she said with a crooked smile.

"Yes, even with that. I would rather this than the life I was living before I met you, and there is no lie in that. Even with death at our door, I've never been happier."

I was shocked to hear those words leave my mouth. I'd never even considered what happiness was, that it was a thing that could still affect me and my life. I thought happiness had died with Carmen, and I guess it had. But now it had come back to life. It was here, it was with Alana. Despite everything, I was happy, and that was fueled by knowing it could only get better. Once we made it out of here, once the coast was clear and we could settle somewhere free from fear, my happiness had no bounds.

"I can't say I'm happy," she said, and for a brief moment it stung. She went on, trying to smile. "I can't say it because it's hard to feel it when I'm worried about so many things. But when I'm with you . . . when it's just you and me, like this, I think I am. I just feel so much, and I wish we could just enjoy it because I think it would be larger than life. The way I feel about you . . . it almost overcomes what's happening. And it's something I have never ever had." She looked down at her hands, her cheeks growing pink. There was something so vulnerable about her that took my breath away. "I just want to be born anew, start again. Free from this. I want to do that with you."

I couldn't help but smile. I was going to give her that, everything she wanted from me, if it was the last thing I did.

"We could start by taking this goddamn thing off," I said, bumping my knuckles along the cast.

"How?" she asked, making a face. "Is it safe to go to a doctor here? Maybe they know it's something I'd do and they've got spies out there in all the hospitals."

I wasn't too sure Este could arrange such a large operation, especially without Javier knowing, but I couldn't tell her that.

"I've got two hands," I told her. "They can do a lot of things."

She smirked at me, her eyes sparkling. "Oh, I know that." She bit her lip for a moment. "Could you seriously take it off? Don't you need a saw?"

"Well, since you've already discovered that little bag of mine, I actually have a saw in there. I could cut halfway and then rip the rest off."

Actually, I didn't know that for sure but I was sure going to try.

She was considering this. "And it wouldn't hurt?"

"I will never hurt you," I told her.

Minutes later, she was lying on the bed underneath a bunch of towels, her cast propped up on a couch cushion. Being as precise as possible, I cut a line through the cast on the inside of her leg, from the top beneath her knee all the way to her toes. The saw worked hard, whining loudly as plaster dust rose and a sickly burning smell mingled with the air.

She winced the whole time. I was certain I was going to cut right into her bone, but somehow I managed to do a pretty clean job.

"This might feel funny," I told her as I set the saw to the side and poised my hands at the top of her cast. Near the knee was the closest cut, pretty much all the way through, and I hoped it was enough to get a nice tear going through the whole thing.

"If you could not re-break my bones, that would be great," she said, doing an impression of the boss from *Office Space*, only with a Mexican accent.

I grinned at her. *"Uno, dos, tres,"* I said, and then tried to tear the cast apart with all my might. My muscles strained, my hands wanted to slip, but with a satisfying crack the black cast split open with a puff of dust.

"Oh my god," she exclaimed as she stared down at her leg. "My leg is so hairy."

I looked down and smiled. Her leg looked fine. She barely had a tan line. It looked a bit skinny and weak, but considering this was the second cast, it hadn't stunted her all that much. It wasn't like she'd been even close to following the doctor's orders and not used it at all. The girl had been running marathons.

"It looks great," I said, slipping the rest of the cast away. "Sexy, even."

She snorted caustically. "I'll give you sexy." Then she went into the bathroom and ran the shower while I cleaned up the remains of the surgery.

She came out twenty minutes later, smelling like coconut soap and dressed only in a towel.

"Ta-da," she said, leaning against the bathroom doorway, her hips swinging saucily to the side.

"Feel better?" I asked, not bothering to hide my roaming eyes.

"I feel like a new person," she said earnestly, coming over

to me. She grabbed the collar of my shirt and pulled me in, kissing me on the lips. "Thank you."

I crouched down and ran my hands over her thighs and calves, both of her legs now bare and smooth and golden. "You're perfect," I told her quietly, running my fingers up the insides of her thighs till they met the silky cleft of her pussy. "In every fucking way."

I tugged at the end of her towel until it fell to the ground, exposing her naked body. I leaned forward onto my knees and grabbed her hard at the back of her thighs, where the soft skin curved into the swell of her ass. She shuffled forward, her hands resting on the top of my head, massaging it slightly. I groaned at that and groaned more as I pressed my face between her legs and ran my tongue up the insides of her thighs. She was still so damp and fragrant from the shower, it was like licking raw coconut.

I teased her pussy lips with my tongue first, slowly running it back and forth until I used my fingers to part her further. She groaned, her nails digging into my skull, as I dipped the tip of my tongue in, probing at first then sucking her into my mouth.

"Oh god," she said, her breath hitching. "You're going to make me come if you keep doing that."

You wouldn't see me complaining. I didn't stop. I kept at her with my tongue and mouth, sucking at her swollen little clit until she was coming into me. Her legs nearly gave out but I held on to her, keeping her upright.

"How about we see what we can do with this new leg of yours," I said to her as I pulled my mouth away, wiping it with the back of my hand. As usual, her taste was to die for.

"Oh, I know what I've been waiting to do," she said, still trying to catch her breath. I stood up beside her and grinned proudly at her pink cheeks, her dilated pupils, and sated appearance.

"Is that so?"

"Take your clothes off and lie on your back," she said. "I was never able to do this with the cast on, but you're about to get ridden by a cowgirl."

I did as I was told, stripping quickly and lying back on the bed. My dick had been hard since the moment she came out of the shower, and I held its thickness between my fingers, stroking the length lightly. She fished a condom packet out of the bedside drawer and climbed on top of the bed with a saucy grin.

"Allow me," she said while she slipped the condom on. I bit my lip, grinning at the sight.

When it was on securely, I tried to grab for her gorgeous breasts but she swatted me away. Since she immediately turned around, her ripe, round ass displayed in front of me like a bronzed peach, I couldn't complain much.

She grabbed a hard hold of my hard, wonderfully hard dick, and then while propped up in a half-kneeling position, slowly lowered herself onto me. Fuck me, she was so fucking wet that it was like I was being covered in the tightest sheet of the world's softest silk.

"Fuck. Oh, fuck," I hissed between my teeth as she began to move herself up and down. I reached up and grasped her soft hips, holding her tight, fighting the urge to fucking impale her on me. God she was so fucking good at this.

"Don't stop," I managed to say. She shot me a look over

her shoulder and began to lightly stroke my balls as she fucked me.

I'd always been good with my stamina before, but this time I had no power, no control.

"I'm going to come so hard," I moaned.

"Yeah, you fucking are."

That was enough. My balls tensed up as I balanced on that edge between pleasure and oblivion. Then I was over, falling, drowning in a million emotions, a million feelings. This was all so much, and as I pumped my cum hard into her, feeling like I couldn't stop coming if I tried, I realized how in deep I was. Not just physically but in every other way.

I had tried to play it cool with her tonight, to skirt around my real feelings. It wasn't easy to admit out loud that I was falling in love with someone else. It wasn't easy to give yourself over when you didn't even know who you were half the time. It wasn't easy to start again when you had lost so deeply.

But this was beyond what was easy. This wasn't something I had a choice in. I was in love with Alana, and it was going to take every part of me, but with any luck, she would give every part right back. She would give me my humanity.

The next time we talked, I would have to tell her. I could only hope my love was something she wanted.

I hoped our love could survive the lies.

The next morning we made our plans. We would stay in Mazatlán two more days, then head up north in a rental car. By then, Esteban shouldn't be looking for us around this area, if he was even looking at all. He would most likely assume we had fled the area, but I liked staying close to the scene of the crime, where they wouldn't expect. We would then take the rental car up to a smaller border crossing going into Arizona, return it there, and catch a bus across. The only problem was that Alana didn't have any ID on her, and it was too risky to call someone like Luz and get them to mail her passport. No doubt her apartment was still being watched and that would only put her friends in danger.

I decided I would email my old friend Gus, someone who owed me a big favor, and see what he could do for her. There were illegal ways into the US that I knew he might help with, too, but we wanted to do everything as legit as possible. Alana wasn't even all that keen on the idea of having a fake identity, but I wanted to at least make sure her last name was changed. If it got out at all anywhere on the news or in DEA channels that she was Javier Bernal's sister, there was a chance she wouldn't be allowed in the US and could even be detained.

While she was out at the pool, determined to tan the shit out of her now free leg, I sent the email to Gus from the free computer in one of the hotel's business stations, mentally crossing my fingers. I hadn't seen the guy since I helped rescue him from Javier's safehouse, all on behalf of Ellie Watt and her boyfriend Camden McQueen, but I hoped he was okay, and most of all, willing to return favors.

I went and grabbed a beer from the bar and came back to the room, glad that no one had taken my spot. I checked my email, thinking maybe Gus had already responded.

There was a new email in my inbox, but it wasn't from Gus.

It was from "A friend" and the subject simply said, "Nice to see you again."

I sucked in my breath. It felt cold in my lungs. I already knew who this was from and what it was about.

I clicked it.

It read:

Hello, Derek, or should I say Hola? You've been living here in the country for so long now, I guess it doesn't really matter.

It was nice to see you last week. You haven't really changed since we last were together, though maybe you've lost a few pounds. Still have that meathead look going for you, though, but I was pleased to see that you knew how to take a shot. Not that you hit me. That was your girlfriend, Alana. Perhaps that explains why you failed to kill her in the first place. Maybe you're not as good as you used to be. Well, you know what they do with old racehorses, don't you? Send them to the glue factory. Yes, I wouldn't mind that happening to you – I'd mail Alana my condolences and use your glue to seal the envelope.

Or perhaps she's the problem. Somewhere between you accepting the job and the money (remember, you still have our deposit), you decided to fall in love with her. Or maybe you fell in love with fucking her. It's all the same, isn't it? I know what it's like. I met a girl once, too, nice thing, had a husband. It wasn't to be but we had our fun. You're having fun now, aren't you? So much younger, different, than that wife you once had. Plus there's that element of danger that gets you all hard. I know all about that. You're fucking the person you were hired to kill. Don't you think that might bite you in the ass one day, like one of those mosquitos you just can't kill? Or maybe not. Maybe this will all blow over. Maybe this will all end and I'll go away. Just like the mosquito does when you fail to kill it.

Only it doesn't, does it? Derek, Derrin, or whatever name you are using right now, I don't think you quite realize what you've done. You think you're helping this poor girl find her freedom, but you're only bringing her to her death. Doesn't she know what kind of person you are? Oh right, she doesn't. Even with Javier's warnings, she still chooses to believe in you, in the person she wishes you were. Sure, you're protecting her right now but you dug her grave the moment you signed on to the job. You may not think you're pulling the trigger anymore but you are. You have been this whole time.

Of course, like last time, I have a backup plan. I was concerned that you wouldn't do the job I hired you to do, and that's why I had the man in the car on hand. His instructions were to hit her if you didn't take the obvious shot then drive away. I would have paid him the remainder of what I owed you.

I suppose the poor soul panicked. That's what I get for hiring the locals. And I really didn't see that vigilante side of you coming out. My, that was like something out of a movie. Well done.

Here's what I want from you. I like you, Derek. That's why I hired you. I knew you were a man who got shit done, and I'd still like to believe that, despite all your hesitations. It's harder now, after all you've done, to still trust you, to trust you're the man you've been building up

*all these years. But I like to believe the best in people. I'd
like to believe that you still can come around and do what
you were meant to do.*

*You have twenty-four hours, Derek. Put the bullet in
her head or something much, much worse will befall the
both of you. You'll still get your money, after all, I'm the
one that's fair here. You'll get to walk away, and then you
can decide if you can be a better person. Though I suspect
you'll end up right where you started. That's the thing
about people like us. The people that do the dirty work,
the dirty deeds. We can't really escape what we are meant
to do. All we can do is become better at it. In the end,
you can be the best by doing your worst. In the end, I
can do the same. In fact, I am.*

*Kill her and kill her now, like you promised to do. It
will all be over soon.*

All my best,

A friend.

It was from one of those email addresses that was just a
bunch of numbers. I was sure that even if I replied, it wouldn't
go anywhere. There was nothing to say anyway, nothing that
even surprised me about this, except that Esteban was even
crazier than I thought he was. Of course there was nothing
here to prove he sent it, but I knew. I knew that face, that
scar, the laid-back attitude that apparently harbored the
world's most dangerous grudge. I should have known the
voice, too, from when I first talked to him, but I'd never even
imagined him in that position.

The man had ambition. Too bad I couldn't find it

admirable. I deleted the email and sat there for a moment, stewing over my options. It was an email and I had opened it. It didn't say anything about where I was. I didn't really think there was a chance he knew where we were, but I couldn't be too sure.

I had twenty-four hours to kill her which meant we had twenty-four hours to get out of here.

We had to do better than that. When Alana got back from the pool, I'd tell her we were leaving tonight, getting a rental car, and heading up north. We'd figure out our steps with Gus from there. We couldn't take any chances here. I didn't know what kind of technology Este had at his fingertips, but if there was even a chance he could trace where the email had been opened, I couldn't take that risk. I'd obviously underestimated him before. I wasn't going to do it again.

I went back up to the room and quickly packed all of our bags. Then I hopped in the shower and tried to think about what to do. I had only been there a minute when I heard someone in the room.

"Alana?" I called out cautiously, sticking my head out of the water.

"Yup!" she called back, her voice muffled. "Hey, why are all the bags packed?"

I quickly jumped out of the shower, dripping all over the floor, and opened the bathroom door. She was wearing a bathrobe over her bikini, holding a margarita in one hand, and staring at the bags with worry.

"I thought we should move on tonight," I told her with what I hoped was an easy smile.

"Why?"

"Better to be unpredictable."

She chewed on her lip for a moment before sighing and taking a huge sip of her drink. "And I was just starting to like it here."

"You'll like San Diego more," I told her. "Trust me."

She smiled at that and I told her I'd be right out.

I got back into the shower and had just rinsed the body wash from me when I thought I heard a knock at the door.

"Alana?" I asked again, turning the taps off and listening.

I heard the front door shut then quickly wrapped a towel around me, heading out into the bedroom.

Alana was standing by the front door, dressed in jeans and a tank top now. She was holding a large envelope in one hand and a stack of what looked like 8x10 photographs in the other. Her hands were shaking.

"Who was that?" I asked, coming over to her. "What is that?"

She looked up at me in absolute horror. After everything we'd been through, I'd never seen that kind of look on her face. It was of utter destruction, of deepest, darkest fears coming true.

"Who are you?" she whispered.

I took a step toward her but she shrieked, "Get away from me!" The sound ripped so loud out of her throat that I froze to the spot.

I raised my hands, everything inside me growing quiet and still, waiting for the blow. "Alana . . ."

She held something up.

It was a photograph of me outside the fence to the Aeromexico employee parking lot. My gun was out and aimed in her direction. It was taken from the side and clear as day.

My attempted assassination.

It was all over.

CHAPTER FIFTEEN

Alana

I couldn't believe it. Of all the things that had happened to me recently, this was the one that was about to push me over the edge. This was the one that was spearing me, stabbing me, burning me deep inside. I felt like whatever good things I had inside me were being torched to the ground and in its place only ugly ash could remain.

I was holding in my hands a bunch of photographs that placed Derrin at the scene of my car accident. Worse than that, it placed him there with a gun in his hand. A gun aimed at my fucking head.

When the bellhop knocked at the door and handed me an envelope he said had come for this room, I didn't think anything of it. I thought maybe it was a package for a local tour or coupons for our stay. Maybe even our bill so far.

But when I opened it, I opened a world of lies and betrayal. I opened the end of us.

I couldn't tear my eyes away, even when Derrin came around the corner. Though his name wasn't Derrin, was it? Of course not. Everything, everything had been a lie. My brother was right.

"Who was that?" he asked. I could feel him pause. "What is that?"

I could barely speak. I looked up at him, and I saw someone totally different. I saw someone who wanted to kill me.

"Who are you?" I asked, my voice weak.

Frustration passed over his eyes and he came toward me.

"Get away from me!" I screamed, panicked, ready to keep screaming, to fight for my life.

He stopped where he was and swallowed hard.

"Alana," he said.

I held up the photograph that showed just who he was. Then I held up another. And another. All taken from multiple angles, all showing him parking outside the chain-link fence to the lot, taking out his sniper rifle, the very one he was going to use yesterday, and waiting. There was a shot of me exiting my car. It felt like so long ago, and through the photographs it seemed like fiction but it wasn't; it was truth. I finally had my truth.

"Why?" I cried out, my hands curling over the photographs in anger. "Why didn't you just kill me then?"

"Let me explain."

I gave him a cold smile. "Let you explain? What can you possibly say that would make this better?"

He seemed to think about that for a moment. And a moment was all I needed.

I threw the photos at him, whipped around, and grabbed the door handle. I ripped the door open, about to slide my body out when suddenly it was slammed shut, nearly taking my arm with it, as Derrin, my assassin, shoved his hands against it.

I opened my mouth to scream for help, but his hand went over my mouth, holding tight over my nose as well until I couldn't breathe. I was just sucking his palm to my mouth. He quickly grabbed me from behind and lifted me up, spinning me away from the door.

I tried vainly to fight, to kick, to get out of his grasp. My eyes darted around the room, wondering what I could use as a weapon. There were plenty of guns and even a knife on the dresser. It was a long shot, but if I could break free . . .

I tried to maneuver my mouth under his hand until it had more mobility, then I chomped hard on the heel of his palm, drawing blood.

He grunted but didn't let go. He pressed his palm harder against my mouth.

"I'm not going to hurt you," he hissed, "but you can hurt me all you want. I'm not letting go, either. I'm going to explain what happened."

I tried to cry out in frustration, his blood now spilling down my chin, but he picked me up then put me down on the bed. I kicked beneath him, trying to knee him in the groin, but his thighs gripped mine like a vice.

"I'm not going to hurt you," he said raggedly as he pushed his hand on my mouth harder, the back of my head being pressed into the pillow. His eyes were wild, crazy. I was afraid of him, I guess as I always should have been. Was he going to rape me? Assault me? Break my neck? I'd found out the truth now, and those who know the truth are always the first to die.

"Alana," he said, his face above mine. I still tried to move but he kept me firmly in place. There was no escape. "Alana, listen to me."

He moved his hand further down my mouth so I could breathe better through my nose. I sucked in air hard, hoping it would give me clarity even though I didn't want to hear what he was going to say.

"My name is Derek Conway," he said, and now, *now* I could see he was being truthful. This was who he was. "I'm from a small town in Minnesota. I grew up playing hockey, had a few chances to make the leagues. Hockey, personal training, those things were my life. Then I decided to join the army. I needed to get away from home, out of the house, out of the life that was slowly killing me. I was shipped out to Afghanistan. Everything I told you about what happened there is true." He paused, his eyes searching mine, beads of sweat dripping off his forehead. I could taste his blood in my mouth. "Are you following?"

I stared at him but didn't give him any other indication that I was.

"I came back home a changed man. I was disillusioned with my country, with everything. I packed up and left it all behind, came down to Mexico so I could start over. And I did. I fell in love with the place, the people. I fell in love with Carmen. I had run out of money and started working for her brother. He was in a fledgling cartel, and I was his bodyguard. It was great at first but then I became more than that. One day there was a showdown of sorts between two cartels. Carmen got caught in the middle. She was gunned down, repeatedly. I saw the whole thing."

His eyes didn't start to water but I could see the pain

reflected in them. I knew he wasn't lying about this, but I wasn't about to let this affect me. This man once had a gun to my head. This man had tried to kill me.

"It was like a second war for me. Again, I changed. This time I let it ruin me even further. I became a gun for hire, an assassin, a mercenary. I would do the dirty work for whoever needed it, and I was loyal to whoever paid me the most."

I felt like an idiot. I should have realized this all along. The fact that he was a white American, and one I was stupidly in love with, had thrown me off.

"And I did the work. I did bad things. Very bad things. I killed many people, most who probably deserved it and some who probably didn't. None of it mattered as long as I got paid. A lot of the work I did for your brother, Javier."

My eyes widened, not seeing this coming at all. I was also scared of what he might say.

"When he split from Travis Raines' cartel," he continued, "there was a lot of blood that needed to be shed. A lot of retaliation. Do you understand? For things that were done. What was done to Beatriz and her family was one example."

Oh my god.

"I put the bullet in Travis' head. It was Javier's order, but I carried it out. Justice aside, that allowed Javier to take over the business. After that, it was the last time I saw your brother. I betrayed him by helping his ex-girlfriend, Ellie, and her boyfriend escape the Raines' compound. It was nothing personal, they were paying me well, and my job with Javier was over." He closed his eyes and his body relaxed slightly. I lay still, wondering if I should make a move.

He went on. "After I helped Ellie, her boyfriend, and her

father out, I was in Acapulco for a few weeks, trying to figure out what to do with my life. I felt like I had done a good thing in helping them, even with the money, and I wondered if I had the strength to move on. To leave the life behind. To return to the United States and find someone else to love, to marry, to raise a family with. I wanted to escape the death. I wanted to kill the person I had become. My own assassination. But I didn't. I couldn't. I was sucked back in for a few more years. Every day was another slog through purgatory and one step closer to hell."

There was so much breaking inside of Derrin's – Derek's – eyes that it was making it hard to concentrate, to get away. But I needed to, I needed to. The more I heard from him, the harder this would be.

"So I did what I did. One day, I was in Cancún, and I got a call from a man I didn't really recognize. He sounded green, new at the game, though, which made me suspicious. He wanted you dead and for one hundred thousand dollars." I gasped against his palm. "He didn't tell me why. They never do. But I agreed to do it. I agreed to kill you." He licked his lips, his breaths coming heavy now. "But then I saw you. I saw you that day, and . . . I knew it was wrong. Then you were hit by the car and suddenly the job didn't matter anymore. Only you mattered, Alana, you and justice and making things right. So I drove after the guy who hit you. I made him pull over and I shot him in the head. I killed him because he tried to kill you and get away with it. I was your so-called angel."

But if the car hadn't hit me? If it hadn't hit me, he would have killed me. The image from the photograph was burned into my mind. That was a picture of a man who aimed to kill.

"Obviously I was set up from the beginning, to be the fall guy if anything went wrong. And it did go wrong. I got another call and the man wanted to pay me twice the amount. Two hundred thousand dollars. Said I could even keep the deposit. I told him no, though. It was messy, it was wrong, and I wanted out. He told me there was no out. Not for me . . ." he looked away, ". . . and not for you."

I could feel my eyes welling up with tears. Suddenly all the fight had drained out of me. It was all true. All of it.

"Alana, please," he whispered, taking his hand away from my mouth. I couldn't even scream. My mouth curled up as my lungs hardened, the tears choking me deep inside. I couldn't breathe, I couldn't do anything but try and keep the horrible sadness inside.

"Please," he said again. "Don't cry. Don't. I know I messed up. I know you think I'm horrible, and I am a horrible person. I'm a bad man. I'm no better than the worst. But please, please know that I couldn't do it. I couldn't kill you, not for all the money, not for anything. I would never hurt you."

"You lie!" I cried out, a sob ripping out of me. "You're hurting me right now, to the bone!" I turned my head away from him, my eyes shut tight as tears spilled out of them and onto the pillow. I felt so stupid, so foolish, so fucking alone. I was alone again like I always was.

The man I loved was only here because he tried to kill me. The man I loved never loved me at all.

I had nobody now. I never did. Not my brother, not my friends. I was as good as dead.

"Why didn't you kill me?" I sobbed. "Why didn't you kill me?"

"I couldn't," he said, his voice ragged. "I couldn't do it."

"You should have. You should have pulled the trigger and ended this!" I screamed the last part then collapsed into sobs. I felt like my body was being torn apart, my lungs and heart and breath all squeezed by the sorrow that was running so violent and deep.

"Alana," he said, burying his face into my neck. He was shuddering against me, trying to breathe himself. "I fell in love with you."

"Liar!" I yelled.

"No," he said, shaking his head. "No. I'm not lying. I love you. I love you, and I would have told you the truth but I didn't know how. I was too afraid to lose you. Alana, please, I can't lose you."

I put my hands up to his chest and tried to push him off me. "You've already lost me."

"No."

I blinked, trying to look through my blurry vision at him. His own eyes looked blurry too.

"Let me go, whatever your name is."

"It's Derek," he repeated, grabbing my arms and holding me tight. "It's Derek Conway and I am not going to let you go. I'm not going anywhere."

"I'll scream," I warned him, not kidding. "I'll scream and get you thrown in a Mexican jail and then what the fuck are you going to do, huh?"

Panic shone in his eyes, their blue color so hard and cold above me. "Alana, listen to me. You can hate me for lying but don't hate me for loving you."

"I hate you because you tried to fucking kill me!"

"But I didn't!" he roared in my face. "And I've been trying to keep you alive ever since! Do you think it's easy to lie, to worry if the person you love loves you or the lie? Do you think I didn't wrestle with the truth every fucking day? Well I did, when I wasn't trying to figure out how to keep us both alive."

His words meant nothing to me now. None of this meant anything to me. He didn't kill me, but in the end it would still come, whether it was from his gun or someone else's. In the end I would still die alone, in a dark, sharp place.

I was empty, I was nothing.

I needed to leave.

But his hold was strong. "No," he said, shaking his head. "I will not let you go. The man who sent you those photos knows where we are. He is Esteban Mendoza, and he's the right-hand man of your brother. I know him, I've worked with him. He's trying to ruin Javier, bit by bit, starting with you. When you're out of the picture, he'll go after Marguerite maybe, or Luisa. But he'll get rid of everyone. He'll do this until Javier is run into the ground."

That got my attention. I was sure I'd heard Javier mention Esteban a few times, but I had never met the guy. If this was true, I had to tell Javier. But Javier would want to know who I'd heard it from, and when that came out . . .

"Your brother has to know," Derek said. "And we have to get out of here."

"I am, without you."

"Don't be stupid!" he yelled, his face going red. "You won't leave here alive if you do. I promised to protect you."

"Yeah well, promises don't mean anything coming from someone like you!" I yelled back. "A liar. A killer. A murderer." I clamped my eyes shut in frustration. "Shit! Shit!" Even though I didn't trust him, I knew he was right. Someone was setting him up, framing him for exposing the truth. They wanted Derek to get in trouble, for me to not trust him. They wanted to put his ass out there. But whatever way it was worded, someone knew we were here. Whether Esteban was the one behind it or it was a lie that Derek concocted to keep me here, I was fucking screwed.

Then I remembered the business card Javier had given to me. I had one more chance.

I swallowed hard and looked up at Derek with pitiful eyes. "Please let me go."

He shook his head. "I can't."

"You have to."

"I will protect you to the very end. Alana, I'd lay down my life for you."

I narrowed my eyes at him, feeling sorrow and hatred and bitterness choke out whatever love I might have felt. I had to snuff it out before it hurt me. Love was only dangerous now. Love would get me killed. "Your life means nothing to me," I said.

He looked like I had slapped him. I felt like I had slapped myself too.

But he had to let go of me.

"Let me get away, Derek. If you care about me at all, you'll let me get away."

"I can't do that. Please. I have to save you."

I let out a caustic laugh. "Save me? I think you're still

waiting to pull that trigger. Now, let me go or I will scream. And if you try and stop me, I will make you hurt me. You say you don't want to but you will if you don't let me walk out this door right now."

"If you walk, you're as good as dead," he said, but there was a resignation coming over his face. I was wearing him down, ruining him as he once wanted to ruin me.

"Then let me die by choice, and let me die alone," I said. He relented and I managed to quickly slip out from under him. Actually, I was surprised that he let me go so easily. Perhaps he had been telling the truth all along.

I stood there, breathing hard and watching him on the bed. For once he looked absolutely fragile, this big beast of a man who seemed seconds from breaking down.

But I couldn't care about that. He was an assassin, a liar, and it didn't matter if he had kept me alive this long. I would have to figure out the rest on my own, with someone I could trust.

I grabbed my duffel bag that had fallen off the bed then quickly reached into his, taking out a small handgun. I aimed it at him. "You know I can shoot this thing now."

He swallowed thickly but nodded.

"Let me leave as is and I won't pull the trigger. I won't scream. I won't get you locked away. I know that even though you were hired to kill me, you have protected me so far. You've at least kept me alive." At that my voice started to shake, and so did my hand. I took in a deep breath to steady myself, blinking fast. "I don't wish you any harm." Now my lower lip was trembling. Damn it. "I don't wish you any harm, but I can't be with you anymore. I can't trust you. I'm sorry."

Derek slowly shook his head. "Please, Alana. I'm sorry. I'm sorry."

And, oh god, I could see that he was. Tears spilled down my cheeks. "Let me get away."

He stared at me, his jaw clenched, his whole body tense. Then he nodded. "Okay. Okay. Keep the gun. Use it well, all right? If you can go to—"

"No," I said quickly. "Don't tell me anything. Let me do this on my own. You stay in here for twenty minutes. Don't come out or I will go straight to security, you understand?"

"Yes."

"Goodbye, Derrin. Goodbye, Derek."

He didn't say anything back, he just stared at me like he was watching me die. And I suppose he was.

With the gun still trained on him, I left the room. The door shut behind me with a heavy click and I was out in the hallway. I waited by the door for a moment, prepared for him to come straight after me. But he didn't.

I couldn't chance it. I hurried to the elevator, and once inside, stuck the gun in my bag. Once I hit the lobby, I glanced around for anyone suspicious, anyone who could have sent the photographs, and when I didn't see anyone, I ran over to a courtesy phone by a bunch of couches.

I picked it up and fished the business card out of my jeans. I dialed the number on it as per Javier's instructions, and then I waited.

"Hello," a man answered. He sounded kind of young. "Who is this?"

"Who is this?" I hoped I didn't have to get sucked into

another one of these stupid games over the phone. There was absolutely no time for that.

"Juanito," the guy said, and I sighed with relief.

"Juanito, this is Alana Bernal."

"Ah, Alana," Juanito said. "Javier will be happy. He was very worried about you. He thought you were going to call last week."

"Something came up. I need to see him now."

"I will go tell him, can you hold?"

"Yes."

I waited about two nerve-racking minutes while Juanito was gone. I kept looking around the lobby, staring at everyone. People were staring right back at me, probably because I looked scared shitless and my eyes were puffy from crying. But these were just ordinary people. They weren't assassins. And they weren't Derek.

Finally he came back on the line. "Alana, where are you?"

"I'm at the Crowne Plaza in Mazatlán."

"Okay, good," he said. "Hold on." I waited while I could hear him typing in the background. "Listen, I'm going to come pick you up but you have to meet me, all right? Just go to the corner of Marina Mazatlán and Sábalo Cerritos. It's a few blocks away. Stay where you are, around people, in the lobby of the hotel. Don't talk to anyone, don't go with anyone. We'll be there in an hour."

"Okay," I said, feeling panicked all over again. What about Esteban? Was Derek right about that? "Will it be you picking me up?"

"Yes," he said.

"Where is Javier?"

"He's not here right now."

"Okay," I said quietly. "What about Esteban?"

"Esteban?" he asked, sounding surprised. "No, Esteban isn't here. I think he's with Javier. Why?"

"No reason," I said, feeling slightly relieved. "Will you take me straight to Javier?"

"Of course I will, those are my orders. He wants to make sure you are safe and I will do just that. He will be happy to know you have called."

"Okay."

"I'll be driving a white SUV. We'll stop and get you. I'll have men with me to watch over you and make sure you're coming alone. These were Javier's instructions if you were to call. We'll bring you back here and you'll be safe, understand?"

"Yes, I understand."

"Be safe," Juanito said, and hung up.

I sighed, and when I tried to return the phone to the cradle, I dropped it. My hands were shaking. I didn't know if I could wait for an hour in the hotel, even if I was around people, knowing that Derek was upstairs.

He hadn't come for me yet, and to be honest, it worried me. I was torn up inside, knowing deep down that Derek would never harm me, not now, but also knowing he was once paid to. Our relationship, my love for him, was built on lies. How could I be sure that the good, brave man I saw was the real him. What if that was the lie? What if all the wonderful things I saw in his soul were nothing but an illusion and I was duped into it by big muscles and hot sex?

My heart told me it was real. But the heart is what gets

people killed. I knew I would die at some point for some reason or another, but I would never let it be over my heart.

I stepped away from the phone and walked out of the lobby and into the sunshine. I decided to wait at the hotel next door instead, which wasn't as nice. Finally, when the time was ready, I headed down the street. I was still surprised to see that Derek hadn't followed me, but then again, it had been his livelihood to stay invisible.

There was barely any traffic on the road, so it was quite obvious when the big white SUV came barreling toward me. Aside from some people at the beach across the street, there were no other pedestrians either, so it was quite obvious who I was.

The driver of the SUV rolled down his window. He had a full face, maybe even younger than mine, but I could tell he was a bit of a heavyweight.

"Get in," he said.

"Are you Juanito?"

I think he nodded. He jerked his head at the back door which then popped open. "Get in," he repeated.

I took a deep breath, put all my faith in my brother, and got in the SUV.

There was a man in the back staring out the window, and another man in the passenger seat doing the same.

I gingerly sat down beside him, and he turned to look at me. He had bright brown eyes and a narrow face, almost lupine in its quality.

"Shut the door, if you please," he said to me.

I leaned over and shut it. The locks immediately clicked and the SUV sped away. I studied the guy more closely.

"Are you Juanito?" I asked.

"Put on your seatbelt," he said. "And no, I'm Benny."

"Benny," I repeated. Meanwhile Benny was looking behind him. "Are you sure you weren't followed?"

I didn't know what to say to that. "Well, I'm not sure, but I don't think I was."

"And the man you're with, you told Javier you had a boyfriend. Where is he?"

I shrugged. "I don't know. Not with me. I left him."

"Why?"

"Because I couldn't trust him."

He seemed to mull that over. Then he sat back in his seat and stared out the window again.

Silence choked the car.

I had a bad feeling. My mind was so frazzled and I was so lost that I was doing, moving, acting without thinking. I was operating on panic now, ever since I left Derek. But the bad feelings, well those were instinctual. Those are the feelings you should always listen to. I eyed the bag I brought with me, thinking about the gun inside. If something went wrong, would I have enough time to grab it? Would I even stand a chance against these three men?

"Where's Juanito?" I asked, trying not to sound as nervous as I felt. I nodded at the man in the front seat. He still hadn't turned around, and I couldn't see his face in the mirrors. "Are you Juanito?" I asked him, raising my voice so he knew I was talking to him.

He turned his head just enough for me to see a scar on the side of his cheek, made all the more prominent by the fact that he was smiling.

My blood ran cold.

"No," the man said. "Juanito couldn't be here, so I decided to help him out today with this little chore." He fully turned his head my way, and I found myself looking into the very eyes of the man I had shot. "I'm Esteban. Esteban Mendoza. And I believe we've met before."

Without thinking, I made a move for my bag but Benny was fast. I felt a heavy crack on the back of my neck and the world went dark.

CHAPTER SIXTEEN

Derek

I was a stupid man. A stupid, broken man.

I should have seen it coming. I should have known the lies would be exposed and I would lose her. I just didn't think it would happen now, before she had a chance to be saved. I figured it would happen down the line, maybe a few weeks, maybe months or years, when my heart would be shattered but at least her life wouldn't be.

But I was a fool. Fooled by love, of all things. And now it had cost us everything.

I wanted to stop her from leaving. I tried. But when she started to cry underneath me, it absolutely wrecked whatever resolve I had. That reserve of sorrow, that darkness that hid deep inside her, the one that came out when she cried in her sleep, lost to nightmares that were once real, was taking over. She was ruined and utterly devastated by my lies, by the things I had done and the person I wasn't supposed to be, and while I saw her heart break open before my eyes, mine was doing the same.

There is no pain like heartache. I thought I had forgotten all about it, left in those aimless dusty days after Carmen had died. But it came back with a vengeance, as bright as day. It was merciless and brutal and cut you from the inside out, making it feel like you never had a heart, that you've always just had this cold black space in your chest. You can almost feel the wind whistling through you when it gets really bad, carving through those hollow places.

Losing love is lonely. Losing it because of something you did is deathly.

And to see it happening to the person who had your heart, there's nothing worse than that. We were both hurting, and hurting so badly. So when it came down to it, I had to let her go. I couldn't make her suffer anymore, and to be more selfish, I couldn't bear to witness it.

What I needed, though, was for her to believe me. Believe that after everything, I had her best interests at heart – that I always had. And that we had a common enemy, one that could never be trusted. Esteban would be after her the second she stepped out of here, so even though I knew I couldn't protect her where she could see it, I would still try to protect her all the same.

I would protect her to the end, just like I promised, or die trying.

See, even though I knew that I was a stupid man, blindsided like a fool in love, I had still planned for something. A few days ago when Alana was on the beach, I went through her clothes and made tiny insertions in the inner side of all the cups of her bras, near the underwire. There I placed a tracking device that was hooked up to an app on my phone. The device could be activated remotely, and when I was pleading with her earlier, trying to mend us back together, I noted she was wearing her black bra with her grey tank top.

The moment she left the room, I started tracking her. I tracked the blinking red dot downstairs into the lobby and then to the hotel next door. By then I was already stealing a Mazda around the corner and waiting for her next move.

It was obvious she had been picked up in a car by her speed on the app, and I assumed it was probably bad news. She'd probably called Javier from the lobby and he sent someone to pick her up. My money was that Esteban somehow intercepted or got wind of the call and stepped in. This theory was only confirmed once I saw her location move away from the highway that would lead toward Culiacán and head toward the marina instead.

Though there were a lot of marinas in Mazatlán, as well as ports for ferries and cruise ships, her blinking red dot went all the way to a large yacht club on the south shore near the lighthouse hill.

Even though Javier had a yacht, I would bet all my money she was being taken by Esteban away from Javier's compound. Out on the seas, a lot of things could happen, and considering Este was frustrated now, I feared that whatever he had planned for Alana was far worse than me being hired to shoot her in the head.

And so this became a suicide mission.

I drove the Mazda all the way to the marina in time to see a large superyacht leaving beyond the jetty. I looked through my binoculars and saw that it was indeed Javier's, ironically named Beatriz. The sailboat was massive mega-ketch, a 187-foot, 550-ton Royal Huisman. The two masts stuck high into the sky while the navy body glistened above the waves. I couldn't see any crew on board at all except someone at the controls. That's how I knew it wasn't Javier. He liked to travel with a large crew, complete with their own uniforms. He was the king of flaunting everything he had.

This was an undercover operation. Javier may or may not have known about Este taking the boat, but in the end it didn't really matter. He had, and he was heading out to sea with Javier's sister.

A part of me wanted to throw caution to the wind and tell Javier that Este had her. But aside from the fact that Javier probably wanted me dead and would never believe me, I had no real way of contacting him. I had to do something, and I had to do it now. I was the only one who could save her.

I grabbed my bag and made it through the locked marina door with ease, strolling through as if I had a proper key and I wasn't just good at picking locks. I continued to walk purposefully down the docks until I saw the right boat. I needed something that was fast enough but inconspicuous, like a fishing boat. Mazatlán was such a major fishing town that even the big shots at the marina kept fishing boats docked here.

I carefully looked around, making sure no one was watching, and jumped down into an 18-foot Double Eagle. This one even had the keys tucked inside the nearest cup holder.

It purred to life and I steered it out of the marina with ease.

In the distance, Beatriz was disappearing over the horizon line, heading in the direction of San José del Cabo and the tip of the Baja.

I maintained my speed, not too slow, not too fast, my eyes on the boat and on the blinking red dot on my app.

I eyed the bag on the chair next to me where the C4 was waiting.

I had a boat to blow up.

I had a woman to save.

I had nothing to lose.

CHAPTER SEVENTEEN

Alana

When I woke up, I was sure I had woken up in hell. My head felt like it was on fire. It was hot and pained, and I swore I could hear the crackling of flames somewhere deep inside my skull. I tried to open my eyes but the pain made me wince, and the world seemed to rock back and forth. My head fell back down to the bed.

A bed. I was on a bed somewhere, but where? What had happened?

Images floated into my brain like a cloud of powder settling.

Derek. I had fought with Derek. I had left Derek. Derek broke my heart.

His name was really Derek.

My chest pinched at the thought, my stomach twisting painfully. The grief was there, just below the surface, competing for the space in my aching body. I had to give in to it, just for a moment, just so I could breathe.

I lay back on the bed, staring at the ceiling above me, waiting for the sorrow to swallow me whole. It didn't matter that I didn't know where I was, that my head was a fiery mess, and I feared something vital had been knocked out of me. That the tiny room I was in with its wooden plank ceiling kept moving up and down and up and down. None of that mattered.

It trickled in slowly. The betrayal. The hurt. The anger and the pain. It was like acid rain on my soul, eating away at me in small doses. And then the memories of Derek flooded me like a raging river. The way he looked at me, like he would give up the world to keep me safe, the way he felt when I fell asleep in his arms, and the kind words he whispered when I woke up from a nightmare. He had ended up being so much more than I ever thought he would be to me. So much fucking more. He had ended up being my man, the one I wanted to see through to the very end, the one that made letting go of my old life okay because it meant starting a new one with him.

And now he was gone, and I was here. And even though the lies still hurt and the truth was even worse, I believe he had loved me just as I had loved him. And I loved the real him, the one he was hiding from the world but showing only to me. The lie was a half-truth in the end, and he was never not the man who became my shield against the world.

I shouldn't have left. Even though it was painfully, stupidly obvious now, I knew I shouldn't have left. I was just so hurt and shocked and confused that I couldn't process it around him. But this wasn't some silly breakup or a fight you have when you're tired. It wasn't a reevaluation of a relationship gone wrong, or "time alone to think." I had treated it all like it happened in my normal, everyday life, not my new life where people were waiting to kill me.

I should have sucked up my pride, swallowed my tears, and put that all aside just for the chance to stay alive. Instead I was a total idiot, such a foolish girl, who chose the righteousness of her own heart and feelings over the chance to live another day. This all should have mattered some other time.

Now there was no other time. He was somewhere, and I was here, taken by the man that had hired him to kill me, the man that my brother considered his second-in-command. I was taken by someone who wanted to use me, hurt me, abuse me, and kill me in order to stick it to Javier where it really hurt.

And now he wasn't going to play games anymore. I'd already shot him. I'd already stolen the man he hired to kill me. I'd already made him look like a fool.

He wasn't going to take that lightly.

I was in for a world of suffering.

At that thought, I took in a deep breath and tried to bury the fear. The heartache was still there, but the fear was growing and taking over. Death was one thing to be afraid of, but torture was another. I had no doubt that my death wouldn't come for a very, very long time.

I don't know how long I stayed in that room, but it was at about the time I decided I needed to use the washroom that someone came to the door.

There was a polite knock at first and then the door swung

open before I could say anything. In the dim light that had been on in the corner of the room, I could see the man's shadowy figure as he loomed in the doorway.

"You're awake," he said. Esteban.

"You're going to kill me."

He chuckled and then stepped into the room, closing the door behind him. The fact that he was backlit from behind and I couldn't see his face properly made it worse. I didn't know where he was looking, yet I could feel his eyes trailing all over my body, sliding over me like an oily rag. I tried not to shudder.

"You're very beautiful," he said, taking a step toward me. He was rolling up his sleeves. "I can see why Derek decided to call the whole thing off."

"Why are you doing this?" I asked, ashamed at how meek my voice sounded.

"Because I can," was his answer. "And not many people can say that."

It was a small room. If he took another step, he would be at the foot of the bed. I tried to shift back, as far away from him as I could go, but the movement made me want to throw up. It was like being hit by the car all over again.

"You're supposed to be my brother's friend," I said.

He let out a large, belly-aching laugh that seemed to shake the whole room. "Oh, that's a rich one, hey? Friend? Beautiful, in this business there are no friends, only enemies you're close with. Do you really think Javier is my friend? He's not. He's my boss. And I'm the little son of a bitch he bosses around." His voice dropped off at the end, dripping with bitterness. "I would have thought you of all people would know what that's like."

I swallowed. "We never really had that kind of relationship."

"And I guess you never will."

I frowned at him. "You're really enjoying this, aren't you?"

He shrugged casually. "I'm not the sadistic one here. You're confusing me with your brother."

"If you're not sadistic, then why am I here?"

He looked around him, and when he turned his head I caught the feverish glint in his eyes. "Who said there was anything sadistic about this? You're on a luxury yacht. Javier's. Have you never been on it before? What a shame. It's a real beauty. Of course, he doesn't know I've taken it for a little spin, and he never will know, but we'll just keep that between you and me." He paused. "Did he tell you he named it after your sister Beatriz? Perhaps his next boat he'll name after you. Something to honor your sorry little memory."

He took a step closer, and as my eyes adjusted I saw a man who didn't really know what he wanted but was going to try and find out anyway. If there was some part of him that truly believed he wasn't sadistic, then I had to find that part and work with it. Maybe I could plead with him, change his mind. It seemed to have worked with Derek, and I hadn't even been aware of it.

"You really are beautiful," he said, his voice lower now. "It's a shame I won't enjoy this as much as you think I will."

Before I could say anything, he was on top of me, pushing me down into the bed with his weight. I screamed and tried to kick, but my head made everything spin, making me weak and disoriented. His hands went for my jeans, trying to rip them off while I thrashed back and forth.

He put his hand over my mouth and leered at me. I stared up at him in utter terror at what was about to happen. I had been in a similar situation with Derek earlier, only Derek's eyes were full of love and a promise that he would never hurt me.

Esteban's eyes were full of bitterness and revenge, and at that moment I knew he would do whatever he had to in order to expel those feelings.

Somehow he got my jeans off, and as I tried to close my legs, he placed his knee between them, keeping them open. I tried to headbutt him but he ducked out of the way, laughing, and his mouth came down on my neck and breasts. His fingers went into my underwear, rough and intrusive and wanting to inflict pain.

"You're so beautiful," he said again with a moan as he undid his fly. "I'm going to fuck the beauty right out of you. Make you as ugly as me. Maybe I'll give you a scar just like mine." His lips came close to mine and he stared at me, almost hypnotized. I felt my body going into shock, shutting down, and I was so angry at it for not fighting back. Maybe if I just went numb, I wouldn't feel a thing.

"Such beautiful eyes," he murmured.

At that, I couldn't help but grin. Even he looked surprised by it. "I have Javier's eyes," I told him. "That explains why you want to fuck me so badly. You're in love with him. You want him."

That got his fucking attention. He yanked his fingers away from me and jerked his head back in horror and confusion.

"What? You're sick. Fucking sick to think that. That is not true."

I kept smiling, loving that I was getting to him. "It explains everything," I said, practically spitting on him. "Why you're so jealous of him. You want him. You want to fuck me and pretend it's Javier. Well, go on. Get your fucking jollies out. I won't tell anyone."

It was a bold move, a brave move. But I had nothing to lose.

It seemed to be working, too. Esteban was beyond indignant.

He straightened up, shaking his head. "You little bitch."

"It can be our secret." I flashed him a big smile.

His eyes blazed with an inferno. "Fucking whore!" he screamed. Then he punched me square in the jaw. The world exploded into stars and fuzzy colors, and I smelled nothing but blood, felt nothing but pure, unadulterated pain.

"You stupid fucking bitch!" he yelled again, and there was another blow to my face, just above my left cheekbone.

I choked on my cries. In my head I sounded like a dying animal.

Then another at my wrist where it had broken. Then my leg that had been in the cast. Then my ribs and my breasts and every other part of me. Esteban kept hitting and hitting, like he was trying to kill me with his fists.

The last thing I remembered was an electric sound, like something being charged, and a zap of light. My body became paralyzed, and for that brief moment there was no pain. There was no anything. I convulsed and shook into a wonderful respite.

Then he removed the Taser and the pain came back so strong it was like every bone in my body broke at once.

I let out a horrific scream until I couldn't scream anymore.

CHAPTER EIGHTEEN

Derek

I trailed the boat into the night. I was so certain it had been headed straight for Cabo San Lucas, but instead it hooked south where it appeared to stop for the night. Not that there was any place for it to anchor, but the speed of the boat had slowed dramatically, I guess to make navigation at night easier. I doubted anyone on board really knew the first thing about sailing; if they did they would have reefed the sails and had them halfway down during the night.

I kept looking at the app to track Alana. She hadn't moved at all from her one spot. I had this sick feeling she could be dead, but I wasn't going to let myself think about that. I was getting her off that boat whether she was dead or alive.

I would not, could not, fail.

When I got the fishing boat within a football field of the yacht, I switched off the lights and the engine and just let it bob around. The night was dark, providing me with the advantage. Their lights were on and I could see into the boat perfectly. They couldn't see me at all.

It turns out there were more people on the boat than I had expected, but it still wasn't a crew. At the controls in the main cockpit at the very top of the boat was a huge guy that had the kind of bulk that could either be strength or laziness. On the next level down, there was a thinner one with an athletic build, and two women. One of the women was topless, and the other was wearing a bikini. They both appeared to be drugged or coked out of their minds, whores rented for the night. I made a silent prayer for them in my head. They were going to be in the wrong place at the wrong time.

But Esteban and Alana, they were nowhere to be found. Even the cabin downstairs was all dark. I had to ignore that wrench in my gut, the one that wanted me to think about all the sick possibilities.

She's dead! it shouted. *She's broken and bruised, raped within an inch of her life! She'll never be that girl again, the one you love. She's not strong enough.*

I had to ignore it. Ignore, ignore.

She was stronger than that.

I was stronger than that.

I was Derek Conway.

And I would save her.

I waited for a few minutes, taking stock of the scene. Then I took off my shirt and strapped the explosives to my chest with duct tape, the putty molding to my skin. This kind would survive getting wet and would be stable until I stuck the detonator inside. I had to put the detonator in a special waterproof pouch, along with the remote triggering device, and strapped that to me as well.

I slipped the shirt back on, stripped down to my boxer briefs, and took off my boots. I didn't even have a place to put my gun. But guns were so impersonal when it came down to it. If I had the chance to come face to face with

Esteban, I wanted to feel his neck breaking between my two hands.

I balanced myself at the edge of the boat, holding the end of the long nylon rope, and dived into the water. I landed with barely a splash and then started doing a fast but silent crawl toward the boat, the end of the rope held between my teeth. If I wanted Alana to get away, she had to have a boat to take her back home, and the Double Eagle would quickly drift away if it wasn't tethered.

Though it was the tropics, the water was cold after a few minutes, and I felt my muscles cramping up. I pushed through it and kept on swimming until I was in the froth of the boat's wake. If the ketch had been going any faster, I wouldn't have been able to catch it.

I reached the small set of stairs at the back and tied the rope around it. Above me was a zodiac, hoisted above the water and ready to be lowered at a moment's notice, but I couldn't count on that to get away.

After I spent a moment catching my breath, I hoisted myself up the rest of the way and ended up on the back deck of the boat. There was a second cockpit here, complete with couches and tables full of spilled champagne, but there was no one around. I waited in the shadows, listening. In the kitchen area on the second flybridge, the party with the hookers was going on. I wanted to go up further than that. I wanted the person at the controls.

Silently I climbed, staying hidden and stealthy until I was at the top level. Turned out one of the women was up here. I could hear her moans. I peered over a seat, and I could see her beside the fat man at the wheel, his dick in her mouth.

Sorry sweetheart. Party's over.

I crept up slowly until I was right behind him. They were both so into it – her eyes were pinched shut – that they wouldn't even notice me if they tried. Without standing up, I slipped my hands over the headrest of the chair, hovering for a second on either side of his head. Then I clamped my hands together and twisted quickly until I heard a crack.

The man's head slumped. I heard a gasp and stood above the woman. She opened her mouth to scream. I drove the edge of my hand into her neck and knocked her out cold. She would die anyway when the ship blew up, but I didn't want to kill her with my hands if I didn't have to.

If I had to, though, that was a different story.

I was about to leave when I had a second thought and searched the dead man's pockets. There were no guns on him but there was a giant pocketknife that could come in handy. I gripped it firmly in my hand then made my way down the side of the boat, slithering out of sight until I was just outside of the kitchen.

The thin man was doing a line of coke with the other woman. He looked like he was going to be a bit more of a problem. Some men fought like unpredictable animals while high, and he looked like the type you didn't want to underestimate. If the fat man had been the muscle, this was the guy who did Este's dirty work. This was how it was passed down in the business. If Este took over Javier's position, this guy would take over Esteban's. Then one day he would betray him in order to rise to the top, and the circle of cartel life would continue.

Unfortunately for them, the circle was stopping here.

I watched the two of them for a moment while scoping out the shadows. Este had to be downstairs with Alana, which made things a lot trickier in the long run, but at least here these two would be easier to deal with.

I decided to go for the woman first. I didn't want to kill if I didn't have to, but she looked as if she liked to scream, in bed and otherwise. I'd take her out first then deal with him.

I moved to the back of the kitchen then slinked inside at a low crouch, hiding behind the island. They were on the white sofas, doing their lines off the coffee table. His back was to me, her face in my direction.

I popped my head up, waiting until she saw me, the recognition appearing in her eyes, then I threw the switchblade. It sailed straight and true through the air then hit her right in the eye socket, lodging itself deep into her brain.

She gurgled and keeled over just as the man was springing to his feet, searching wildly for a gun that didn't seem to be on him.

I leaped up onto the kitchen island, picked up a bottle of wine, and broke the end of it off while he tried to tackle my legs. I jumped up again, out of his grasp, and brought the jagged end of the bottle down on top of his head. It dug into his skin and he yelled, but he was a tough cookie.

I landed on the ground and rolled away to the couch, yanking the knife out of the woman's eye then throwing it at the man, but he was already ducking behind the couch. The knife landed hard into a wood post instead.

I jumped at the man and made a few punches which he blocked, then he tried to knock me off of my feet. I twisted backward and ducked as he came at me, then I plowed forward at an angle until he was slammed over the back of the couch.

While he was falling, I spun around and plucked the knife from the post. This time I wasn't going to throw it; this time I was going to stab him.

The guy quickly balanced himself and picked up the couch cushion right as I came at him, slicing the cushion all the way through, the air exploding into a flurry of feathers. I kept at him until my shoulder was shoving him down, and he landed on his back on the coffee table, the glass shattering.

He managed to pick up one of the shards, and with bleeding fingers, sliced open the side of my arm. I brought my knee down into his groin which bought me a moment of stability before I was able to chop my hand into the side of his elbow on one of the arms that was trying to hold me back.

He cried out, arm buckling, then I put my weight on it until it twisted with a crack underneath.

While he struggled for purchase, I headbutted him until his head cracked against the table again, then I quickly dragged the blade across his throat, opening a gushing wound. His eyes rolled back, his body jerking, trying to fight, to live, but not today.

"I should have known."

Esteban's voice from behind made me leap up and pivot, knife held out in front of me.

Naturally, he was holding a gun. But that didn't mean I would lose.

"Where's Alana?" I asked loudly, hoping she could hear me.

He smirked, and with one hand, brushed his long hair behind his ears. "She's going to be out for a while. I don't think she's as strong as you believe. In fact, she broke much like a flower between my hands."

I swallowed down the rage that threatened to consume me. This is why I was good at what I did. I had to compartmentalize. I had to focus on the task at hand before I could focus on her.

I had to kill Esteban.

Even if he thought he was going to kill me first.

"This works out in my favor, though," he said, coming toward me, the gun still trained on me and just out of reach. He reached for the wall and pressed a button. The back of the boat shuddered and clanked. He was lowering one of the zodiacs into the water. "I'll get to go back to the compound and tell Javier the sad truth. You were hired to assassinate his sister. It worked. And you both perished. Perhaps I even tried to save her life by killing you."

I kept my eyes on him, trying to figure out what to do. If he came just a step closer, there was a small chance I could fly at him and knock the gun out of his hands before he fired. He wasn't a very good shot to begin with.

But he didn't come closer. In fact, he was moving a step backward, and from the way his eyes were focused on my chest, I knew that if he missed he would fire until he didn't.

There was too much pride in him to lose again.

"I hope you've atoned for your sins," he said to me with a small smile. "Sadly, you'll never be redeemed."

He fired the first shot. I was already twisting sideways as he did so, anticipating his move. But the next shot would be too fast for me.

Everything went in slow motion. He grinned. Finger tightened on the trigger.

Then Alana appeared behind him. She looked broken, battered and beaten, and close to death. But she was holding the base of a lamp, holding it above her head.

She brought it down with one brave burst of strength, her bruised features straining from the effort. My heart ached in response.

It shattered on Esteban's head just as he pulled the trigger. The second shot grazed me, hitting the side of my chest and knocking me back to the ground. I lay there for a moment, my ears ringing, trying to go through the checklist of my body to find out how close I was to dying.

Suddenly Alana, with her blood-crusted face, was above me screaming, and I stared up at her. Her hands were feeling around my side, and I managed to sit up and look. There was no blood anywhere. I quickly lifted my shirt. The bullet had nicked the edge of the C4 putty. Contrary to popular belief, the shit did not blow up when hit by a bullet. Thank god.

"You bitch!" Esteban screamed, grabbing his head and trying to get to his feet but failing. His gun had been knocked out of reach.

I got to my feet first and grabbed Alana's arm. "You need to head to the boat. He's lowered one to the water and I have one out there, attached by a rope. Get in it and go, now!"

"What about you?"

"I've got something I want to do," I told her. I grabbed her face, conscious of Este in the background. "Grab a life preserver, too. A jacket, a ring, anything that will keep you afloat and wrap it around you, okay?"

"Derek . . ."

"Go!" I screamed, and at that she quickly limped away to the back of the boat.

I was going to deal with him once and for all. I picked up the gun but saw there were no bullets left in it. For what I was about to do anyway, I wanted him alive until the very last minute, until it was too late and the heat tore apart his bones. I went over to him and pistol whipped him hard on the side of the head until he fell over to the side, unconscious. Then I quickly took off my shirt, pulled out the C4 and the waterproof box, and stuck a piece of it at the base of the propane stove. I stuck in the detonator and then stuck two more pieces on opposite sides of the bridge. I could hear chains clanging and water sluicing and hoped that Alana was finding her way onto the boat. I was planning to leave with her, but we wouldn't have much time.

I ran down the stairs to the bottom level where the engine room and all the bedrooms were. I wasn't sure if I had carried enough C4 with me – I had never anticipated using it on a ship, let alone one of this size – but if there was one place that would take well to a boom, it was the engine. I stuck the last pieces all around the block, planted the detonators, and then ran back up the stairs to the second level. I was about to head toward the back, toward where I assumed Alana was, when I looked back at the kitchen.

Esteban had moved. He was nowhere to be seen.

Before I could comprehend that, someone ran at me from behind and I went sailing over the railing. I grabbed the edge of the rail, trying to hold on to that and the remote control trigger at the same time.

Este appeared over the side, blood running down the side of his face, pried the trigger out of my hand, and tried to stab my fingers with a knife.

I let go of the railing before he could cut my fingers off and fell down, down, straight into the water. From that height it had knocked the wind out of me so it took me a moment to act. I quickly kicked up toward the surface and looked around. The Double Eagle was almost on top of me, the current having pushed it close, so I grabbed hold of the side and hauled myself up and over as quickly as I could.

I expected to see Alana on board but there was nothing. In fact, the boat was quickly drifting away from the yacht, the rope having been severed at some point.

Suddenly the air filled with the roar of an engine. I saw the zodiac speed away into the night, a dark shadow at the helm.

Please let Alana be on it, please.

But of course it wasn't.

Another movement caught my eye, and I looked up at the top of the boat. I could see Alana's head bobbing as she ran along the side. She was still on the fucking boat!

"Alana!" I screamed, panic tearing through me. "Jump!"

She disappeared behind part of the bridge but I didn't hear a splash. It looked like she had been about to run down the stairs.

"Alana!" I screamed again. "Please!"

Then my scream was swallowed instantaneously.

There was a burst of light, smoke, a ripple in the air. Then a split second later the whole world exploded. I was knocked flat on my back, my head striking the captain's seat of the fishing boat as I went down. Debris rained down on me but I couldn't even cover myself. I just let the sparks and bits of flaming boat hit me.

Alana.

Alana.

Alana.

Not again.

No, not again.

Somehow, though I don't know how, I managed to sit up. My head felt like it had been filled with gel, my hearing blocked, my eyes stinging. I crawled to the edge of the boat and looked out at the water.

The Beatriz had been broken up into three pieces. At least those three pieces were all that was left of it and were quickly sinking down to the ocean floor. Everything else was just a mess of debris and flaming water. Near the edge of the fishing boat I spotted the fat man's severed arm floating beside a pillow.

Alana.

Alana.

"Alana!" I yelled, my voice catching in my throat. "Alana!"

I yelled and screamed and cried her name over and over and over again. I don't know how long I had been doing it for but after some time it turned to tears. Then more screams. Then a combination of the two.

She didn't survive it.

No one could have survived that.

Este had escaped.

I had escaped.

But Alana was dead.

The job had finally been fulfilled.

She was finally dead.

And it was all my fault.

I had failed Carmen, I had failed Alana. I had failed myself.

Esteban was right.

There was no redemption here.

There never really was.

Not for someone like me.

The ones who do the dirty deeds can never really be washed clean.

I swallowed down the ugliest sorrow I had ever felt in my life. I felt it eat at me as it went through my body, consuming all the love I had, my hopes and fears and dreams. Oh those dreams I had for us. Those wonderful fucking dreams.

I lay back in the boat, staring blankly at the night sky as the fire crackled faintly in the background, and prayed for death.

I prayed for the morning sun to come and bake me, for birds to peck at my flesh and sharks to eat my bones. I prayed to drift off to sea forever, until there was nothing left of me.

I prayed until I fell asleep.

And prayed I would never wake up.

In my dreams I saw Alana and Carmen, sitting on a beach and talking to each other. They were so beautiful in the sun, so different yet so much alike. No wonder I was so taken by each of them instantly. They were a breath of fresh air, a force of light and nature.

I walked out of the sea and stopped in front of them, salt water dripping down my body.

They both turned their faces toward me and smiled, happy to see me. It was blinding.

"We are finally free," they said in unison. "You'll be free, too. Free and unafraid."

I woke up to see a brilliant night sky.

But I was afraid.

And that had been a dream.

CHAPTER NINETEEN

Derek

Alana's funeral was held at one o'clock at a cemetery on the outskirts of Puerto Vallarta. It was dangerous for me to go, stupid even, but I had to. I had to take the risk. I had to see with my own eyes and know for myself what the truth really was, even if it was damaging.

So much damage had already been done.

I pulled my cap down over my eyes and made my way through the overgrown brush on the side of the cemetery. Everything was so well-groomed and taken care of for the dead, but the moment the cemetery lines stopped, nature was waiting. It wanted to take back the land, for roots to grow deep and suck life from bones, to bloom from death. The mess, the wildness that suited the graves more than mown lawns and wilting flowers.

I took my binoculars out of my back pocket, crouched down and crept, soundless and smooth through the bush, stopping at the edge. In the distance I could see people gathered for her funeral. There were even more than I had imagined, but Alana had been a popular girl, more so than she once thought. The solid white casket was at the front of the crowd, a priest beside it, reading something out and over the grave faces.

Everyone looked destroyed, and that in turn destroyed me. It was a good thing that Alana couldn't see this – it would hurt to know the pain she was inflicting on the people left behind.

Luz and Dominga were sitting on fold-out chairs near the front, tears running down their faces, hanging on to each other while what seemed like their family members tried to console them. There were a lot of people her age, women mostly, whom I assumed were employees of Aeromexico. And at the very back of the chairs, standing at attention, was Javier.

His face held barely any expression, but what was there was nearly heartbreaking. I was surprised. It's not that I didn't think he cared about his sister – I knew that he did – but after losing so much of his family already, I didn't think it was possible for him to be affected any more. In some ways, I didn't think he had the capacity to really feel.

But the look on his face . . . it was the most controlled version of utter devastation that I had ever seen. This was going to ruin him.

That had been the plan, hadn't it?

Sure enough, coming up behind Javier, was Esteban, as well as Luisa. Like Javier, they were dressed in black, their expressions strained. There was something about them, though, the way they were walking together out of Javier's sight, Esteban's hand briefly at the small of her back before lifting away, that made me pause. Now that I knew who the villain was, I was starting to see another motive at play. This wasn't over, not by a long shot. Esteban was going to take away everything that mattered to Javier, one step at a time.

Alana's death was the first step. The dominoes would follow.

Luisa was next. But in what context, that I didn't know.

I eyed the surroundings, wondering if anyone else was going to show up, if anyone was watching – anyone like me. But it seemed I was alone. Javier had so much control over the state, but sometimes I wondered if he was almost flaunting it. His power was making him lazy, and that laziness was going to cost him. The man who wanted him out of the picture, the man who was his biggest threat, was standing right beside him, forced to mourn while making eyes at his wife.

I could see how this was all going to go down. Luckily, I wasn't going to be around to see it. I had plans to get out the country, to get as far away from all of this as possible. If Esteban was going to slowly take down Javier, win people's trust, and take over the cartel, then it was Javier's fault and no one else's.

I almost felt sorry for him.

It's too bad that Alana and I had been brought into it and ripped apart at the seams. Every fucking day I regretted taking that damn phone call from him. But for all the grief and trouble, I knew that if I hadn't, I never would have met her. I never would have been free of my sins and this life. I never would have found love again, or even happiness. I never would have found my redemption.

Now I was starting over. Alana's death was bringing me a new beginning. Bringing us a new beginning.

I watched as the priest continued his talk, and then people

slowly came up to the podium to give their eulogies. I wondered about Alana's sister, Marguerite, and why she wasn't there, but then I realized Javier would never allow that. For her safety, I was sure that Marguerite would never be allowed to step foot in Mexico ever again. The only Bernal sister left.

Surprisingly, Javier came up to speak. He was the last one. People stared at him in shock, having not noticed him in the back, probably still processing the now wildly-known truth that Alana's brother was head of one of the nation's largest drug cartels. It was because of him that she had died.

I couldn't hear what he was saying, and I could only see the side of his face as he addressed the crowd, but it was apparent he was getting choked up over his words. He left it short then disappeared into the back of the crowd again.

The casket was lowered into the ground, and the priest threw dirt.

Alana Bernal, as everyone knew her, was laid to rest.

I swallowed hard, feeling their sadness waft across the graves and penetrate my bones. I had felt that utter horror just a week ago when the explosion first went off. That grief, that fear, that big black hole of hell in your heart – it was still all so real for me. Loss. The world was cruel with what it gave you and what it took away.

I stayed in that spot until it was all over. Until the last people to stand over her grave were her brother, Esteban, and Luisa. I watched as Javier mouthed words to the freshly-turned earth then walked away. I watched as Esteban put his hand on Luisa's shoulder and whispered something to her. Her expression wasn't impressed, but his was as cunning as a wolf. Then they followed behind Javier, Luisa walking quickly to catch up to her husband.

This was a detonation waiting to happen. But it wasn't my problem to worry about. It was Javier's. And I had a new life to lead.

When everyone left, I turned and headed back through the jungle for about a mile until I came to a road where I'd parked the truck, the dirt stirred up by a hot breeze. The houses here were little more than rustic shacks, but the face of the old man staring at me from the overturned bucket on his porch told me they were happy.

That would be me soon. The money I got from Alana's hired assassination – that deposit, it wouldn't last me forever. But the happiest people seemed to be the ones with less to lose.

I waved to the old man, and he waved back, content to smoke his cigarette as chickens pecked at the dirt path, and got in the truck.

I didn't stop driving until I reached Guatemala City in Guatemala. I hadn't been here for a long time. Not since the last time I had been involved with Javier, helping to take down Travis.

I had no wish to stay here, but it was an easy meeting spot.

My blood pumped heatedly in my veins as I handled the busy city streets. The closer I got to the hotel – to the first hiding spot – the more anxious I became. The darkness here, the scattered city lights, thrummed with promises.

The hotel was right downtown, and a rather fancy one at that. It was about being unpredictable, now more than ever. Until the danger was far enough away, we had to be careful

– we could never ever let our guard down. Even after death, someone would watch the grave. Someone would always wonder what was.

Was that body lowered into the ground today Alana's? Had there been anything to bury at all?

Someone out there was asking themselves that. Maybe not about to follow up on it, but it would be simmering at the back of their head, waiting for someone to slip up one day. You couldn't tempt fate. We had tempted it enough.

I parked the truck a block away then walked over. I got a few stares as I often did – I'd feel better once my hair started to get long and I looked less like myself – I was always going to be paranoid.

I walked into the hotel, glad I had worn a crisp shirt and tailored pants, my watch glinting under the bronze chandeliers that lined the lobby.

"*Hola*," I said to the well-padded clerk behind the front desk. "Do you speak English?"

He nodded. "Of course."

"I have a reservation for Dalton Chalmers," I told him, and when he asked for ID, I pulled out an American passport with the name on it, a perfect forgery I had gotten from Gus.

"Someone called earlier, asking for you," the clerk said once he'd run my credit card, also belonging to Dalton Chalmers.

"Oh?" I asked.

"A woman," he said, as if he was telling me a secret.

I guess it kind of was. I managed to smile at him. "Well, well," I said, and the clerk grinned in response.

He gave me the key and I went up to the room, my feet light on the velvety stairs. I felt like I was walking on the moon, the thin metal key with the brass sun pendant heavy in my hand. It had been three days.

It had been too long.

I found my room and stuck the key in the door, opening it to a simple but brightly colored room: polished wood furniture, orange and green bedspread, red walls, a bronze sun with a circular mirror at the center.

It was empty. I knew it would be, but even then my heart sank a little. This was what could have been.

I went and sat on the end of the bed, waiting. There was a marching band in my chest.

Then, a knock at the door.

I took in a deep breath, and for a split second I almost dropped my guard. I made sure my gun was loaded, my safety off, my grip on it firm.

I edged toward the door, wishing there was a peephole of some kind.

I waited, my head gently pressed against the wood, listening. I couldn't hear anything.

"Derek," she said softly.

Dalton, I thought, but at that moment I didn't care that she'd forgotten.

I unlocked the door and eased it open a crack, looking at Alana's face.

She barely looked like herself. Her hair was sleek, shoulder-length and light brown, and laced with shades of sand. She had lots of makeup on to cover the bruises Esteban had left, but it was pretty seamless. She was wearing all black, even carrying herself a bit differently. But that smile – that gorgeous smile – was all hers.

"You made it," I told her, trying to contain myself.

She held her chin at a saucy angle. "I'm a better spy than you thought. I was in the lobby, hiding behind a newspaper, watching you."

"Won't you come in then, Anna," I said, emphasis on her new name. I opened the door wider as I put my gun away.

"Right, Dalton," she said, remembering her mistake from earlier. "I guess I'm not as good of a spy as I thought."

She came inside and walked to the middle of the room, looking around. It took all that I had not to throw her on the bed and bury myself deep inside of her, feeling that she was finally here with me, that she was real, that she was alive.

Alana was alive.

Everyone else thought she was dead.

We had escaped Mexico.

We were starting over.

She set her leather carry-on bag down on the ground. I locked the door and went straight up to her, wrapping one hand around her waist, the other at the back of her head.

"You're like the sun returning to me," I murmured, my grip tightening, so afraid to let go, so happy she was here.

"And you're my big, powerful sky," she said back, her golden eyes trailing to my lips.

I kissed her, so hard I thought I'd bring her pain. But she moaned and melted into my mouth, wanting more.

I gave her more. I gave her everything I had.

I stripped away her clothes like a child on Christmas morning, feasting on her neck, her shoulders and her breasts, while she took off mine. The way she looked at me made me feel like she was seeing me for the first time.

Maybe this was the first time for both of us. The first time born anew. The first time at a second chance.

This time was forever.

I scooped her up in my arms and placed her on the bed, torn between wanting to take this slow, to feel every inch, to make the seconds stretch, and needing to have her quickly and all at once, for this frenzy, these flames, to engulf the both of us.

We compromised. While she was naked beneath me, wet and willing, needy and greedy, I thrust into her. She was tight around me, so beautiful that I had to close my eyes to take it all in. While we skipped the foreplay, I wanted to make sure I could prolong our lovemaking for as long as possible.

I leaned on my elbows on both sides of her head, my fingers disappearing into her smooth hair, my eyes staring deep into hers as I slowly, tantalizingly pulled out. My breath hitched and I buried my face in the soft, warm crook of her neck. She smelled like flowers and fresh air.

"I was afraid I wouldn't see you again," she said, her voice whisper-sweet, caught between moans. "I was afraid . . ."

"You don't have to be afraid anymore," I told her. I pushed in again to the hilt and she gasped before letting out a strangled cry. I wanted her to believe it. We would always be cautious, but we would never be afraid.

Esteban, Javier, everyone had to believe that Alana had died during the explosion, or she would never really be free.

"I love you," she whispered to me just before she came.

Her head went back, her eyes squeezed shut, her back arched, so vulnerable, as if she was offering herself to me.

I took her hungrily. Soon I was coming inside of her, and for once I felt like I wasn't trying to fuck something out of me; instead I felt like I was trying to take something from her. Love. Her soul. Her everything. Whatever it was, it made me better.

It washed me clean.

I pulled out of her and gently pulled her into my arms, kissing the top of her head. Light from the city filtered in through the gauzy lace curtains, creating a kaleidoscope of shadows on the wall.

"Are you going to tell me what happened?" she asked, her voice hushed in the room. "Today. My . . . my funeral."

I exhaled, kissing her again. "Do you really want to know?"

She nodded against me. "Yes. Did you see Javier? Marguerite?"

"Your brother was there," I told her. "Marguerite wasn't. But I assume that was for her own safety."

"Was he upset?"

"Yes," I said. "He was."

"And Esteban?"

"He was there too. Right by his side. I have no idea how the boat explosion was explained but I'm going to assume that Esteban feigned ignorance over it. The crew had all died. There's nothing to place him there at the scene of it all. Maybe he'll have some damning evidence about me if push comes to shove. We don't know. But I think that's why I was brought in in the first place. He needed someone to take the blame, the fall, just in case. He's trying to overthrow your brother. I wouldn't be surprised if he went after his wife next. And I don't mean in a murderous way."

"Luisa?" she asked, craning her head back to look at me with wide eyes. "Luisa loves Javier. I know this. She would never go for Esteban."

"I'm not saying that she would. But it looked as if that might be the next step. Take out the sister, take over the wife, ruin Javier until he can't rule no more . . . take over the cartel."

"But why me?"

"Because," I told her gravely, "whether you believe it or not, you mean more to your brother than you think. The man I saw today was a destroyed man. Javier will be changed after this. I could see it."

She closed her eyes and shook her head slightly. "I can't stand him feeling that way, to think that I'm dead."

"But it's the only way. You said so yourself."

"I know," she said, her voice choked up. "I know I did, and it's true. If I show my face, if I even give him a hint that I'm still alive, I'll never be free. Not as long as Esteban is in the picture. I can't risk it. I can't risk us. What we might have."

"What we *will* have," I corrected her.

There was a pause and then she asked, quieter now, "And Luz and Dominga?"

I squeezed her to me. "They were there. They were taking it pretty hard."

She sniffed, and a tear rolled down her cheek before she buried her head into my shoulder. "They were everything to me. I can't imagine how they must be feeling."

"I know," I said.

"It doesn't seem fair. To just let people hurt when they don't have to."

"It's not fair. And it's not fair that you had to leave them too. But I would rather you be alive, living a life that's unfair than be dead and not living at all."

"Maybe one day I can let them know the truth."

"Maybe," I said. "Until that day comes, though, they must believe that the body in the coffin was you."

"Whose body is it anyway?"

"I'm not sure," I admitted. "Someone else. One of the prostitutes on the boat, I'm guessing. Whoever it is, though, it fooled the police, or whoever was hired to be the police that day."

And it had fooled me. When the boat exploded and I saw Esteban disappear into the distance, I really thought Alana was dead. There was no way she would have survived that, and it was all my fault. I was the one who put the bombs there. I had let my emotions get in the way, and in a moment of weakness, I messed up. I should have made sure Esteban was dead before I did anything else, I just wanted him to burn alive so badly.

I had lain back on the zodiac for some time as the debris rained down around me, and smoke and flames filled the air. I was so close to jumping off and letting myself sink to the bottom of the sea with her. So damn close to dying.

But then, in the middle of the cold, dark night, something bumped into the boat repeatedly, and when I finally found the strength to see what it was, I discovered Alana, hanging on to a life preserver in a state of semi-consciousness. She had listened to me in the end, making sure she had something that floated to hold on to, and jumped before the boat exploded.

It was still a miracle, but it was one I would gladly believe in.

"And Esteban escaped into the night, wiping his hands clean of everything," she said bitterly.

"Yes, he did. But so did we."

"Our hands aren't clean."

"No," I smoothed my palm over her head. "But in time they will be."

That night she fell asleep in my arms as Anna Bardem. When we woke up the next morning to a beautiful sunny day, we started our new life together.

EPILOGUE

Utila, Honduras – one year later

Alana (Anna)

It's funny growing up in a place like La Cruz or Puerto Vallarta, a land of sand and palm trees, margaritas and blue waves. It's where so many people come to vacation, to forget their troubles, their cares, their everyday lives. It's paradise.

But it's never been my paradise. Home never really is. At least that's what I had thought. When you have the fucked up childhood that I had, home becomes a scary place, and paradise has no business mixing with fear. While tourists – whether they be Americans, Canadians, even Mexicans – came to Puerto Vallarta and the Bay of Banderas to relax and have fun, I lived their paradise like I was trapped in a cage. A cage built of violence and terror and that looming threat that at any minute, I would be taken from this world in a horrific way, just as it happened to my family.

Throughout all that, though, the years of promoting paradise through Aeromexico, or watching foreigners get drunk on the sandy beaches, I always dreamed of my own slice of heaven. It wouldn't look like Mexico, though. It would never be Mexico.

I had finally found it. We had finally found it.

After my fake funeral, Derek and I (I still can't call him Dalton), headed through Guatemala, up to Belize for a bit, and down through Honduras. We were thinking we would head to Costa Rica or Panama, perhaps even set our sights on Chile. We were looking for a place where we could be safe, free, and live a long and happy life, one that didn't rely on large sums of money or guns or lies.

We really meant to keep going, but as we were driving through Honduras – a place where Derek had been before – checking out the beaches, we stumbled across a place that could only be called paradise.

The tiny island of Utila.

There, with its talcum powder beaches, golf-cart transportation, tiny towns, and a vibrant mix of Spanish and English, we were able to put down roots, to find ourselves.

With the money Derek had saved in his account, we bought a beach house on half an acre. It's waterfront with its own dock, and we have a fishing boat. On weekends we use it to go diving – I'm certified now, and of course Derek always was. We also go on fishing trips. In the evenings we grill up the fish on our deck and watch the sun go down on the horizon. Sometimes we even have friends over too – it's easy to make them in a place where everyone is smiling.

During the week, we both have jobs. I work as a barista of sorts at a local café and juice bar. It's really low-key and most of the week it's just me by myself. I get paid in cash, and I'm often tipped quite well. It's nice, honest work and a hell of a lot easier than being a flight attendant.

Derek works as a personal trainer at one of the gyms.

Sometimes he drives our golf cart around the island – gas is expensive, roads are narrow, cars are rare – and trains people at their homes. He likes his job a lot. I can see it in his face when he comes home, the feeling that he helped someone today instead of, well, murdering someone.

Of course, no one here knows who we are, what we did. The past is behind us, hidden beneath many layers I hope no one ever uncovers. It's not easy to forget the life I led. I miss Luz and Dominga dearly and often spend my nights staring at the star-filled sky, wishing they could hear my thoughts, saying a little prayer for them. Maybe, somehow, they know I'm still alive.

I miss my brother, too. But more than that, I feel sorry for him. It sounds silly to want to protect someone like him, but I feel like someone has to. He's suffering, I know it, from my death, and he's probably leaning on all the wrong people. But Javier has wronged so many people in his lifetime, perhaps this is just the way the world works. It's unfair, but sometimes it can still be just.

Derek is almost like a different man. Almost. He still gets moody every now and then, becomes quiet and withdrawn. I see this spark in his eyes – they harden and become menacing. I know then to leave him alone. He's atoning for his sins. He's thinking of the wife he once lost because of the violence that controlled him. He's thinking about the war and the things he saw and how futile it was to think he could ever escape it.

But he did escape it. He broke that life, that cycle. He's still a tough man and he can seem emotionless even when I know he's not, but he's a better man.

He's my man. I love him and he loves me. Without a doubt, that man loves me.

"How was your week?" Erin asked me.

I looked over at her, snapping out of my wayward thoughts. We were sitting on the roof deck of our house, watching yet another unbelievable sunset as the sun slipped in an orange and pink path toward the distant shoreline of mainland Honduras.

Erin was one of the first people we'd met on the island. Actually, she was the realtor who sold us the beach house and got us a screaming deal. Though she and her partner George were a bit older than us, we fast became good friends. George and Derek often played golf together, although Derek usually returned from those games embarrassed. For a man with a lot of steely resolve, he seemed to lose his shit when he played golf. I found it adorable.

"It was good. You know, the usual," I told her with a smile, reaching for my wine. Derek and George were downstairs in the kitchen, preparing some fish we'd caught yesterday.

She looked pleased, her freckly cheeks beaming at me, as if she'd been part of our integration. In some ways she had – aside from the house, she'd introduced us to a circle of friends who were fun and easygoing, embracing the island lifestyle.

"I'm so glad, Anna," she said. I still found it jarring every time someone called me by my fake name, but at least I was good at hiding it. It hadn't been the same with Derek. After I'd called him that a few times last year, we decided to just tell everyone that Derek was his middle name and that he was used to that. It's not like Derek Conway really existed out there in any form except for an ex-military soldier who went off the grid.

At least, that's what we hoped.

Soon, Derek and George brought up the platters of steamed fish with lemon dressing, Caribbean rice, and sautéed vegetables that I'd picked from our garden out front. Another bottle of wine was uncorked. Local acoustic music from the bar down the street wafted up over the azaleas and palm trees, catching a ride on the sea breeze.

This was paradise. I was home.

Later that night, Derek and I settled into bed. Well, we didn't so much settle as collapse, drunk and exhausted. The two of us had too much wine at dinner, which, after our guests left, led to hot monkey sex in the kitchen, on the couch, in the shower, before we finally succumbed, wet and sated, to sleep.

It must have been the middle of the night – the moon was working its way across the sky and filtering in through the window in silver beams – when I heard the noise. Despite my aching head, I stiffened immediately, my senses flaring up. Derek was already out of bed and by the door. In the moonlight I could see the gun in his hand.

He motioned for me to stay put, stay quiet, but I couldn't. I never could. As he eased our bedroom door open and eyed the dark hallway, I quietly crept out of bed, holding my breath, afraid that the hardwood floors would creak.

While he stealthily entered the hallway, I brought out my own gun from the bottom dresser drawer. I hadn't looked at it since I put it there the day we moved in. There hadn't been a need.

Now I was afraid that our past had finally caught up to us. We were so careful, but someone else had probably been even more so. We had really started to believe that we'd left all of that behind us, that the people we had once been couldn't touch us anymore.

It was worth it, though. If I hadn't touched the gun for a year, that meant it was worth it. Paradise, Derek, freedom — they were worth everything.

I cautiously followed Derek out the door, seeing him go down the stairs at the end. We had made a plan, an escape route, if things went terribly wrong one day. I was to head to the office at the end of the hallway and go through the sliding glass doors that led to the deck. From there I could go up toward the roof, or down toward the ground.

But even though that was the plan, I couldn't go. I couldn't stand the thought of leaving Derek behind. I knew he could more than take care of himself, but even then, dark, horrific thoughts teased at me. I could almost hear a gunshot going off, imagining Derek gunned down, his life seeping out through his blood while I escaped to freedom. That didn't seem fair, and my life had its own share of injustice.

So I followed him down the teak stairway, even though he was shooting me a hard, intimidating look over his shoulder, telling me to stay put. I wasn't listening.

Now that we were on the main floor, the sound had stopped. Upstairs in the bedroom, it had sounded like someone trying to open a door, or perhaps someone accidently banging into something. There was nothing now.

Then the motion detector outside went on near the back door, which looked out onto the beach. If anyone were to break in, there was no fence or real property line in the back to deter them. Plus it was darker back there, just the garden, sand, and sea, and no one to witness a thing.

I looked at Derek, the cold light showcasing the hard, masculine planes of his face as he edged toward the back door, his hand moving toward the handle. I wanted to yell out for him, to tell him not to open it, to keep us locked in our ignorance, but my voice choked in my throat.

It all happened so fast. Derek took in a deep breath then the door flew open, and he jumped out in a low crouch, gun drawn, eyes focused dead ahead.

There was a terrible thud just out of reach, like something hit the side of the house and then a hoarse, vibrating cry that reminded me of a cornered animal or a dying donkey.

Derek froze, not pulling the trigger. Then his face contorted in shock before breaking out into a smile. What the hell?

"Alana," he said, turning to look at me.

I was already at the door and stepping out beside him.

On the back patio there were two donkeys. One of them was looking mildly surprised at our intrusion, the other one was busy eating out of the compost bin they had knocked over.

Donkeys. Motherfucking donkeys.

I looked at Derek with wide eyes.

We both burst out laughing.

Not just giggles, but full-on, gut-bursting laughs that were sure to wake the neighbors. We keeled over, holding our stomachs, our faces growing red, tears streaming down our cheeks. I nearly fell over.

Meanwhile, the donkeys paid us no attention and went

back to eating and occasionally stomping their hooves on the deck.

Derek came over to me, his smile as big as the moon, and pulled me into his arms.

"Talk about paranoid," he said, kissing the top of my head. He let out another laugh. "In all my years, I've never pulled a gun on a donkey before."

"Good thing you didn't shoot first and ask questions later," I said, trying to catch my breath.

"You're right. I guess I'm changing, aren't I, sunshine?"

I smiled at him, my heart feeling so unbelievably full. "You are. But you haven't lost all of yourself."

His brow furrowed. "Hopefully I've kept the sexy parts."

I pinched his side. "You did. And then some."

He put his arm around my shoulder and I leaned my head against his chest as we watched the donkeys for a few moments.

"I wonder who they belong to," I mused.

"Probably wild," he said. "Don't you be getting any ideas."

"The only idea I'm getting is that we may need a fence. Then again, I like that they came here. Wild but not afraid."

"Just like you."

I gave him a grave look. "But I was afraid. Back there, in the house, I was afraid."

His lips twitched into a half-smile. "And yet you still stood by me. It's okay to be afraid, Alana. We'll always be afraid to some degree, I think, and that's a good thing. You need fear to stay sharp. You need fear to keep your wildness in check. But just a little bit. Just enough to feel alive." He paused. "I think we're more alive now than we've ever been. Just this life here, this beautiful little life with you and this island and everything, is all I want for the rest of my life."

Hot tears tickled at my eyes as I was lost in the sincerity of his words, in the confidence in his eyes. I reached up and kissed him sweetly, wanting to remember this moment forever.

A loud bray from one of the donkeys was the only thing to interrupt us.

We waved them goodbye, deciding to clean up after them tomorrow, and went inside, and back to bed.

During the week that followed, I felt happier than ever. You'd think that would correspond with feeling lighter, but for some reason I felt weighted down, bloated, irritated, and heavy. It didn't help that I had missed my period, either. Finally I had to bite the bullet and face what could really be going on with me.

So I went to our rinky dink local drugstore, and once I was back at home, took a pregnancy test.

It came out positive.

I wasn't really sure how I would react – waiting for that pink line was so nerve-racking that I had no idea what my thoughts were. But the moment it became true, it became real, I felt a happiness bloom inside me like a flower I'd overlooked.

When I told Derek, his reaction was the same – pure joy. We cried and laughed and did a funny dance around the bedroom. We let the news sink in over and over again, and smiled until we were sure our faces wouldn't crack in two.

No more wine (except a glass on occasion), no more fish. Lots of healthy vegetables and grains. The whole island seemed to know I was knocked up, and it was like I suddenly had a giant family rejoicing with me, a family that seemed hell-bent on making sure my child was raised as happy as can be.

Some days I laid on the roof deck and stared up at the sky, hand on my growing belly, and thought about the future. Now it wouldn't just be Derek and me. We would have someone else in our family.

Someone else to love.

Someone else to run wild with.

Someone else to call home.

Get ready for the
Dirty Angels Trilogy . . .

Mexico is lawless. It's lethal. It's scorching-hot.

It's dog eat dog in the world of the drug cartels.

But sometimes, forbidden love can blossom
from poison.

And when it does, you've got to guard it with
your life. You've got to watch your back.

Available from

headline
ETERNAL

You haven't lived 'til you've visited the wild world of The Artists Trilogy . . .

You'll meet a Mexican drug lord, a beautiful con artist and a damaged tattooist.

You'll play a lethal game of cat and mouse, of life and death, of love and revenge.

It's dark, dangerous and deadly.

It's time to buckle in and lose your inhibitions.

Available now from

headline
ETERNAL

headline
ETERNAL

FIND YOUR HEART'S DESIRE...